Praise for *Lette*

Miriam has woven a beautiful, heartwarming, realistic picture of life, loss, and love in the late eighteenth century, proving that life may be different in the twenty-first but the feelings stirred through love and loss remain constant. She gives us a true sense of how complex, complicated, and yet rich marital love can be. *Letters to Emily* is a story to be shared.

—CE Hilbert, author of *The Wooing of Jane Grey*

This homey story will delight your heart. Miriam Ilgenfritz vividly depicts the harshness of life in rural Pennsylvania in the 1700s, where times are challenging and emotions raw. Walk by Hannah's side as she faces each new day with its joys, sorrows, and incredible challenges—from pig roasts to *hog maws;* from yellow fever to thunderstorms; from barn raisings to difficult births.

In *Letters to Emily,* you'll experience the daily life of the early settlers, feel their pain, share their sorrow, and rejoice in their victories. A heartwarming glimpse into another time and the struggles faced by one family.

—Sharon Dow, author of *Antipas: Martyr* and *Pergamum: Satan's Throne*

Letters to Emily is a heartwarming story of a woman struggling to adjust to marriage and frontier life. Hannah's raw honesty with herself and her feelings about her husband will endear her to readers as they relate to the challenges life throws her way. Real life isn't fairytale-perfect and without the grounding of faith as a compass, tragedy can send relationships spinning. Ilgenfritz grounds her characters in faith, yet keeps them brutally real.

—Tara Fairfield, licensed psychologist, speaker, and author of *Makai Queen*

Letters to Emily is the poignantly crafted debut novel of Miriam Ilgenfritz. With superb historical detail, she captures the realities and hardships of late 1700s in America. Deeply felt characters in an authentic rural setting when faith and family carved the beginnings of a great nation. To read this book is to experience the heart and soul of our heritage.

—STAN BEDNARZ, author of *Miracle on Snowbird Lake*

LETTERS *to* EMILY

LETTERS *to* EMILY

MIRIAM L. ILGENFRITZ

Deep River
BOOKS

Letters to Emily
© 2014 Miriam L. Ilgenfritz

All Scripture quotations are taken from the Holy Bible, King James Version. Public domain.

Hymns quoted or mentioned in *Letters to Emily* are as follows:

"A Mighty Fortress." Words & Music: Martin Luther, 1529. Public domain.

"When All Thy Mercies, O My God." Words: Joseph Addison, in The Spectator (London: August 9, 1712). Public domain.

"Rock of Ages" Words: Augustus M. Toplady, 1763. Public domain.

"How Firm a Foundation." Words: attributed variously to John Keene, Kirkham, and John Keith. 1787. Public domain.

Published by
Deep River Books
Sisters, Oregon
www.deepriverbooks.com

ISBN-13: 9781940269016
ISBN-10: 1940269016

Library of Congress: 2013951923

Printed in the USA

Cover illustration by Lisa Marie Browning
Design by Robin Black, www.InspirioDesign.com

DEDICATION

To my husband, Mark, who always believed I could write a book;
to the many children in my life who inspired humor and dialog;
and to Lydia, who read my rough draft while sitting in her creek
one hot summer and encouraged me to pursue publication.
I love you all.

AUTHOR'S NOTE

To all readers, especially those who may bear the name Zartman, I wish to assure you, my characters are entirely from my imagination. While I am aware that there were several Hannah Zartmans down through the years, I picked the name Hannah merely because I like it, and any resemblance my Hannah may bear to any real Hannah Zartman is coincidental.

After I named all my characters, I visited a local cemetery and discovered several Zartmans buried there bearing the same names as some of the children in my story. Again, I would stress that none of the Zartmans in my novel are factual.

I have tried to stick with history as I could discover it with the research means at hand. And while my characters are invented, many of their trials did happen to others in Pennsylvania during the time periods covered by this novel.

As far as the village of Dornsife, it was here, but not as a town with that name. David Dornsife was a Hessian mercenary and married a woman named Elizabeth, and they lived in this area, but the town was not named as such until later.

As far as I can tell, the homestead I write about was purchased in 1768 by Jacob Zartman. He bought 122 acres and seven years thereafter, another 100 acres. His son Henry inherited it, and at one point it was referred to as "Henry's Delight." At the time of Henry's death in 1803, the homestead comprised 312 acres and included a church.

It was necessary to alter these facts somewhat for the telling of my tale, but the reader should be aware that this farm actually was a Zartman possession prior to the date in the novel; and while there were Zartmans who were mercenaries, the family who resided here came by other means.

Contents

1

THE PROBLEM WITH PIGS

"Mama, Mama," rang out through the humid afternoon. The way the air felt, there must be a thunderstorm building up.

"What in the world do they need now?" Hannah pushed her long, unruly brown hair back behind her ears and kept on churning the butter, perspiration trickling down the sides of her face. Too bad this job always took longer on humid days—butter was a better barometer than the old glass instrument her husband, Georg, kept on the sideboard.

"Mama, we need you!" The young voice sounded again, and recognizing the voice as that of Clara, one of her more responsible children, rather than one who cried wolf, Hannah wearily straightened her back and considered giving the butter up as a wasted effort. Unfortunately, they needed it and there wasn't any more cream. Well, time to think about that later, she'd better see what the problem was.

Holding her long skirts in one hand, she pushed open the wooden door and stepped outside. The unusually warm spring sunshine blinded her for a moment, and as her eyes adjusted, she could see not just one but eight of her nine children running down the hill to meet her. While they were in a hurry, no one seemed to be bleeding and they didn't look scared as they might if a stranger was approaching. As they ran through the apple orchard and then past the double red outhouse, they all tried to get her attention at once.

"Mama, it's Peaches," said one of her boys, brushing his blond hair out of his eyes. "She's having her piglets, but we think she's having trouble."

"Mama, she's crying," added Margaret, her chubby three-year-old.

"Pigs don't cry," scoffed Hans, yet another slim blond boy.

Hannah shook her head and reflected on Peaches's last three litters, all born smoothly and with no help from human hands.

"No wonder she's upset. You know not to bother an animal when she's giving birth. Let her be."

"Mama, you don't understand. Peaches never looked like this before."

Peaches was the only sow Hannah and Georg owned, and her piglets would provide meat this winter. They couldn't afford to lose her, and a crowd of small squealing orphan piglets would be difficult to keep alive.

With a weary sigh, Hannah checked quickly on her napping baby. Then she tucked up her apron and dashed up the hill for the pigpen, wondering for the hundredth time why this farm had been built on all these hills. There weren't any level places, and it was an effort to get anywhere quickly.

Sure enough, Peaches was lying on the ground just inside the pigpen gate. Mud was caked all over her lovely black and red patches, and she looked completely miserable. Her curly tail drooped into a puddle where she had spilled her dented tin water pan, and she was panting rapidly in the heat. From time to time she tensed up and strained intensely, but there were no results; and each time Hannah watched her strain, she seemed a little weaker.

"Get me some bear grease," she ordered all the children at once, and thirteen-year-old Benjamin ran off. He returned a minute later with a small bowl of grease. Hannah rolled up her sleeve, wrinkled her nose at the pungent smell and then quickly smeared her slender arm to the elbow while ignoring the noisy children clustered outside the pen and the smell of pig inside the pen. She was glad Peaches was quite gentle, as she was a huge sow. If she had been an angry, laboring mother pig, Hannah never would have dared to climb into the pen. Peaches seemed to realize help was on the way and let Hannah reach up.

If Emily could only see me now, she thought as she squirmed around on the muddy, reeking straw with her arm pinched inside the pig. Her sister, who still lived in New York, would never believe this. She could barely believe it herself.

Sure enough, she could feel little bitty pig feet. She gently grasped the tiny legs and waited for the next contraction. It didn't take long. She pulled out a huge pink-and-black baby squealing in protest at its rude entry into the world. She laid the piglet gently next to its mother. "That pig just didn't want to be born," Hannah gave Peaches an encouraging pat on the neck. "Now this big one's out of the way, the rest should be okay."

As the children waited and wiggled and admired the husky new arrival, Hannah remembered her butter. It was probably ruined after all this time. They would just have to eat molasses on their bread again tonight. One of these days, everyone would be older and she would catch up with all her work.

The children waited and waited, eight pairs of eyes in every shade of blue peering over the rails of the pen, but no more piglets appeared. Despite her prediction, they must be stuck. Finally, Hannah greased her arm again and again and eventually delivered ten healthy piglets, to the great relief of Peaches.

"I don't know what your problem was," Hannah said wearily to the pig. Then she smiled despite her aching arms and reminded herself how thankful she was that the pig was still alive and all the babies seemed healthy. If they had died, Georg would have been furious even though it wouldn't have been her fault.

"All right, everybody. The excitement is done. Let's leave Peaches here alone. Whose turn is it to milk the cow tonight? Clara, I think it's you." She ruffled her slender ten-year-old's fine blond hair. "Go get the bucket, and let's all finish up the chores so we can have a nice meal with Father when he gets back."

The children scattered in all directions.

If he gets back tonight. How many days did it take to deliver a load of lumber to Philadelphia anyway? Ten days, more or less, to get there, several days to do business, ten days or less to get back because there would be no heavy load. Say four weeks on the outside, and Georg had been gone almost five weeks. Their wagon was practically new. Surely it couldn't have broken down. And both horses had just been shod again, so the trip should have been fairly easy. She pondered Georg's unusual lateness as she poured the ruined buttermilk into a bowl for the pigs to eat.

By the time she had heated some water, washed up, and put on her only clean dress, it was suppertime. Scrambled eggs would fill everyone again tonight.

"At least the chickens are cooperating," one of the older boys said.

"Well, just wait till winter. Then we'll get pork and sauerkraut again." Frederick, at seven, was old enough to know what the successful birth of ten piglets meant to his family.

Leaving Samuel, Clara, and Hans to clear their old wooden table, worn smooth by years of hard use, and scrub the dishes, Hannah dropped wearily into a chair. Perhaps the children would let her have fifteen minutes to let her thoughts wander before someone needed her. The plump baby, Daniel, who was just learning to walk, stumbled across the tongue-and-groove floor and crawled into Hannah's lap, putting his heavy head down.

As she sat, Hannah surveyed her small domain. Her husband had displayed unusual ingenuity in building their snug little cabin, and Hannah felt a surge of thankfulness every time she stopped and looked around her small home. The kitchen was built right over the top of a small spring and boasted a trough faced with stone along one end. It was the perfect place to store milk and butter in the hot summer, as the spring ran cold all year long. Also, she never had to walk anywhere to fetch water. It was handy every day.

On the next wall was the fireplace, which kept the whole kitchen warm in winter. Above the fireplace was a sturdy wooden mantel, where Hannah kept her prize possession: a chiming clock her sister had given her and Georg as a wedding gift.

Hannah looked at her clock and smiled. This was her one link to her past life, growing up in a moderately wealthy home. This little farm in Pennsylvania was almost entirely hard work, building for the future of their family. Back home there had been time for small bits of luxury. Emily knew her life here would be a hard one and gave the clock to remind her that it was not always so. However, Hannah knew many settlers lived harder lives than hers.

She even had a smooth stone floor in the kitchen that was cold in winter, but every now and then in springtime the spring overflowed, and the stones were much easier to keep clean than the hard-packed dirt in so many frontier cabins.

"Mama, you put the baby right to sleep," observed Clara, passing the rocking chair as she stacked the plates in the one cupboard they owned.

And almost myself as well. She awkwardly got to her feet, trying not to wake the baby, and carried him up the stairs to the second of their two small bedrooms. Gently she laid him in the boys' bed, next to the wall so he wouldn't roll out in the night, and went back downstairs to help the rest of the children finish their work before bedtime.

Hannah whisked the rest of the supper crumbs off her apron, tied her unruly hair back, up and gathered everybody to the table for some reading, and then set the older ones to working sums. With no school in this secluded part of Pennsylvania, her kitchen was her children's schoolroom.

While they worked quietly, she retrieved her letter to her sister to add today's adventure to the collection she already had.

Biting the end of her pen didn't seem to hasten her thoughts any, so she took a minute to picture her sister, at home still with her mother and father. Emily would be dressed in whatever the latest fashion in New York was now, curls tied up in a matching ribbon, snuggled up in their immaculate living room reading a letter from her sister in the wilderness. Since no sudden inspiration reached her even then, she just began jotting down her thoughts from the day.

May, 1798

Dear Emily,

You would never believe what I had to do today. Georg isn't back yet, and the pig—remember Peaches?—was having so much trouble delivering her piglets that I had to help her. If Father could have seen one of his fine daughters down in the mud, he would have had one of his fits of anger. And Mama, she would just weep and say, "I can't believe you've come to this."

At first I felt the same way, but when I saw all ten little piglets, fat and pink and black and nursing heartily, I couldn't help but feel I had accomplished something important.

Emily, I've been so worried lately. Georg has to haul so much lumber back to Philadelphia to pay our farm expenses that he doesn't have time to work the farm properly. I try to help, but some of the jobs are just beyond my abilities, and the big boys can't quite do a man's work yet. It has been quite hot this spring and so the new pasture grass is barely growing, the cattle look skinny and sad, and I don't know if Georg will have time to till up any new land like he wanted although we have space for more fields now with cutting down the timber.

I know that Georg loves this land. This is the place he has always wanted. He is a free man here, not like he was in Germany where you owe your service to a lord. I can't imagine how he lived before he came here, and I cannot bear the thought that we could lose this place if our finances don't turn around.

On the other hand, if we weren't on this farm, maybe life would be easier for Georg. I hate to see him working so hard, it seems he could work himself into an early grave and then where would be my dreams of happy ever after? I'm just so torn. I'm waiting for him to get back, and I don't know what I want to tell him when he does get back.

The children are all growing so fast. I know I always say that, but you haven't seen them since the baby was born, and I can hardly keep up with sewing clothes to fit them. I am going to start teaching the girls more sewing skills. They can hem well, and Clara has made many beautiful samplers and helped me with quilting. If she could learn how to cut out fabric without so much waste, it would be a big help in keeping the boys properly dressed. Most of them don't care too much if they have holey pants or their wrists and ankles stick out but everything wears out fast here so it's even hard to hand things down to the next boy.

I have to bake bread again tomorrow. I could bake six loaves a day and they would all get eaten. I guess growing up in house with all girls like we did; I never realized boys could eat so much food. I am thankful that we have a big barrel of molasses left for the bread. Today the butter all got ruined because I had to go out and help the pig. Then we had eggs for supper because there simply wasn't time to cook anything else. I guess that was the good part about Georg not getting back yet. He hates eggs for supper. He always wants some kind of meat and potatoes if we have them. He even planted a big potato field up above the house so we'll have another good supply this fall.

Benjamin and Frederick are working on digging a ground cellar to keep all the potatoes in so they don't freeze or sprout too much over the winter. And we even planted some apple trees so in a few years we'll have our own fruit if we can hang on that long.

I don't know when this will get sent to you, but writing is almost as good as having a face-to-face visit. I hope Georg brings me back some more ink. We just killed a goose last week, so I have plenty of quills; but if I run out of ink, I would feel so sad—for how else can I tell you how life is in the wild?

Your loving sister,
Hannah

Gathering up her tablet and pen, Hannah announced, "It's time for bed, children!"

While they often mumbled and found excuses, tonight everyone seemed tired; after a quick cleanup of slates and tattered books, they shuffled wearily off to bed. Hannah found herself lying in bed, still alone, and listening to the rumble of thunder in the distance. The whole afternoon and evening, the cabin had remained hot and humid. A good storm would clear the air and bring welcome rain, although she hated to think of Georg camping out in a storm. Her thoughts seemed to roam every which way as she waited for sleep. Finally she drifted off with one ear open in case the baby should cry, only to be awakened an hour later, first by the gentle chime of the clock downstairs and then, as her fuzzy mind cleared, to the welcome sounds of rain on the tin roof. Lightning flashed through the glass windowpanes, and thunder shook the house, but all the children slept peacefully and so Hannah finally drifted into a restless sleep again as well.

A crash of thunder closer than the rest woke her again, but she thought she'd heard something else too. She jumped out of bed and grabbed a shawl and squinted through the glass toward the barn, trying to see past the blur of rain hammering on the window. A light glimmered, went out, and shone again briefly. She had a sudden panicky thought that the barn was on fire from a lightning strike—and then the pieces fell into place. Georg was finally home and putting the horses in the barn. He must be exhausted, drenched, and freezing. She ran down to the fireplace, stirred the coals, and threw two more logs on. At least there would be hot tea when he got in.

It wasn't too much longer before her tall, blond husband burst through the door. "I'm home, Hannah, I'm finally home!" he shouted joyfully in his deep voice, disregarding the lateness of the hour and the fact that everyone should be asleep.

She flew into his arms, but before she could even begin to ask all the questions bustling around in her head, the children began tumbling down the steps and everyone seemed to be shouting at once, "Papa's home, Papa's home."

Much to her astonishment, Hannah began to weep. She hadn't realized how much Georg's absence had bothered her while he was gone, but now that he had returned, she could stop being two parents and the farm manager and be just a mama and a wife for a while.

Together they settled the children back to sleep and then made their own way to bed.

"Georg, I prayed every day for your quick and safe return. I was beginning to think God couldn't hear me out here in the mountains, but now you are back," she bubbled, exhausted but more thankful than she'd ever imagined she could be.

There was no answer. Her husband had given in to the softness of the feather bed, and Hannah could hear the gentle snore that she had been missing. Hannah too waited for sleep to overtake her. She rolled on her side, curled up, put her feet on Georg's back, and promptly felt her worries emerge from the corners of her mind where she had pushed them. *Suppose we can't pay the mortgage, suppose the crops fail, suppose the drought continues and the cattle all have to be sold.* Hannah rolled over again. Her thoughts felt like bees buzzing angrily in her mind, each demanding a turn to be heard.

Finally Hannah put the pillow over her head, and the stuffiness began to lull her to sleep. Tomorrow was time enough to hear all that had taken place on the road and in Philadelphia.

2

CIRCUIT RIDER

The pink light of early dawn was just creeping over the hills to the east of the farm when Hannah woke up. The loud, uncertain crowing of a young rooster had roused her much earlier than normal. Unable to go back to sleep, she slid quietly out of bed, pushed open the wooden shutter that closed their one small window, and gazed at the hills surrounding their cabin. The air was fresh and smelled like early April instead of hot May, which had arrived three weeks earlier. A few tattered clouds scudded by in the breeze from last night's rain, and every bird in the area sounded as if it were rejoicing over the fresh air.

Hannah crawled back under her soft, faded quilt, pulled it up to her chin against the cool air, and lay still for a while beside her husband, savoring the quiet. Her thoughts drifted back to the day she and Georg had first met, in 1778. She had been traveling by coach with her father, a merchant living in New York City who had business in Winchester, Virginia. While she had been only fourteen years old, each of her four sisters had gotten to travel with their father once in a while, and now it was her turn.

They had passed an enclosure full of men. Her father had told her that they were German prisoners from the war. To her astonishment, he also told her that they were not really treated as prisoners, and some Americans were trying to convince them to desert the army and remain in the new country as citizens.

As the horses clopped past, she had noticed a very young prisoner lounging against the fence. What attracted her attention first was the way the sun shone on his shaggy red-blond hair and the self-assured way that he held himself. He looked almost cheerful and certainly not intimidated by his circumstances even though he was a prisoner.

Now that's the kind of man I would like to marry, Hannah told herself. As their eyes met, she shivered. Handsome was one thing, but her Father had no liking for Germans who'd fought for the British. Young girls have silly thoughts, Hannah told herself sternly and put the young man out of her mind completely.

Imagine her surprise five years later, when on a second trip with her Father, she had run into this same tall man in Pennsylvania. She and Emily, her closest sister, had been invited to visit relatives in Reading. Since Hannah and Emily both loved to dance, it was only natural that they attend as many fetes as possible during their visit.

While their father viewed dancing as a way to exhibit his considerable wealth and social standing—as well as his young beautiful daughters—Emily and Hannah much preferred to sneak out and go to the barn dances where there were not so many social regulations to conform to and a girl was free to just enjoy the music and the company. They always made sure to sneak back to the more formal dances before their father noticed they were gone, but since he spent most of his time discussing business and politics or playing cards, he hadn't noticed their frequent absences from the dance floor.

At a visit to the punch table, at a particularly lively barn dance, she had turned around hastily right into a tall young man, spilling punch all over both of them.

"You're in a bit of a hurry," he had said in a heavy accent, seeming to enjoy the awkward moment.

"Have I seen you somewhere before?" she had asked as they mopped up, knowing she had but wondering if he would remember such a casual thing as a glance. Her heart did a quick flip-flop, but she tried to look relaxed and mature.

"Yes, I saw you in Virginia."

His smiling reply made Hannah's cheeks flush, and her heart jumped again. So it was him and he did remember. She paused for a second look. He was much taller than she was, had broader shoulders than she remembered; but he had been so young then, blue eyes that seemed to look right into her heart. What would she do with this information? "How did you get to Pennsylvania, then?"

"The prisoners were brought here, and when peace came this year, some of us decided to stay in this new country. I have no wish to return to Germany where my life is not my own. I was taken away from my family and I was not even fifteen years old, forced to fight in a war that I had no concern in, and no, I will never return. I plan to find a farm here and stay."

Hannah shivered with excitement. What a fascinating man.

Their romance had been secret and quick, a courtship conducted at the dances, which often were the only entertainment available for young people. By early 1784, against the wishes of her family, she was a married lady of twenty.

By the time she was twenty-four, she and Georg had three children and were on their way to central Pennsylvania, where he had found the land of his dreams, a parcel of three hundred acres. Formerly owned by William Penn, it had been given to a German family before the war but was now being sold again, as the first family was moving further west.

The land had a cabin, but most of it had burned the previous winter even as the owners were contemplating a move. The fire confirmed the original owner's plans; it also enabled Georg to get a better price when he purchased it.

The farm nestled against low-lying mountains with a stream running through it, just a few miles east of the Susquehanna River. All it needed was a rebuilt cabin and a willing family to work the land.

Hannah had never heard of the area but knew there were several towns nearby, including Fort Augusta, so she bolstered her spirit of adventure and helped pack the three wagons that brought all their worldly goods to their dream farm. The hardest thing had been moving further from her favorite sister Emily, but seeing her husband so happy and finally owning his own piece of land had compensated for that sorrow.

Now here they were with nine children instead of three, the farm that was to be the answer to their prayers if they could sustain it, and a collection of adventure stories to tell the grandchildren—if she lived that long.

The rooster crowed again, louder and closer to the cabin, jolting her back to the present. This was enough thinking. If she didn't soon get up, there would be no quiet time left to accomplish some work before she had to awaken all the children. Georg was exhausted, so she would sneak out and let him sleep.

The children would all be grumpy today after their papa's late arrival. Well, maybe not. They would be so excited to hear of his trip that perhaps they'd forget their tiredness. On the other hand, that rooster would need some attention. He crowed every two hours starting at midnight. Yes, he was young, but surely a rooster could tell when morning was near. Perhaps today would be a good day to have roast chicken. She did have several other roosters who were more sensible than this one.

The fire wasn't even very low yet, since their late night tea. It was quite easy to get it blazing, and efficiently she stirred up a pan of biscuits. They still had a little bacon left hanging in the smokehouse, and everyone would enjoy waking to the smell of biscuits and gravy instead of the usual cornmeal mush.

Sliding the cast-iron skillet full of biscuits into the hearth, Hannah decided to dress quickly while they baked and then finish off the gravy in time to call the children. She tiptoed up the stairs and was just brushing her hair when Georg whispered, "Come over here, Mama. Let Papa see you before all the children need you."

Hannah blushed even though no one was around, but she went over to give Georg a morning kiss. He grabbed her around her still-slim waist, kissed her hungrily, and hugged her tightly. "I missed you so much," he said huskily. "I could hardly wait to get back home to you."

"I can't stay," she protested, trying to wriggle out of his grasp. "The biscuits will burn."

"Well, let them, then, I haven't seen you in forever." He kissed her again, and Hannah simply couldn't think of a way to rescue the biscuits without making Georg think she didn't want to be with him, so she kissed him back.

The rooster suddenly crowed again, next to the house, and Daniel began shrieking for his mama.

"Well, I see nothing has changed around here." Laughing, her husband set Hannah free to attend to her smallest child and the almost-burned biscuits. "I'll still be here tonight." He chuckled and pulled the quilt back up around his broad shoulders. "Wake me up when the children are all up. I brought a present for everyone."

Hannah smiled. The trip must have gone well if they could afford gifts. Picking up the still-shrieking toddler, she woke the boys and then set about drying Daniel and dressing him. His blond hair hung down into his big blue eyes and reminded Hannah that it was past time to cut the boys' hair. They were all looking shaggy these days. Today would be a good day for a lot of things—including dealing with that pesky rooster.

It was Frederick's turn to milk today. He was fairly new to this chore, and Hannah hoped it would go all right. Some of her boys were hefty lads, but Fredrick was short and slight and just turned seven, and the cows seemed to know they intimidated him. She kept telling him to sing to them and they would give more milk, but the boy also seemed afraid someone would hear him and tease him about his singing ability. Well, his papa couldn't sing either. Maybe having him home would keep the teasing to a minimum.

Deftly, Hannah finished whisking the lumps out of the gravy. She had a few minutes before everyone came back in and quietly got out the family Bible. Every day, if she had time, she tried to read a passage to think on as she worked; and when Georg was gone it brought her comfort. Other times, she read it and wrote down questions for the circuit rider. Her father had brought the family up attending church, and after each service, they would all discuss the message as they walked home. Here there was no church building, but Hannah clung to her belief that God was with her wherever she was, church or no church. Still, a church in the area would be a wonderful thing, although that could be years away.

She scarcely had time to read one verse from the psalms before eggs were set on the table in a dusty basket, a pail of milk dripped across her floor, and all the crowd of hungry children piled into the kitchen, clamoring for breakfast.

Breakfast was festive with Papa back at the head of the table. Hannah looked around with pleasure at all the blond and dark heads chattering at once, vying for their father's attention. He seemed younger than when he left; perhaps the fact that he was so cheerful made him seem more youthful. When they'd parted, a world of care seemed to be lying on those broad shoulders, but today it was gone.

I shall enjoy this day to the fullest, Hannah said to herself. It has started out well, and whatever tomorrow holds, today is good. She could almost picture herself back when she and Georg had met, fallen quickly in love, and determined that no parent or lack of land or anything else would hinder their getting married.

"And I got exactly what I wanted," she told herself.

"What, Mama?" asked ten-year-old Clara as she shoved another biscuit into her mouth. "What did you want?"

"Oh, I'm just thinking out loud, and what I wanted was your Papa and here he is."

Georg winked at her from across the table, and Hannah felt the heat on her face reach all the way to her hairline. Why did he always have to show so much affection in front of the children? Her mother and father were so restrained that even after fourteen years of marriage, she still felt funny when Georg did such things. The children didn't seem bothered, though, so she decided to ignore those funny feeling and vowed once again to enjoy the day.

As soon as the dishes were cleared, Georg announced that he had gifts for everyone. Amid cheers and laughter, he brought out his saddlebags, which had been hidden under the bed, and dramatically began handing out his treasures. First, he had a small bag a of maple sugar candy for each child, and for Hannah, a small bag of marzipan because Georg knew she had loved the almond flavor as a child and there was none to be had out on a farm.

The children were so unused to gifts that they all became speechless as their father produced one toy after another. For Daniel, there was a beautifully carved and brightly painted wooden top; even though he was too small to figure out how to make it spin, he was thrilled to have his very own toy. Margaret and Magdalena, who were three and six and looked like twins with dark curls like Hannah and big blue eyes like their papa, each got a small doll with a carved wooden head and a cloth body.

Johann, Frederick, Hans, and Samuel each received a bag of glass marbles, while Clara exclaimed over a small box filled with her own sewing supplies: a thimble, several needles, and even some cloth for stitching samplers. Finally it was Benjamin's turn.

"Well, Son." Georg grinned. "You were supposed to be the man of the house. I know you are only thirteen, but I brought something I hope you will use for many years." Reaching behind the door, he brought out a smooth-bore rifle with a curly maple stock and handed it to the disbelieving boy.

Benjamin was speechless. Finally he found his voice. "Papa, you bought this for me?"

"Somebody better start hunting when I'm gone, and these little boys surely aren't going to shoot that well just yet. I bought this from a gunsmith who made it for his son. Now that son is grown up and needs a larger gun. This one looked just your size. Besides, I always take my gun when I travel, and I thought we ought to have one here too." He gave their eldest son a sly look, humor glinting in his eyes. "I guess if you're not ready for it, I could teach someone else to shoot it."

"No, Papa, I just could hardly believe it."

He stood there silently, gently rubbing his hands over the beautiful wood. Hannah thought she saw tears in his eyes, although she knew he would never admit such a thing. Finally all the children began shouting, "What about Mama? Didn't you bring her a present? What's for Mama?"

With another broad smile, Georg reached in his bag one last time and brought out two flowered pieces of calico and a thick, tattered envelope. Frowning at the envelope, he shoved it quickly back into the bag and then turned to Hannah, who couldn't hide her own bright smile, with the gaily colored fabric.

"Hannah, I think it's high time you made yourself a new dress or two," he said, "and one can be for Sundays. I know there's no church, but you could dress up just for us when we gather to read the Scriptures."

As speechless as Benjamin, Hannah hugged the fabric to her and buried her face in it. She fingered the flowers gently and could already picture her first dress taking shape. Finally Georg shouted, "All right, everybody, let's go see how the animals and gardens are doing."

They all trooped out, including Georg with his saddlebags, so Hannah had no time to ask about the letter. She was left alone to finish up the dishes and dream of making new dresses.

The dishes done, she grabbed her letter to Emily and wrote quickly to capture her whirling thoughts before they escaped.

> *Emily,*
> *You'll never believe it. After I wrote you last night, Georg returned. You may have seen him if you were in Philadelphia, but he didn't say. Emily, he is so cheerful, not at all like when he left. It's like having my carefree soldier boy back again.*

With that, she folded up her precious thoughts, replaced them in her small bureau, and grabbed her apron on the way out the door to find her family.

The air was still cool and fresh from last night's rain. Hannah could hear the voices of her children over in the cornfield, so she grabbed her sunbonnet from where it hung on a nail on the porch—as she fingered the frayed edge, she decided she might even have enough fabric to make a new bonnet, too—and headed up the hill to join them. The children were all clustered around Georg, who was examining the spindly light green shoots of corn. They hadn't been up out of the ground long, and the dry spring had not been kind to them; but if the weather cooperated, they would still recover and produce a good crop by October.

Hannah whispered a quick prayer, "God, I know you have the weather in your control, and maybe it's not right for me even to ask for you to make it nice for us, but we need a good crop this year so badly. Would you see fit for a rainy spring and nice hot summer for our corn?"

By the time she was done, she had reached her own little crop of farmers. They were all on their way to admire the piglets, and everyone was telling Georg at once how Mama had brought the babies safely into the world. He simply chuckled and said, "I always thought you had it in you to be a midwife."

"Well never again for pigs, I hope," she retorted.

From piglets, they checked on the cattle and then the pasture grass, which was still slender and new. Finally they were ready to head back to the house.

"All right, everybody," ordered Hannah, "Let's gather up all the hoes and weed the vegetables."

"Ohhh," groaned several children in unison. "Do we hafta?"

"Yes, indeed, or the weeds will take over and there won't be anything to eat this winter. Now march!"

"Hannah," reproved Georg, "I can decide what needs to be done next. I could see the garden needed weeding when I got up this morning."

"Well, I couldn't keep up with everything," answered Hannah defensively. "There's too much work here for one adult. I needed to keep things moving."

"I'm not scolding you for your lack of work, darling, but now that I'm back home, I'll tell the children what needs to be done unless it's kitchen jobs."

Resisting the urge to point out that she had done a man's work in addition to a woman's work the whole time he was gone, Hannah bit her tongue and headed off to the chicken coop to see how her hens were doing. Before she could reach it, Clara started shouting for her. Hannah sighed. "I will never teach that girl to be a lady. She is as loud as the boys."

Then she saw the reason for Clara's excitement. The circuit rider was plodding up the road. You could recognize him from far away because he always rode a big white mule instead of a horse, and the mule, Zaccheus, was so old that it had only one gait left—slow. No one knew how old he was, but the preacher refused to give him up for any faster method of transportation. No wonder we hardly ever see him, thought Hannah. It takes Zaccheus so long to get around to all the settlements.

Well, no time to worry about that now, he probably expected a big meal in his honor and perhaps would even spend the night. And then he could take her letter with him because he would be in Philadelphia before long if the mule didn't die of old age first.

Hannah rounded up Benjamin and sent him to catch the rooster that had been so annoying this morning. Then she sent Samuel after another rooster. It would never do to run short of roast chicken with the preacher present. There still wasn't any butter, but they could eat molasses on biscuits, and there were plenty of dried beans left from last year. She put a bowlful out to soak and ran down to the garden to pick some of the early peas for the children to shell while the chicken cooked. Georg had made her a handy spit, and it wasn't such a bad job to turn the chicken if one's siblings sat all around and shelled peas and told stories.

The circuit rider, who always went by his full name, John Martin Henry Claybaugh, was a fat, jolly little man with a fringe of gray hair He slid awkwardly off Zaccheus and gave the reins to Frederick to take the mule for a drink of water and some fresh hay.

"Reverend Claybaugh, welcome back," said Georg. "I hoped when I passed you on the road the other day that you wouldn't take long to get here. Hannah always looks forward to your coming."

"Well now, I just take my time, but I always get here." The reverend beamed, shaking hands with all the children in turn. "And look how Daniel has grown. I hardly knew him."

"And I hardly know my garden," said Georg, "with the weeds taking over. Please excuse us while we get that job done. Hannah will get you a cold drink out of the spring."

"I surely would appreciate it. Even after a rain, riding is dusty work, and you have the best spring water for miles and miles."

Tension still thick between them, Hannah got the water dipper without speaking to or looking at Georg.

Once the reverend's thirst was quenched, he went down to the garden to watch the children and visit with Georg, and Hannah scurried into the house. What a day for him to come. She hadn't cleaned up or made the beds or anything. Well, that's what comes of leaving your work until later, she reminded herself sternly. The grass would still grow, the flowers would bloom, but Mama better get her chores done before enjoying a spring day, otherwise someone was sure to drop in for a visit.

Once things were straightened up, she felt better and rejoined those children who were still outside. Things seemed to be under control, and all the peas were snapped, so she took a turn next to the fire, turning the spit. The chicken was starting to brown; juice dripped down and sizzled in the fireplace, and Hannah wiped her forehead with the back of her hand. This was a hot job any time of year; the children did get tired of it—and it was her dinner, after all.

The delicious smells brought the children back in, so she mopped her sweaty face with her apron again and left Hans with the spit while she mixed up some biscuits. Biscuits twice in one day were a treat.

"Clara, please sweep the floor, and then see if my tablecloth is all right. I hope no mice got in my chest and chewed on it." Their only tablecloth was indeed still in one piece with no holes, so they spread it over the boards they usually ate on and got out their wooden plates and pewter cups.

Hannah took great delight in actually having everything in order by suppertime. The animals were fed, the garden weeded, the house had gotten clean enough to please the most discriminating preacher—which Reverend Claybaugh was not—the supper was done, nothing had burned even though it was all cooked over the hearth, and the table was set. Grabbing their big brass bell, she went outside and rang it vigorously, calling children and men from all directions. Georg had gotten her a large bell so no one had the excuse of not hearing the supper call, and everyone came running to fight over whose turn it was to wash faces and hands first in the basin she had set outside the door.

Finally everyone was sitting around the table in great anticipation of a feast. Used to being in charge of a meal, Hannah didn't wait for Georg but said, "Reverend Claybaugh, will you please ask the blessing?"

"Of course," he replied, and while Hannah thought she noticed a frown flit across Georg's face, she decided it was just her imagination.

After a lengthy blessing, the fragrant chickens were carved and plates handed round filled with fresh vegetables and the dried beans she had soaked and boiled earlier. Biscuits and molasses made their way around the table as well.

"Georg, you are going to need a bigger table when all these children start getting married," teased the reverend.

"A bigger house too," added Hannah.

Georg seemed unusually quiet during the meal, but he was probably just tired from his journey home and all the activity today. A good night's sleep should fix him.

As the conversation wore on, her husband got quieter and quieter.

I don't think he's tired, Hannah thought, something's on his mind. I wonder if it's that letter he had in his saddlebag and when he is going to tell me about it.

Well, the preacher would soon be going out to sleep in the shed, the only place there was room for an extra bed, which was really just a soft pile of hay with warm blankets spread over it. Since it was spring and warm for the season, Reverend Claybaugh had assured them he would be just fine. Hannah would have a chance to finally talk to her husband.

Eventually everything was cleaned up, the children tucked in, the reverend made comfortable, and it was time to retire to their own bed.

Hannah brushed her hair and then deftly braided it so it wouldn't get knotted in the night. She folded the quilt neatly at the end of the bed, all the while waiting for her husband to break the silence. Finally she broke it.

"Georg, why are you so quiet?"

Georg, already in bed by now, stiffened. "Well, how could I say anything? You were busy all evening ordering everyone around, giving directions, telling the boys what to do. You'd think you were the man of the house."

Hannah was speechless. Her fists balled up at her sides, and she took a deep breath. Afraid her husband might interpret her lack of response as an affirmation, she stammered, "I . . . I wasn't trying to order everyone around, I just wanted everything to be perfect for the minister. And I guess you were gone so long on your trip that I got used to telling everyone what to do."

Hurt by the unjust accusation, she burst suddenly into tears, to her own surprise, and judging by his expression, also Georg's.

"I try so hard to do everything the way you want me to," she sobbed. "How can you come home and say those things to me?"

There was no answer. Georg had gone to sleep.

Hannah lay for a long while, wondering how a day that had begun so beautifully ended with them in a fight over something so silly. How could her husband even think she was trying to take over? What would she want with being a father or the head of a house? It was hard enough being everyone's mama. And what in the world was in that envelope Georg had? It looked like it had traveled across the ocean, it was so crumpled and dirty.

Full of questions, Hannah finally gave in to sleep. Her last thoughts were hopeful ones of resolving this the next morning before the minister and all the children woke to find them angry at each other. She and Georg had promised each other the night they were married never go to bed angry at each other, and until today they never had; but here he was just back from a long journey, and she was angry that he made these accusations and then went off to sleep. No doubt he was angry too.

"God," she prayed sleepily, "please help me figure this out. I desperately want to be a good wife, and I don't understand why I keep failing Georg and having these foolish quarrels."

3

Deep Waters

Morning arrived much earlier than Hannah wanted, but at least the rooster wasn't crowing and driving Georg crazy. Her tension from the night before had faded, and she decided maybe she could let the matter rest instead of trying to point out that she hadn't intended to usurp her husband's authority. She was curious about that letter, though, and decided to bring up the subject once breakfast was over. Georg's return meant they had a fresh supply of coffee, and she tiptoed downstairs to stir up the fire and boil some water.

To her surprise, when she finished washing up out at the basin and came back into the cabin, she could smell coffee. Georg was already sitting at the table, running his long fingers around and around on the wood worn smooth by years of use. He looked grim. Did his expression have anything to do with last night's argument, or was something else wrong?

Georg noticed her. He sat up straight and took a deep breath. "Hannah, there's something I have to tell you," he said abruptly. "I wasn't able to sell the lumber at a very good price, and I am not sure we will be able to pay everything that we owe."

Hannah stared at Georg for a minute, unsure she had heard him correctly. "I don't understand. You brought home all those gifts for the children and never said a word all day yesterday. Why did you spend all that money?"

Georg's face darkened, his shoulders tensed, and his jaw clenched. Hannah recognized the signs he hated to discuss this. "I was gone so long, and it seemed like I left so much for you and the children to do, that I wanted to surprise you all. I love seeing everyone's face when I bring presents home. I was so sure I would get a good price that I arranged for my purchases ahead of time." Georg's shoulders slumped now, and his stiff spine seemed to melt before her eyes as he told her the news. Defeat was written all over him.

"Oh, Georg, I can't believe it!" Hannah buried her face in her hands. Against her wishes, her eyes filled with tears. Georg reached across the table and gently pried her hand away from her face. He kissed the tears on her palm and smiled at her perplexed look. "We'll make it, Hannah. You have to trust me."

Just then she heard Daniel whimpering upstairs. Swallowing hard, she ran up to get him.

By the time she returned, Georg had poured the coffee into two old pewter mugs. The handle of hers was so hot, she wouldn't be able to drink it for a while, but her favorite porcelain cup had broken last year, and pewter was all that was left. The older children were up by now too and getting ready for their morning chores.

Samuel, who would rather be outdoors than anywhere else, ran down the stairs. "Father, could we go canoeing today? It's perfect. We had some rain, and the creek is high enough. Please, please, please?"

Hannah was on the verge of forbidding such an expedition when she remembered her determination not even to look like she was taking over. She closed her mouth, waiting for Georg to break the bad news.

"I think that's an excellent idea, I'll go along with you," her spontaneous husband answered.

"But, the water's too high for these boys, and what about the garden, and the circuit rider is still here and . . ." Surely her children were too young for such a trip, even with their father along.

Georg had that firm set to his jaw that meant, "Don't argue with me," and she remembered her resolve for the second time in five minutes. Instead of arguing, she turned her back so she couldn't see her husband, got her cast-iron kettle off the hook, poured water in it, and pushed the hook over the fireplace. It didn't take long to boil, and as she stirred the cornmeal into it slowly so as not to get lumps, she said under her breath," God, please give me grace not to say the wrong thing."

She heard the cabin door bang as Georg headed out for his morning chores and suddenly remembered the letter she had seen the day before.

She was still bursting with curiosity whenever she thought about the envelope. It was true that her husband often told her she was too nosy for her own good, but mail was so rare, it must be something that concerned them both. She waited for the right moment when she knew he would be alone, left the mush to cool, and followed him out to the forge to ask her questions with no children around.

"Georg, when you gave us all gifts, there was a letter that came out of your saddlebag."

He sighed. "What letter are you talking about?"

"The one that was all crumpled, it sort of fell when you got my fabric out, and then I saw you look at the envelope and stuff it back in. Was it important?"

"Hannah, what is this about? Can't you see I have work to do?"

"I thought perhaps you forgot about it, and if it was important, you should tell me about it."

Georg ran his hand through his hair impatiently. "Hannah, that letter was of no concern to you, but since you asked, there are some rumors about a new tax, and some farmers feel the government has taxed us enough already. If this tax is made law, the farmers want to protest, and they also want to know if I will add my voice."

"And will you? I mean, how will it affect our family? Will you be gone again, and can we even afford another tax?"

"I don't know, yes, and maybe yes. Hannah, I don't know yet what will happen. That's why I didn't bother sharing it with you. It could be important, but it may not even become law. No sense bothering you with something that may not ever matter."

"I just wanted to feel more a part of what you think about." Hannah bit her lip in frustration and tried again. "You used to share everything with me. Now I feel like I'm outside, looking in at your choices, yet I have to live your decisions too."

"Life was simpler then. I will let you know if anything much comes of this. Now if you are satisfied, I have a little work to do before breakfast."

Hannah was not satisfied, but seeing this was all she would get out of her husband without angering him, she left the forge, wondering just how much of a man's business should also be his wife's business.

Her cornmeal mush would have cooled enough to eat, so she called everyone to breakfast.

Reverend Claybaugh joined them, and they all poured molasses over their hot mush. Gone were the festive meals of yesterday celebrating a joyous homecoming. The whole farm looked different to Hannah today, grayer somehow, even though the sun was out. After a prayer from the reverend and the reading of a psalm together, the plump circuit rider rubbed his hands together and announced briskly, "Well, I must be off. I have to travel far today. Shall we sing a hymn together?"

Hannah loved to sing and brightened up instantly. "All the children know 'A Mighty Fortress.'"

The Reverend laughed, making his round belly jiggle. "Well, that's a Lutheran hymn for sure. Let's see how good you all are at singing."

The rousing song lightened the atmosphere. When the song was done, the whole crowd of children trooped outside to wave farewell to the preacher and Zaccheus, who looked well rested after his day in the pasture yesterday.

Georg turned to Hannah. "Come on now, we deserve a little rest, don't you think? Everyone worked hard while I was gone, and yesterday they all worked hard again. What could one day of canoeing hurt?"

Unable to argue with that logic, Hannah returned to the house to pack some venison jerky left from winter. It was time to use it up anyway, and it would make an easy lunch.

Benjamin was a pretty good shot with a bow. Maybe he could bring it with him and shoot some squirrels along the way. There was nothing quite as tasty as squirrel in broth with potatoes and thick homemade noodles.

"Just who all is going with you?" Hannah couldn't decide if she was glad Georg was spending time with the boys or disappointed that he didn't want to work around the farm and spend the day with her.

"I guess Benjamin, Samuel, Hans, and Frederick," her husband replied. "With me along, that will fill the canoe."

Johann instantly started wailing. "I want to go with Papa too."

"Hush," said Clara. "You're too little and you know it. How many five-year-olds can paddle canoes anyway?"

"I could just sit real still while Papa paddles," sniffed Johann, but there was no more room in the canoe. Disappointed, he shuffled out to sit on the step and gloomily watch his brothers get ready for the expedition.

The cheery creek just down the hill from their farmhouse would be swift today after all the rain. The spring that their house sat over bubbled downhill into a runnel and gathered the trickles of several smaller streams before joining the creek, which then wound around for several miles and emptied into the Susquehanna River. It was a nice length for a day trip with young boys.

The boys carried the canoe with Georg giving a helping hand and carrying the lunch as well, and they all waved energetically as they walked down the path. Hannah waved in reply, although not with as much enthusiasm, and then went inside.

There was enough cream by now for another attempt at butter, so she took the pan of skimmings and poured it into the churn. "Magdalena, come here, please. It's time you learned how to make butter," she commanded the chubby dark-haired six-year-old hovering near the door.

Magdalena never hesitated. Her round little face beamed with delight. "Oh, Mama, of course. I want to show Papa how much I can help. I'm growing up."

Hannah laughed. Six was far from grown-up, and making butter lost its appeal quickly, but today it would be done cheerfully. That job assigned, Hannah turned her attention to the remaining children.

Clara took charge of Johann. "We can go look at Peaches and make sure all the piglets are doing well. Margaret, you come too. I'll hold your hand."

With everyone busy at least for a few minutes, Hannah set Daniel on top of the table so she could sweep the floor while she watched over him. He couldn't go anywhere that way, and he was at the age where someone had to be with him at all times to keep him safe.

"Mama loves you," she said and kissed his fat cheek before grabbing the broom from its hook behind the door.

The morning passed swiftly. Magdalena soon tired of churning, and Hannah took over, salting the butter when it was done and pressing it into the wooden mold Georg had carved for her some years before. She set the butter and the buttermilk back into the trough for the spring water to keep cool and took the younger children outside to shell peas. Everyone was soon laughing and eating more peas than they shelled as Hannah told them stories to make the job more fun until finally no one was even hungry for the noon meal.

When the peas were finished, Hannah took them inside. The cabin seemed dimmer than usual today. Perhaps it was time to think about making new candles. On the other hand, the sun was so bright outside and the air was fresh smelling as only late spring air could be.

"I think we deserve a break today too," she told the children, bringing the two milk pails back outside. "Let's go see if the wild strawberries are ripe yet."

"Hooray!" shouted four young voices, while the smallest voice piped up, "I luff stwabewies," and everybody laughed as they set off up the hill to the pasture to hunt along the stone fencerows for the wild strawberries.

All the pastureland lay on the side of a mountain, where over the years, men and boys had gathered the stones from the pasture area and piled them in rows along the borders. Picking rocks, the children called it, and every spring, new rocks seemed to ooze out of the ground and wait for a day when one of the children said, "I'm bored." Then everyone got sent off to pick rocks. By now, a two-foot-high wall meandered along the north end of the pasture, and wild strawberry plants grew all over the ground and crept up the wall.

Hannah was careful to keep one ear open while they picked. There were still black bears in the area, and they were just as fond of berries as her children were.

Several hours of hunting rewarded them with a pail full of small wild berries in all shades of red, scratches everywhere because berries hid close to the wild roses, and a thirst for a cold glass of buttermilk. With a last glance at the profusion of white blooms from the wild roses, everyone set off for the cabin. Reaching home was quicker than setting out for picking because everyone could run downhill.

Daniel stayed with Hannah, who was carrying the berries so they wouldn't spill in the wild race and had one hand free for the toddler. Before they were halfway down the hill, Hannah heard shrieking off to the left.

"Magdalena, stop! Don't move!"

"Oh no," whispered Hannah, hurrying to see what the danger was. "Please don't let it be a snake."

A few more steps brought her around the edge of the rosebushes, where Magdalena was in full view. Not fifteen feet away loomed a massive black bear looking right at her. The other children, further down the hill, had frozen. Clara looked anxiously at her mother, and Hannah motioned them to go down the hill, knowing Clara would go slowly and not alarm the bear. Hannah still had Daniel by one hand. The only question was how to get the bear to leave without causing Magdalena to panic. She could see her shaking.

"Daniel," she murmured, "go around to Clara, very carefully. Shhhh. Don't let that bear see you."

Hoping the bear's attention was firmly on Magdalena, she put the toddler down and bent over gradually, keeping her eyes on the bear all the while. She picked up a large stick up in one hand, and grasping the berry pail firmly in the other, she inched her way toward her daughter.

"Don't move until I yell," Hannah spoke calmly and clearly, "then run to the cabin as fast as you can."

Magdalena barely nodded her head, and Hannah crept closer. When she thought she was near enough to distract the bear, she began screaming and banging the pail with the branch. The bear turned his attention upon her, Magdalena suddenly took off running, and the bear began to amble toward the source of the noise. With all her strength, Hannah threw the pail at the bear. It came close enough to rain berries all around, and when the bear stopped to investigate the tasty smell, Hannah bent low to the ground and headed down the hill. Circling around where the bear had been, she stood up and could see Clara with Daniel in hand and Magdalena close behind them. Looking back despite her fear, she saw the bear still eating berries, and she found speed to close the distance between her and the children. Tripping and falling, they fled down the hill, ran into the cabin, and slammed the door.

She leaned against the door, her chest heaving, and made sure all her children were inside.

The bear was probably long gone, and now one of her good pails was gone too. As the shock wore off and thankfulness for their safe return set in, so did the tears. All the girls were crying, most everybody was scraped from falling in the headlong flight, they had no berries, and Hannah had lost her milk pail.

The fear of the last half hour suddenly turned to anger at the stress of the last several weeks.

"I wish Papa hadn't gone away today. We should never have gone berry picking without someone with a gun. I'll be right back," she said through her tears. "Don't anybody go outside until I come back down." She flung off her apron and stormed up the steps to her room, shut the door, and fell onto the bed. She rarely had the luxury of a good cry, but this time she couldn't contain the sobs that racked her body. At last her weeping gave way to hiccups. She felt drained and empty except for an occasional sniffle and a few last trickles down her cheeks.

When she finally cried herself out, she sat up and listened for the children. It sounded like Clara was telling stories, so she picked up her Bible and opened it to one of her favorite psalms, the eighteenth. "For thou wilt light my candle: the Lord my God will enlighten my darkness . . . . It is God that girdeth me with strength, . . ." *This is what I need to remember. God is my strength.* She wiped her face with her dusty sleeve and went downstairs to wash her face and regroup. Tomorrow one of the big boys could go out and get her pail. The bear would be long gone. Surely things weren't as bad as she felt right now. The children all looked up as she came down, but no one seemed as upset as she had been, so she simply washed up and retied her apron around her waist in preparation for the rest of the evening.

"I'd better think about supper," Hannah remarked, trying to keep her voice natural.

"Your papa and brothers may be returning soon. Magdalena, go gather the eggs, I am going to make a big bunch of noodles. Hopefully they'll bring home some squirrels, and tomorrow we can have pot pie. Tonight we can just eat the soup that I made from the leftover rooster. By tomorrow my noodles will be dry enough for cooking."

A dozen eggs combined with flour from the barrel and a little salt made a dough that rolled out into thick, delicious noodles that Hannah had seen many German housewives make when she and Georg had first met. The dish they called pot pie was more like a thick meat, potato, and noodle stew; but it was filling, and her whole family was glad she had learned to make it.

The soup was hot by now and smelled enticing. The sun was low in the sky. Coming out of the cabin, Hannah looked to her right and scarcely had to shade her eyes. The clouds piled up against the hills, diffused the harsh rays, and gave the air a pink tint. It would be a beautiful sunset, but where were the boys? She needed one of them to chop some kindling for her. If Georg hadn't been home, she never would have let them go canoeing right after a big rain when the creek was so full. What was he thinking anyway?

She sighed and decided she'd better chop the kindling herself. If her men were too much later, all the chores would need to be done, they would forget about chopping wood, and by morning, she might not have a fire to cook with. "Boys," she sighed and trudged up the hill to the barn to find a small ax that she could handle.

That chore completed, she stirred the soup, checked again to make sure Daniel hadn't escaped from Clara's watchful eye, and brought her pen and paper out into the late-afternoon sunshine to write a few lines while she waited for her men folk to return. It did seem women were always waiting for men, but perhaps that was just the way life was.

"May 1798," she wrote again.

Dear Emily,

I'm so thankful Georg is back, but honestly it seems like all we do is spar at each other with words. I want to do things one way; he does them another. Georg thinks women don't need to bother about business matters, but Emily, this is my home and family as much as his. Why wouldn't I be concerned?

I hope tonight he and I can talk; and I'm going to pray for grace not to speak my mind but just listen. I do think God could help me with that. I had to bite my tongue so many times today before they left to go canoeing—with the water so high! I want to be the best wife I can to Georg, but there are days I think I really could give some good advice, and if I do, we immediately get into an argument.

I took the little children berry picking, and Magdalena was almost attacked by a bear. Now don't tell Mother, she would weep so, and I already did all the weeping when we got back safely. When Georg hears, he will be furious with me for forgetting a weapon. It seems like when he is gone, I miss him so I can hardly stand it; and when he is home, we find everything to fight about. He just got home, I cannot have fighting already.

I wish you were here to tell me I'm a good wife. There are no other women around close to us to tell me whether I'm doing this job right. I need some old grandmother here to tell me how she did it back when she was a young married lady.

Oh, listen to me go on. I'm going to feed the little ones, and now that I wrote all this down, I feel better. I love you, Emily. Maybe next year, we'll have enough saved up that I can come and visit you.

Folding her letter up, she went slowly back into the cabin, climbed the steps to her room, and replaced the letter in the wooden box where she kept her pens and ink and small supply of paper.

The children were already gathered around the table. "Clara, thanks so much for setting out the bowls. You are so grown up lately. I didn't even have to ask."

"Well, everyone was so hungry, Mama, I thought you probably weren't going to wait anymore for the boys."

"No, I'm not. We have soup, and they'll just have to get theirs when they get back. Daniel, this is hot, so let it cool first."

"Hot, hot," said Daniel cheerfully. He loved to eat, and his plump hands and feet were evidence of that fact. He waved his wooden spoon around in the air. "Hot, hot."

The other four children blew on their soup and began hungrily slurping it up before Hannah stopped them. "Don't you think we should stop and thank God that we are all safe and we have food to eat?" she reproved them. "I know Papa and most everyone else are gone, but we are still thankful."

"We're sorry." Johann's blue eyes filled immediately with tears. "We were so hungry, we forgot."

"I'm sure God understands." Hannah smiled. "Now don't cry. It's my fault dinner is so late. I was waiting for the others, but let's just enjoy the soup, and they'll be back soon."

Before they were done eating, it was close enough to dusk to light the candles. Summer was on the way, and they would go to bed when darkness fell, but spring still brought a need for candles before all the chores were done.

Hannah wondered where the men folk were so long. She hoped it was a good day of hunting that brought them home so late; she kept her worries to herself because she didn't want to alarm the children with other possibilities. She ran upstairs to her chest and gave Magdalena one of their few books, given her by her father. "It's your turn," she told the six-year-old. "You can practice reading aloud. Johann and Margaret can listen, Daniel can sit up here on top of the table, and Clara and I will clean up the dishes."

Magdalena hadn't stumbled through more than three sentences when the sound of horses' hoofs on the track outside caught Hannah's attention. Who in the world would be coming at this hour? She could hear the excited voices of several people. Actually, some of those voices sounded like her boys. Grabbing up Daniel from the tabletop, she opened the door and stepped onto the porch, followed by the four other children. Sure enough, here came all her boys in a wagon. Georg and someone she couldn't make out in the dusk were walking next to the horse, and the canoe was perched on top of the wagon. The tight knot in her stomach unclenched as she counted all the heads.

When the smaller children realized a stranger was along, they turned instantly shy and ran back inside, causing Hannah to smile and then turn to her late arrivals. Whatever had happened, they were all together. Her children drowning in the creek was one of her worst fears. She hugged each of the boys hard, and then lightly shook Benjamin's shoulders. "I was so worried about you," she scolded. "You're so late. Don't you think about us at home waiting?"

"Hannah, enough!" said Georg brusquely. "We are all here, and we are exhausted. This is Martin Reitz. He was on his way to Fort Augusta and stopped to give us a ride. It's too late tonight to make it that far. Can we give him some supper and a bed?"

"Of course we can." Hannah regretted her angry words instantly. "Welcome, Martin. I'm sorry to greet you all in such a manner. I've been fretting for hours about my family."

She put her hands on her hips and glared at Georg's back as he turned to hug Magdalena, who was pulling his arm and loudly proclaiming, "Papa, Papa, I made the butter."

Martin, a tall, thin, blond fellow topped with a crumpled felt hat, stepped forward, touched his hat, and then swept it off his head. "It's not a problem," he said. "I have a wife too, and she worries about me as well."

Glad to have a little sympathy for her distress, Hannah smiled slowly. "We just have soup tonight, but it's hot still. I kept it close to the fire. Come on in everybody. Did you bring me any squirrels?"

Benjamin, who had been talking quietly to Clara, jumped guiltily and ran over to the wagon. "They're already cleaned, Mama. Maybe we should boil them tonight so they don't get bad."

"Nonsense, I'll put them in a dish and set them in the spring tonight, and tomorrow we'll have pot pie." Chilly, wet fur brushed her hands. "Why are these squirrels soaking wet?"

Uneasily, Frederick and Hans glanced at each other.

"They fell in the water," Samuel blurted out. "We all did."

Even though it was dark by now, Hannah noticed Hans kick Samuel on the leg, and he fell silent. Hmmm, she thought, there's a story here that I need to hear about, but not when there's a stranger standing outside my door.

"Come on in," she said again. "Let me put the bowls out before you all starve to death."

Once again the kitchen was full of life, excited voices, the clunk of wooden spoons on bowls, men talking, Daniel fussing since it was way past his bedtime; and Hannah in the center, serving soup, and wondering all the while what had happened on the expedition. From the looks of things, she would have to find out tomorrow. Johann was falling asleep in his chair, and Hans looked ready to slide off the side of his. He could barely keep his eyes open as he shoveled the soup in. Daniel was so sleepy that he had gotten silly and was dancing round and round the little kitchen, jumping up and down and making the girls laugh.

"Time for bed," she finally ordered. "We'll just have to wash up tomorrow. Martin, Georg can show you the shed. There's a bed out there and a washbasin. The outhouse is up the hill, and please, just make yourself at home."

Finally all was still, and Hannah and Georg made their own tired way to bed. Once again Hannah's questions were unanswered. She hadn't dared bring up the subject of bears, but as she drifted off to sleep, wrapped in Georg's strong arms, she determined to ferret out some answers and make things right in the morning.

4

TROUBLING NEWS

Gray, thought Hannah when she woke next morning. She shivered and noticed no bright May sunlight escaping past her faded calico curtains. No matter, gray suited her mood anyway. She had been so exhausted when she went to bed the night before that she determined to sleep until someone demanded her attention. She had awoken briefly earlier this morning, thinking to wake up Benjamin for the milking. When she heard him creep downstairs and heard the *clink clank* of the milk pail, she knew things were under control and rolled over for a few more minutes of rest.

And now what time was it? She couldn't remember hearing the clock chime. The house was quiet, but Georg wasn't in bed. She couldn't smell anything cooking. All the children were probably still worn-out. Suddenly she sat straight up in bed. They had company out in the shed. Martin was probably being polite and waiting for the family to awaken, but he had to get to Fort Augusta on whatever his business was, and he would probably like breakfast first. What kind of farmer's wife slept in late anyway? There were always things for her to do.

She jumped out of bed and threw on her wrinkled dress, which reminded her it was past washday.

Every Monday she built a fire in the yard, and the bigger boys helped her put the large cast-iron butchering kettle over the fire and filled it with water. Georg had returned Sunday night. Monday they were so busy with presents and the circuit rider, and then yesterday, the canoeing trip.

Whatever was she thinking these days? Every day had a routine so all the work was done by the end of Saturday—and she had just spent two days falling behind. It was a wonder any of them had clothes to wear. Most likely they were all in dirty clothing since hardly anyone had more than two work or play outfits. Frustration at her forgetfulness stirred in her. She would get started on the wash as soon as the children were fed. And now to find everyone.

No one seemed to be downstairs in the cabin, but she could hear giggling outside. She cracked the door open and peeked out. Sure enough, there were Georg and Martin. Now she was embarrassed that her guest knew she overslept. The children were all clustered around their daddy, who had built a big fire out where they heated the wash water. He was skillfully frying eggs in their largest iron skillet. Every child had a plate, and they were eating eggs as fast as he could fry them.

Georg shouted cheerfully, "Who wants a dippy egg? Here are a couple hard ones. Anybody like scrambled?"

Right next to Martin on the ground was the coffeepot, and there were three mugs, so they were counting on her. Annoyed with herself for being annoyed, Hannah went resolutely out to join them, mentally preparing herself for being teased about her sleeping habits.

Georg smiled gently, which flustered her further. He never said a word about her lack of hospitality but simply acted as if he always made breakfast for the family.

"Here's your coffee, Mama," he said with a smile and a little bow. "Frederick, pull up a log for your mother to sit on so she can join us."

Hannah took her coffee, grateful it gave her something to do while she pondered Georg's good mood and her thankfulness that breakfast was underway. Perhaps she wasn't as indispensable as her children seemed to think.

The children were still eating eggs as if they were starving, and Georg handed Hannah a plate with a smile. "Sorry, the children devoured the last biscuits. Don't you feed them when I'm not home?"

"Well, you know boys." Hannah smiled back. "They eat like it's the last meal they'll ever see." She attacked her own eggs then, and a peaceful silence fell over the group.

Martin hitched his horses up immediately after breakfast, saying he had business in Fort Augusta that couldn't wait.

"There's an inn up the road if you have trouble and are delayed again," said Georg. "It's called Penn's Tavern, and it's right along the river where the ferry comes over from the west."

"Thanks, but I have to arrive today." Martin clucked to his horses and rattled out of the farmyard.

"Here it is Wednesday already," said Hannah briskly. "Georg, could we talk a little while the boys get the wash water ready? I didn't wash on Monday, and soon there will be nothing clean left."

"Hop to it lads," ordered their papa. "Your mama has much to do and so do we."

He got up and stretched his lanky frame. He had never filled out, probably due to his continual hard work, and he was still handsome even after fourteen years of marriage and life on the farm. Gathering up the pewter mugs, he carried them toward the door, and Hannah followed with the frying pan, leaving Clara to bring the plates and Magdalena to watch Daniel.

"Now," said Georg firmly, "sit down and I will try to explain about my trip to Philadelphia before I forget it even happened. I had no news of your family. I know your father often travels that way, but of all the people I saw, no one had seen him for a while. He is getting older so maybe he's not traveling so much, but don't fret. If there had been any bad news, your family would make sure we heard of it."

"I know that," said Hannah. "I just hoped maybe someone would have had a letter for me. So many store owners know we moved out here, and they often keep letters until someone is heading this direction. And what about the lumber? You worked so hard cutting trees and hauling logs and loading the wagon. Why didn't you make much? I thought lumber prices were high and lumber was in demand for all the building."

She jumped up again. "You talk while I scrub these dishes, or I'll never be ready for the washing."

"Sit down, Hannah!" Georg commanded. "I can see you are frustrated, but washing dishes while I talk makes me feel like you aren't even listening."

Hannah sat and twisted her apron into little rolls and pleats while trying to listen, and all the while her thoughts were racing about trying to figure out ways to solve the problems before them.

"First of all," said Georg, "the trip took so long because the roads are especially bad right now. Some of them are nothing more than cart tracks, and other areas further east have gotten so much rain that they are more swamp than track. I know Pennsylvania is supposed to have the best roads of anywhere in this new country, but on this trip I was beginning to doubt it.

"The wagon was so heavy with all the lumber that I actually left the horses at a farm I passed and borrowed their oxen. They pulled the weight better, but they are also a lot slower, and these oxen didn't know me so they caused me quite a bit of effort to keep them going."

"So that was another expense?" asked Hannah.

"No, I suggested to the fellow where I left the horses that we just exchange animals until I returned. Our horses are fine for plowing and lighter work, so he had the use of them both while I used the oxen."

"Thank goodness for that. I don't think we could afford to have the trip cost any more."

"Then," Georg continued, "four fellows came into town right when I did. They all had lumber they had cut from land they were clearing.

The other two times I've gone, I brought all the lumber there was, so I could ask more. Also, there is some sickness going around, and it seems building has slowed up. There are even families leaving the city while they wait for it to pass."

Hannah caught her breath. "Oh, you didn't meet up with anyone who was sick, did you? We are not prepared for illness. What is going around?"

Georg shrugged. "Some are saying it's the yellow fever, but it's not been there long, and people frighten too easily. In any case, I couldn't get the price we had counted on."

Before the discussion could go any further, Magdalena and Margaret ran in.

"Mama," they cried in unison, and then they both giggled.

"The water is boiling," said nine-year-old Hans, coming in behind the girls. "They were racing to see who could tell you first. And I found a hen clucking on a nest of eggs in back of the old hay. Do you want her to hatch them out, or should I collect them all?"

"That hen's been missing for almost three weeks now." said Hannah thoughtfully. "The eggs are probably about ready to hatch, and we surely don't want to eat eggs that have been under a hen that long."

"Eeuuu," cried Margaret, wrinkling up her little nose. "I can't even think about that. Remember last spring when Samuel found all those eggs and they were rotten?"

"Well, these won't be rotten," said Hannah. "They will be new hens for me when some of these hens I have now are too old to lay eggs. Just leave her alone, and as soon as they hatch out, we'll put her in the coop so hawks don't get the little ones. Good work, Hans."

Hans beamed all over his round face, and his dark eyes shone. He ran out as quickly as he had run in.

"Well," said Hannah, "it seems there's never enough time to tell me all the news. I know we've used up all our money, and while bartering works fine with our neighbors, I am still wondering how you bought gifts—and wouldn't it have been better to use what little we had to bring down some debt? Having all this debt scares me. What if the crops do poorly, and what if we need something before the crops are in?"

Georg bristled. "I told you yesterday that I was gone so long, I wanted to reward the children for their hard work. And you, I brought you fabric. Didn't you like it?"

"Of course I did, and you know it," Hannah retorted. He wasn't going to make her feel guilty that easily when she was in the right.

"Since I am the one cutting and hauling trees, I think I can decide how to spend some of my labor. This discussion is over."

Hannah frowned. Their money discussions always ended this way. She might as well not start them. Gathering up her basket of muddy aprons, petticoats, breeches, and stockings, she retreated out to the fire and began battering the clothes up and down on the washboard.

Georg stared after her awhile and then shrugged his shoulders.

"Women," he said to no one in particular as he passed the wash pot and went out to the pigpen to see how Peaches's piglets were coming along.

Once her clothes were beaten thoroughly, Hannah spread them out over the bushes by the house to dry in the sun and set Johann nearby to keep birds and bugs away and make sure no breezes blew away some item she had worked hard to make and could ill afford to lose.

Daniel was taking a nap by now, so she snatched up her basket of quilt patches and dragged her rocking chair outside, up the hill, and under the apple tree. There she could sew, keep an eye on the children, think about their situation, and maybe even calm down enough to enjoy the late spring sunshine.

The gray of the morning had given way to bright blue skies and even a soft breeze. The apple trees were still in bloom; their delicate fragrance surrounded her, and the peacefulness of sitting outside under flowering trees slowly began to work its magic. Hannah sat still, fingering her quilt.

Everyone seemed cheerful doing work except her. On the other hand, no one else knew what having no money meant to the family.

Georg probably knew, but he seemed oblivious to the whole matter and never took her premonitions seriously.

Realizing she was making no progress, she stabbed her needle up and down through her patches and rocked violently. The last several days had been so up and down for her. She needed some time for events to smooth out and life to resume its steady, even pace. Then she would be ready to deal with this news. She had the nagging thought that perhaps she should pray, but she was too angry to do it.

Maybe she should make some mental notes of their condition, and her perspective would be restored.

They had the farm. Over three hundred acres belonged to them, enough to farm and give some to the boys as they grew up if they didn't decide to move farther west like many she heard about these days. They had two good plow horses and an old but sturdy plow. They had their Conestoga wagon, which made hauling timber a good venture—providing every man in the state didn't haul his timber to the city the same week. They had two guns now that Benjamin had gotten one, so they should have plenty of venison and other game to dry for jerky over the winter as well as fresh meat. They had a big garden, and their spring was strong; so even if it didn't rain much, they could haul water and keep things growing. They had clothing to wear. Much of it was patched but serviceable enough until winter if they were careful and the boys didn't get too rough.

On the other hand, they had borrowed money from Georg's family to purchase this farm, and he was supposed to make payments on a regular basis. Even family expected one to keep up with agreements. Money was scarce everywhere and the loan of it was like a gift. They never could have bought this farm without help. Bartering was useful, but they had an obligation to get some cash somehow or they wouldn't be able to keep the farm—and then where would they be? Who would have a place for nine children if their life remained on its current course?

Of course, some of the boys were old enough to be apprentices, but it was unthinkable to her to let them leave the family already even if it was a common enough practice. That was one reason she had agreed to move here so many years ago. It seemed the best way to keep everyone together.

Then too, if there was yellow fever in Philadelphia, no one would be thinking of building. When such an illness struck, as many as possible left the town, usually until fall or winter halted the spread of disease. So the cutting of timber might be a wasted effort. There weren't any towns large enough to sell one's lumber in any closer. Georg could spend his time here, then, getting the farm back in order.

Hannah suddenly began to feel like an ocean wave, tossed this way and that. Maybe it was better not to think so much. There was nothing she could do today anyway.

Suddenly a new thought struck her. No one had explained yet why the canoe had returned in a wagon or late or why all the canoers were soaking wet. There was something here that the boys were keeping from her. Hannah quickly decided that Benjamin was most likely to give her a straight answer if she asked questions the right way. She would have to be careful how she asked about the trip because none of them would want to betray their Papa if Georg had told them to keep quiet.

Hannah jumped to her feet. She had sat here thinking long enough. It was time to cook the squirrels for pot pie, and if she could find Benjamin she would get some answers. Plus, she hadn't spent any time at all today reading her Bible. Maybe that was her problem. She often found comfort in her reading and it was the best way she had found so far to quiet her spirit when she felt such unrest. That and singing hymns to the cow, but it was too early for milking.

Returning her quilting to the sewing basket, she set it on the seat of her rocker and carried everything back to the cabin in a better frame of mind than when she had dragged it out. She stirred up the fire again. It was hot enough to cook outside. The squirrels were put on a spit and Frederick agreed to turn them while she cut the potatoes and pulled an onion out of the garden.

It didn't take long for the smell of roasting meat and potatoes and onions boiling to bring the children around.

"It's not time to eat yet," said Hannah firmly, "but there is plenty of time to do some reading. We haven't spent much time doing sums either, the past couple days. You children have all been on holiday and it is time to get back into our routines before you forget everything I've taught you. Samuel, run inside and get the Bible. Everyone can take a turn reading aloud while we turn the meat."

Obediently, Samuel ran indoors and Hannah realized with a start how tall he was getting. With his blond hair, he looked more and more like Benjamin. He soon returned, reverently carrying the big Bible back outdoors where everyone was gathered.

"Let's try Proverbs," he said. "There are not so many big words there."

"Very well, start right at the first chapter. While you read, I want to talk to Benjamin."

Benjamin's face fell immediately and Hannah knew she had picked the right person to question. He couldn't be dishonest if he tried, his face always gave away guilt, and he did try very hard to be an honest young man. He left the spit and followed Hannah up the hill behind the cabin to the chicken coop where they stood admiring Hannah's plump red hens, out of reach of any interested ears.

"I guess you know what I'm going to ask you?'

"Well, maybe," Benjamin replied reluctantly.

"Yesterday, you came home soaking wet, your papa was wet, and the squirrels were wet. You can't hide that from me." She was angry now, the anxiety of their late return catching up suddenly with her questions and making her voice harsh.

"Well, there was a little problem. You know where the creek bends and the banks are steep?"

At her uncertain look, he hesitated. "Where we swim in summer when it's dry."

"You mean where it gets so deep in spring?"

"Ummmm, yes, well, a tree fell over the creek, and the current was so fast. Are you going to tell Papa I told you this? He'll be so angry at me."

"I don't know yet," said Hannah. "Please just tell me what happened."

"Papa said we should learn how to paddle right, so Samuel and I were paddling. When the water got fast and deep, Papa didn't have time to get one of the paddles from us. We couldn't keep away from the log, and the canoe got stuck, then the current tipped it up, and we all went in the water. I was hanging on the log, but Samuel, he got sucked under the water, and Papa had to try four times before he could pull him out. Then we had to pound him to get him to spit out all the water."

"And just where were Frederick and Hans while this was going on?" She was surprised at how under control she felt. Maybe she should be screaming at somebody, but who was at fault?

"They were holding on the canoe," Benjamin answered. Now that he had started telling the story, it all spilled out. "Papa got Samuel over to the bank, and then he got them, and then he helped me swim over too. After we rested a little, Papa and I swam back to the middle and got the canoe tipped back upright. Before we left, we had tied everything down to the thwarts, even the squirrels, so even though it was all wet, everything was safe. That's because Papa is careful when we go out, and I don't think this was his fault."

No, thought Hannah, he just encouraged the idea. She would have forbidden it yesterday. Well, she could thank God they were all safe. If she could just figure out how to deal with all the turbulent emotions she was feeling. One or all of them could have drowned, and her whole life would be different today. A shiver ran down her spine as she contemplated the upheaval if one of her children had not come home last night. Suddenly, she felt like she couldn't deal with these thoughts at all and tried to shove them to the back of her mind.

"Where did you meet Martin, then?"

"We portaged the canoe downstream, partly because the water was so high and partly because Papa said the work would warm us up. The creek was so chilly. Anyway, where the cart track curves around, we saw Mr. Reitz. He was passing by on his way north to Fort Augusta and when he saw how wet and tired we were, he turned back and offered to bring us home, and then it was so late, that's why he stayed over."

Hannah shook her head and felt the tension knot her shoulders. Just relax, she told herself. They all came home safely.

"I'm just thankful you are all safe. I should have heard this last night. I won't speak of this to your father just yet. I'm too upset and I can't think about what happened. Thanks for being honest with me." She gave Benjamin a quick hug. He hugged her back awkwardly and they both headed back toward the cabin.

She noticed then that Benjamin was getting taller too. At only thirteen, he was ready to pass her up in height. Everyone was growing so quickly. Soon there would be men in her family instead of boys. She hoped she was ready for this change.

Benjamin's voice would change next and her sweet firstborn baby would disappear forever. The man he was becoming looked to be a good one but he had so much to learn yet. Georg never seemed to have these doubts about his ability to raise young men. Maybe she was just lacking some confidence today.

She stopped, took a deep breath, and looked about her. There was beauty on every side. There were bright green hills to the southeast and behind her. Her father called them mountains but his family was from Holland where everything was flat. Georg, who had seen mountains in Europe when he was a young boy, assured her that these were hills.

In any case, the old trees were covered with young leaves. The pasture was greener every day. The grazing cattle looked content. Now that the grass was up, they weren't bawling with hunger every morning. The chickens scratched and pecked happily as well. There were plenty of bugs to go around as summer approached. No, she had nothing to complain about. Life was good. Sure they had money worries but what settler around here didn't. And all her children were healthy. She should spend more time being grateful.

After checking on the progress of the roasting squirrels, she went indoors, bringing the Bible in with her. Placing it back in its place of honor on their dresser, she thought again of Emily and her letter. It was time to finish that epistle so the next passerby could speed it on its way. Giving her unruly hair a quick brush and rewinding and pinning it up on her head, she grabbed the letter with one hand and her favorite quill with the other. Georg had forgotten to bring her ink, but she could make ink with soot from the fireplace and some of the apple cider vinegar still left from last fall. It wasn't nearly as nice to write with, but it was better than not writing.

> Emily, I am trying to finish this quickly. Georg said there is sickness in Philadelphia. Father always knew when to keep us close to home. He seemed to have some sort of instinct that way.
>
> Life isn't as rosy as I thought it was when I wrote the other day. The trip went badly, and there was hardly any profit. I hope Georg bartered something for our gifts instead of using credit, but as you know, cash is still so hard to come by. When I asked, he said he handled the finances, and it wasn't a wife's business to meddle. I am truly getting worried. He works and works, and things don't always go as one plans, especially on a farm where we must depend not only on our own skills but the weather as well. I think we are sinking deeper and deeper into quicksand, and I see no way out.

Then there is that "mysterious letter" as I call it. I have been told I'm too curious, so maybe I should forget that I saw it, but it could affect all of our family.

Emily, I know you can't do anything about these things, but somehow just writing about them makes me feel better, and I do talk to God about it too.

Remember how Mother used to always say, "Tell God, He cares for little girls too"? Sometimes I wish I were still a little girl and life was easy.

After I heard all the news about the failed trip, I found out, by some careful questioning of Benjamin, that the reason the boys got home so late from their canoeing trip was due to an accident. My heart almost stopped as he told me about it.

These boys are growing into men and take these things in stride, but I am still Mama with little ones hanging on my skirts, and I am not ready for this. I was always the one to tell them how to behave and what to do when Georg was gone. Now they feel as if they are old enough to make their own choices, and some of those choices are not safe.

Emily, I just feel like I am not ready for these changes. You know me, I never liked change anyway, even good changes. I feel frightened when I should be excited to have more men in the family to help Georg.

On the other hand, there are mornings when I wake up and feel desperate, like I must do

something to fix our problems. It weighs on me
so. I know its Georg's responsibility, but what if
I came home and took up work as a seamstress?
I could never ask Father for a loan, and I did
make this choice to marry Georg, who I love, but
I can't stop what I see—we are sliding into a pit
on this farm, and I don't know if we can climb
back out.

I'm sorry, Emily, to burden you with these
crazy thoughts. Why don't you just pray for us
here in Pennsylvania, and I will try not to complain
so much.

How are things in New York? Are Molly and
Betsy still close to you since they've gotten
married? And you, Emily, when are you and William
going to decide to get married? He's been courting
you for ever so long. Do write and tell me all
about the things I know and love back home, and
I will sit under my apple tree and picture you all.

I do love my husband and my life, so please
don't worry about me. Now I am putting this letter
safely into a packet. If anyone comes on a trip east,
I want to send this to you. I love you, Emily.
    Hannah

5

YELLOW FEVER

The end of May arrived swiftly. Bees buzzed everywhere. Now that they were done pollinating the fruit trees, they had moved into the garden to do their work among the plants.

The clover was in full purple bloom in the pasture, keeping the cattle happy and the milk sweet. In early May, the pastures were full of wild garlic and the children were much fonder of milk when the cows ate clover than garlic.

The peas were over, but the potatoes were growing well and today the children were all outside making mounds of dirt along the potato rows before the next anticipated rain storm. As with so many of the garden chores, no one was thrilled with mounding potatoes in the warm sun, but the anticipation of plenty to eat in winter and the threat of Papa's displeasure kept them at it.

Hannah had the wash done and hanging on the line Georg had finally strung for her between the cabin and the outhouse. She loved the smell of clean clothes when they were brought in at night and Clara helped her fold them up. Nothing was better than climbing into a bed with fresh sheets that smelled of sunshine and green grass.

Their hay field had grown so quickly this year that Georg had gone out to see if it was ready to cut.

"It looks as if we could get three cuttings of hay this year," he had told her just this morning. "That's a sure way for this farm to make some money."

Making hay involved everyone in the family, and any passersby were pressed into service also if at all possible. The hay had to be cut with scythes and then raked. It needed to dry and be turned over with rakes several times to ensure that it dried everywhere. Hay that was piled up damp could mold and catch fire later on, destroying all the work and possibly barns as well.

All of this took several days, and then it had to be loaded onto the wagon with pitchforks and stored out of the weather until it was needed in winter to feed the animals. If a thunderstorm blew up in the middle of the process, it would ruin the hay crop, and then they would have to hope for the second cutting to go better. The hay also needed to be cut before it went to seed, as it got tough and the cattle didn't care to eat it.

Hannah usually left a child watching Daniel and helped in the fields too, unless it was close to mealtime. In hay season, she would fry eggs and put them between two pieces of bread as a sandwich and carry a huge platter out to the pasture so the workers wasted little time with a meal. The smaller children took turns carrying a bucket of water back and forth, since making hay was thirsty work.

Hannah thought this would be a good week for hay if the clover was tall enough. It looked to be dry all week, and today was only Monday. They could get their two fields done by Friday or Saturday if all went smoothly.

Sitting outside on a stump, drinking a late morning cup of coffee, Hannah enjoyed the sun on her hair as she watched the children at play. Hans and Johann had dug a pile of dirt, and Daniel was happily digging in it, pretending to be a bird catching worms under the indulgent eyes of Margaret and Magdalena.

The older children were about done with the potato mounds. Hannah knew they would soon be looking for a cool drink. Her trip inside for water was interrupted when the sound of galloping hooves to the north made her look up suddenly. A man she had never seen before was coming from the direction of Penn's Tavern. The ferry stopped there, and perhaps there was news from further west. There were scarcely any Indian problems in this area anymore, so she didn't think it would be anyone bringing warnings of uprisings.

"Whoa." The rider jerked his horse to a sudden stop as he caught sight of Hannah. "I'm looking for a family by the name of Zartman around this area. Would you know where they live?"

"We're the Zartmans," Hannah answered, "but there are other families of that name in the area. Which Zartmans?"

"Hannah Zartman, it says on this letter I have."

"That's me," said Hannah, wondering why she was getting mail from the west. Her few letters came from the east.

"I guess someone came over on the ferry, and then was in Fort Augusta. They left this mail there." The man must have guessed her thoughts. "Must not have passed by here or not known where you were. One of the men at the fort, man by the name of Martin Reitz, said some Zartmans lived down this way."

"Yes, Martin, he helped my husband a couple weeks ago."

"Anyway, I'm in a hurry, but he asked if I could drop these off for you. I know how scarce news and mail is in these parts, so I was glad to oblige him."

"Thank you," said Hannah hurriedly. "I've been waiting for news of my family. They live in New York. Would you like to come in for a cool drink?"

"I just have a minute," said the rider, "but my horse would appreciate a drink, and I'll step in for one myself."

"My husband would be glad to speak with you," offered Hannah. "Should we run get him?"

"No, I'm returning from an errand, politics and taxes, you know, and there's a wife waiting for me who will soon be giving birth. I want to get back home before her time is too close. I need to head back to Philadelphia." He climbed off the horse and led him to the water trough.

"Come on in," Hannah urged again, "I've got cool water right in the house. And I've got a letter you could carry to Philadelphia for me. Someone will get it to New York then."

Only a few minutes passed before the dusty rider came into the kitchen with two letters that were indeed addressed to Hannah.

"These were both at Fort Augusta. Someone must have gone north of here and dropped them off. No telling how long they would have been there if I hadn't passed by. Oh, and Martin gave me this crock and a recipe from his wife for you. It's an old sourdough recipe that someone gave her. He seemed to think you might be tired of biscuits."

Hannah laughed. "I guess he wasn't sure what we ate around here, but I would love some sourdough starter. I haven't had any for a long time."

She set the brown-and-white crock next to the sink and picked up her letters. She was so excited, her hands were shaking. The first letter was in Emily's handwriting, but the other looked more like her father's. That was odd. He never wrote. Not only had he been angry when she and Georg married, but then they had moved into the wilderness, and he had gotten angry again that they hadn't consulted him. Well, maybe her papa was finally reconciled to their differences and would put them behind him.

Her guest drank quickly and went off as speedily as he had arrived, leaving Hannah free to wait for Georg and with two letters in her hands. Knowing Georg wouldn't mind her reading the mail immediately, Hannah slit open the first letter. It was dated May 1798.

"Dear Hannah," she read.

Maybe you have heard by now that the city of New York has been stricken with Yellow Fever.

Oh no, this was to be a missive of bad news. The desire to read it and the desire to just put it aside until later warred within Hannah, but in the end, she decided she had better read on.

We always have fevers that go through the city in summer as you know. This one has hit more people than ever. Many have left the city hoping to avoid catching it. We would have gone too, but Father was gone when it hit, and no one recognized what it was for a while.

By the time he returned, Mother had caught the fever. She is very ill even as I write this and we decided to stay here. She is too ill to transport, none of your sisters are allowed to come back home to help lest they or the children catch ill, and so I am doing my best to bring some relief to her.

I am not afraid of the fever, but I do fear for Father. He is not ill, but he has never done well around sick folk and now that it is Mother who is sick, he is impatient and cross, mostly out of worry for her life and his feelings of helplessness.

Hannah, you have no idea how fortunate you are to have all your children alive and healthy. Every day, we hear of someone else who has lost one or more children. Our neighbors down the road lost all five of their children within days of each other. How can a mother stand that kind of sorrow? I don't know how to comfort her even if I wasn't so busy with Mother. I cannot write more now, I must go to her; but there is a man

traveling west tomorrow that Father knows, and he will take this to you. Pray for us. I will write again when I can. I love you!
  Your sister, Emily

Hot tears stung Hannah's eyes. Mother sick? Suppose she would never see her Mother again. She knew she took that risk when she left for this little farm, but it had never seemed such a real threat as now.

How long did yellow fever last, she wondered, and when would she know whether the outcome was good or unthinkable? There was the second letter waiting for her. Where was Georg? Maybe she would wait until he came back and ask him to hold her while she read the second letter. Perhaps it was news saying Mother was recovered. She could only hope for the best.

"God," she whispered, "You have kept us safe through so much. I don't even know if it's right to ask this, but please don't let my mother die. I don't know how Father would get along alone, and I don't know how I could handle it knowing she's not there anymore."

She knew she couldn't wait for Georg to read her other letter. She simply had to know if it was written before or after Emily's and if the news was good or bad. At first, her tears blurred the words, but she wiped them away with the edge of her apron and determined to read the whole letter.

  My dear daughter,

Oh, Papa always called her "dear daughter" when he was in a serious mood.

  I fear I am the bearer of bad news. I know Emily wrote you two days ago that Mother was very ill, but I have to tell you that she is no longer with us. God has called her home.

It is too soon to know what I will do. Your mother kept things in order and loved me so well that I may be lost without her. Oh, I know some of your sisters are close by, and they will help me, but it is not the same as one's own beloved wife.

Then too, you and Georg and your Mother and I did not part on the best of terms. I regret that, even though I have forgiven you this rift as had your mother, we have never expressed it properly, and now it is too late to make it right the way I wished to.

"Oh Father," Hannah whispered through new tears. "Always so formal. I always knew you forgave us, but I never told you and Mama I was sorry for the way we left for this farm without your full approval. We didn't even respect you enough to ask your advice."

Hannah,

I am well and Emily is well, and so we are trusting God to see us through this time of difficulty. I will write more when I have sorted out my thoughts better. Just know I love you.

Your father

"I must go and help him," said Hannah determinedly. "Molly and Betsy won't be a bit of help, and they have their own families. Emily will need me right now. I've got to find Georg and see how I can get to New York."

Going outside into the warm breeze, she grabbed her sunbonnet. It wouldn't do to go to New York all brown and looking like a farmer's wife—even if she was one. The society her family moved in wouldn't understand.

She headed toward her closest child. "Benjamin, I need to find your father. He's somewhere out in the pasture. Please watch everybody until I get back."

"Mama, who was that man that rode in here?" asked Samuel. "He didn't stay long."

"He was just passing by on his way home," answered Hannah. "He had some mail for us. Now no more questions, I need to hurry."

"Mama?" said Clara, who was much more observant than the boys. "Are you okay?"

"No, I'm not really. I had some bad news, but I will explain as soon as I find Papa."

Without waiting for any more questions, Hannah ran off up the hill, her letters crumpled in her hand. If she had to explain too much more, she would weep, and she always kept control of her emotions in front of the children. She ran until her legs ached and she had a pain in her side. She stopped for a moment and pressed her hand against her side. Now she knew she was going to cry.

"I'm in control," she told herself sternly. "I will find Georg, and I don't need to cry."

As she panted up the hill, she kept trying to think of how to explain to Georg that she needed to go home. Tears kept threatening her, and she ran faster as if she could outrun her own emotions. Her husband wasn't in the first field she reached, so she took a minute to catch her breath and try to think where else he could be. The vines and brambles all around her distracted her from her grief for a bit. The wild raspberries were almost ripe. She would have to make sure the children got them picked for drying and preserving. The blackberries were still covered in flowers, and didn't ripen until later in July, but it looked like a good crop this year. Benjamin would have to go along with his gun so there would be no more bear incidents.

Hannah pushed her hair back behind her ears and began walking slowly again, still trying to catch her breath. These hills made it difficult to go anywhere in a hurry. She finally reached the top of the second hill and could see Georg up near the woods. He seemed to be looking at a tree. But she was too far off to tell what he was looking at.

"Georg," she called. "Georg, I need you."

He turned slowly, and she thought how handsome he looked standing with the sunlight glinting on his hair and a silly grin on his face as he caught sight of her. I do love this man, she thought, all our quarrels have to melt away when we stop and look at our many years together. She had almost caught up to him by now.

"Georg," she panted.

"What is it that brings you running up the hill so fast? Is one of the children hurt?"

"No, I got a letter from Emily and one from Father."

"If your father wrote us, it's bound to be bad news," Georg said grimly as his smile faded away. "Sit down here and tell me about it."

He grabbed her elbow and sat her on a fallen branch. "I just found a honey tree while I was out, and I don't want to lose track of it, but I also want to hear your news." He sat down next to her, and the branch creaked alarmingly but held his weight.

"It's Mother. Emily wrote that she had yellow fever, but Father wrote after that, and . . . oh, Georg, she's dead, and I never even told her I was sorry we left on such bad terms. I know she forgave us, and I knew when we left I might never get back, but now that something has actually happened, I feel so guilty, and I need to go see Father."

"Hold on, Hannah, what do you mean, 'go see Father'? He's in New York."

"Well, of course he is," she blurted out. "I'm not dumb. I just meant he will need me now, and Emily could even be sick. She took care of Mother. I just have to go."

"Whoa, now, back up. Emily is with your Father, and your other sisters are close by."

"Well, they're married and have families."

"So do you, in case you haven't noticed," reminded Georg. "Why can't they take care of things?"

"If you knew those girls any better, you would understand. They're likely to just moan and wring their hands and not be any help."

"I'm sorry to be the one to refuse you, Hannah, but there is simply no way that we can afford for you to travel right now even if finances were the only issue. But they are not. There are all the children."

"I could take Daniel with me."

"And have him catch the fever. You are not thinking clearly. Then there is all the work you do. Clara is not big enough to take over your responsibilities."

"Georg Zartman, that is not fair! Who takes over your responsibilities every time you have to leave this farm that you wanted? It's me. I do the work of two people, and I miss you terribly, and then you come home and we fight over foolish things, and I feel frustrated all the time and I can't keep the children under control and—" her vehemence surprised even her, and she stopped suddenly and began weeping.

"Now look at me. I wasn't going to yell and I wasn't going to cry and I can't even control myself. Sometimes I wish I had never come here."

"Hannah, Hannah, calm yourself. You don't know what you are saying. I understand this news is overwhelming, and I understand your wish to go home, but we just cannot afford it." Georg gathered Hannah into a hug, but she beat her fists against his chest and then pushed him away, refusing to be comforted, even though she had sought him out for comfort.

"Hannah, now get yourself under control," he said sternly. "If you are just here to argue with me, take yourself back down the hill and check on the children. I have made my decision, and it is final."

Hannah stared at him, speechless. Deep inside, she knew she was overreacting, but she couldn't seem to help it. She turned around without a word and marched back down the hill. If that was the way he wanted it, she would just refuse to talk with him at all. As she stomped down toward the house, she fumed and fussed, repented of her angry thoughts, and then they immediately returned.

This farm was such hard work; they seemed to be sinking ever deeper in debt; why had she ever let Georg bring her out to this wilderness anyway? Now because she had listened to him, her mother had died without her daughter close by, and where was God in all this turmoil?

Hannah was afraid to go all the way home, lest the children see her weeping and out of control. She set off along the path toward the creek. The farther she walked, the more of her anger drained away. Finally, she sat down on a rock. This was no way to live her life. She had always been taught that God had a plan for her. Now she was somewhere in the wilderness, seemingly without God. She had plotted and planned to marry Georg, and they had both agreed to buy this property. It wasn't fair to be angry at him when they had both wanted to have this adventure.

The way he spent money without even discussing it with her or borrowed against their property all without her knowledge was a different issue.

Then there were her beautiful children, all the result of her love for Georg and his for her. She couldn't turn her back on all she had just because she was full of guilt for her relationship with her parents that now was too late to mend.

"Dear God," she prayed aloud, "I can't seem to hear You anymore. I know You are here, but I have to hear something. Send someone to our cabin to help me understand this conflict in me, or do something, anything, to help me figure this out."

Hannah wasn't sure how long she sat on her rock waiting to hear some sort of answer. Finally, she shivered. It was getting cool out, and dark clouds were gathering overhead. Thunder was rumbling in the distance. Even though it was only early afternoon, it grew darker and darker, and the birds had stopped singing.

"It's good we didn't cut the hay yet," Hannah said out loud. "I'd best be getting back to the cabin before someone misses me. I wonder just how late it is anyway."

She gathered up her long skirts and began walking rapidly in the direction of home. Lighting and thunder could be dangerous out in the woods next to a stream, and she had no desire to hide out in one of the caves she knew were around. The bear would probably come and join her.

As the thunder got closer, Hannah began running. Long skirts were so clumsy, she thought, and suddenly tripped over a log. Picking herself up, she heard in the distance her own name being called.

"Hannah, where are you?"

"Mama, Mama?" That would be Benjamin.

The big boys and Georg were probably out looking for her before the storm struck. She ran again and caught sight of the cabin just as the first big drops of rain began to fall. Georg and both boys were not far away, calling, and she called back, "I'm over here," as she ran for the door.

As soon as everyone was safe inside, Georg grabbed her. "I can't believe you ran off for so long. We were looking all over."

"I'm sorry," gasped Hannah, scarcely able to breath in his tight embrace. "I just needed to think things out."

"Well, please think closer to home next time. You didn't even take a weapon."

"Georg, I am sorry. I didn't want the children to see me crying, and I was angry. It won't happen again."

The children were all crowded around Hannah. "Mama, look at your hands and elbows. You're all scraped and bleeding," said Johann. "Daddy, can you fix Mama?"

"Of course I can," answered Georg. "Now, children, your mama has had some very bad news, and she is upset today. I don't know why she was afraid to cry in front of all you. You cry in front of her when you children get hurt or sad."

He looked at Hannah as he talked to the children, but she refused to look at him. He gently cleaned her hands, and then he said, "All right, everybody. Mama got a letter today from her father telling us all that Grandmother has died of yellow fever. Now I know most of you were very small the last time you saw Grandmother, and some of you probably don't remember her at all, but she was your mama's mama. So I want you all to be especially helpful, and that may help your Mama feel better. Mama wanted to go to New York to see Grandfather, but we don't have enough money for that, so she will have to stay here even though Grandfather might need her."

Hannah smiled lopsidedly. "Yes, children, this is a sad time for me, and I would like to go to New York to help Grandfather for a while. I guess I will just have to write to him and tell him how I miss him. We can all pray for him and Aunt Emily and the people in New York. There is a lot of sickness there right now, and a lot more families than us have lost mamas and papas. Now, how about I fix you all some popcorn while we wait for the storm to blow over, since I never made your lunch today?"

"Hooray for popcorn!" was the unanimous response. Hannah had learned long ago that she could hide turbulent emotions in keeping busy, and she decided today would be no exception.

6

INDEPENDENCE DAY

The remaining spring days passed swiftly into the heat of late June. The children reveled in the warm air. The boys tramped into the woods one hot day and cut long poles from the young maple trees and spent hours digging in the moist soil next to the pig-pen for night crawlers. Georg fashioned hooks for them from scraps left from the forge so they could go fishing in the creek.

Fresh fish was a welcome change from chicken and venison. The children fairly drooled when they smelled Hannah's trout roasted over the hearth with fresh butter and the wild garlic that grew profusely on the farm. When they grew tired of fried trout, Hannah sent them back to catch fish to dry on racks that Georg built beside the house. The late June sunshine was perfect for drying fish, and winter would be the perfect time for dried-fish chowder. The garden flourished, the weeds as well as the plants, so every morning before it was too hot found Hannah and everyone except Daniel out pulling weeds.

Daniel spent his time stumping unsteadily around the outskirts of the garden where everyone could see him, or playing with small wooden toys that Samuel had whittled for him in a pen built by Georg to keep babies contained. It had been used by almost all the children, and Hannah could still picture her taller sons and daughters sitting in it and playing in years gone by.

This morning had dawned hot and clear, and excitement was in the air. Today was the fourth of July, and although fifteen years had passed since the end of the war, everyone planned great celebrations. For Georg, it was a reminder that even though he had entered this country unwillingly, he had become part of it—and that was cause for celebration.

Hannah was still grieving, but quietly, in her heart; not violently as she had when she first learned of her mother's death. She had thrown herself into the work of the farm in retreat from her feelings of loss.

Since there were no nearby neighbors with whom to celebrate, the children had begged and begged to go to Fort Augusta, where they knew there would be a parade and cannons. To their dismay, Georg refused. Such a trip would be costly and long, needing the wagon to haul everyone; and then there would be no one left home to milk the cow and take care of the animals. To help assuage their disappointment, he had promised them a pig roast.

The family had one pig left from Peaches's litter of the previous year, and so the boys made ready to help prepare it.

"Clara," Hannah called, "bring all the children in now. I don't want them watching when Papa kills the pig. Benjamin and Samuel will have to help, but everyone else needs to come indoors. We will work on the rest of the food and eat outside tonight. It will be a grand picnic celebration. Come quickly."

Clara had no argument with that plan. She hated butchering days. They all enjoyed meat, but these little piglets had spent their whole life here being taken care of by the children and now one had to give up its life. She gathered everyone and herded them toward the cabin.

"Oh Mama," Hans complained, "I'm big enough to help."

"No matter," said Hannah. "One shouldn't enjoy the killing of animals. Now come on in here, and don't argue with me."

"Yes, Mama." Hans stuck his hands in his pockets and scuffed his toes along the floor.

Benjamin raced past him on his way out, carrying his new gun. "Papa said I should shoot the pig, Mama. I need to improve my hunting skills."

"Well, don't brag about it." Hans scowled. "Mama won't even let me go outside."

"Come on, Hans." Clara put her hand on his shoulder. "We need your help."

"That's girls' stuff." Hans shrugged off her hand impatiently, but he sat at the table anyway and grabbed a small knife. "What do I have to do?"

"Well, to start off," said Clara, enjoying this role of bossing the boys around, "yesterday Mama and I picked all the apples off that yellow tree that gets ripe early. If you boys peel the apples, we can make pie for supper. That will be great for our celebration. Maybe almost worth missing the cannons."

"I can peel too." Johann ran over to the table. "We haven't had apple pie since last winter when we made the Christmas pies out of those old shriveled-up apples. Mama said this year we might get enough apples to dry them, and then we can have pie longer." As he reached for another knife, Clara smacked his hand. "You need to wash first," she reprimanded him.

Johann slipped out the door to the basin, and Clara wrapped an apron around her waist. "I can't wait for pie all winter."

"As long as the sugar holds out," remarked Hannah, coming up behind them. "If you stop talking and start peeling, we may have time to get the pies baked."

"Well, Papa found a honey tree," said Hans, glad to be the bearer of good tidings. "He said we can start our own hive and then we'll have honey when the sugar runs out."

By this time Magdalena had come in from gathering the eggs, and everyone big enough to handle a knife sat down to peel apples. Hannah didn't know what kind they were, but all the children cared about was that they were large, yellow, and came ripe in July instead of September or October like most apples. It wasn't long before the table was covered with sticky apple juice and flour crumbs from the crust Hannah was rolling out. Daniel wandered around eating the apple peels and soon had juice running down his fat cheeks, making little trails in the dirt. Margaret looked almost as messy, but laughing at the two together enjoying apple peelings helped the older children forget the events going on outside.

It wasn't long before the apples were loaded up into the piecrust with sugar. Hannah liked to bake pies in her iron skillets, and Clara was given the job of watching them in the hearth as it was easy to burn anything baked in the fireplace.

Samuel came running in. "Mama, Papa wants to know where we should put the heart and the pig stomach."

"Here," said Hannah. "Take the bucket. Benjamin finally found it up in the field. Put everything we plan to eat in here, then bring it in the cabin, and I'll clean it up."

She chuckled to herself as she remembered the first time she encountered the German dish called hog maw. She had actually eaten and enjoyed the savory meal before asking what it was and learning that it was a roasted pig stomach stuffed with potatoes and sausage, onions if they were available, and herbs.

Wanting to learn to make this food that her husband enjoyed so much, she had asked one of the German settlers that Georg knew to show her the tricks and was now adept at the process. The little children didn't like to watch the smelly, messy job, and after a quick sweep of the floor, they went outside to play. It was a holiday after all.

Hannah found herself with the kidneys, heart, and stomach. She rinsed the kidneys and heart and put them in a bowl to soak in saltwater and set the whole bowl in the spring water trough to keep cool. The stomach, she rinsed and turned inside out. Emptying the half-digested grass inside was a disgusting task, but she held her breath and tried to think of other things. A second bowl was soon filled with the smelly grayish-green mess, and she called Frederick to come get the bowl and get it to the chickens. He wrinkled his nose as well.

"We can't waste anything," said Hannah. "The chickens will eat this, and it will be good for them. Just run out quickly and try not to smell."

Easier said than done—even she felt nauseated from the odor and the heat as she quickly separated the muscle wall from the inner lining. Only a thick, clean white muscle wall would be left, which could be stuffed with a mixture of meat and potatoes and then sewn up and baked, resulting in a meal they all enjoyed. They would have to plan that for tomorrow, as the stomach wouldn't keep any longer even in their cold mountain spring water.

The smell of apple pie soon covered the scent of raw meat, and Hannah's stomach quieted down. Georg had already dug a large pit and filled it with rocks that had been heated in the fire. While not heavy, the pig was awkward to handle, and the boys helped him lower it into the pit and covered it with leaves. Over the leaves they heaped more heated rocks. Then they covered the whole pile with dirt. By evening, the entire pig would be roasted to a tenderness not produced by any other cooking method and devoured by the family.

After washing her hands, Hannah wiped them on her apron and went outside to determine what else needed to be done for a successful family picnic. Georg's refusal to let them go to Fort Augusta still rankled. Even though she hadn't been set on going, it would have been such a special event for her children.

While they had all thrown themselves into picnic preparations, she knew there was grumbling among the older children. Benjamin, Samuel, and Clara knew enough not to complain in Georg's hearing, while Fredrick had spoken up and received an angry glare in return. Hannah had started to speak in his defense, but before the words left her mouth, she thought better of them. Now her feelings were bottled up inside. She wished something would ease the tension and lighten the mood.

She sat down on a log to gather her thoughts. The warm breeze played with tendrils of her hair that had escaped from her bun, and she swept them back into place absentmindedly. The preacher hadn't been back through since May, and she was beginning to feel cut off from the outside world. If only Georg had let them take a trip, what change it would have been for the whole family.

"Daniel, come back here!" she heard in the distance, and then the unmistakable sound of Daniel screaming. "No, no, no."

He didn't sound hurt, so Hannah didn't run, but she could hear the rest of the children, and it sounded like they were chasing after Daniel.

He soon came running around the outhouse. There was something in his hands, but it was too small for Hannah to make out at this distance. Daniel was short and fat and it didn't take long for Johann to catch up to him and grab his wrist. Since this seemed like a good moment to intervene, Hannah quickened her pace.

"Daniel, let go, I say," yelled Johann.

"It's my mousie," sobbed Daniel. "I want to hold it."

By this time, Hannah had reached the children, who were all crowded around Daniel. Clenched in his dirty, chubby fist was a tiny mouse. Its eyes weren't even open yet.

"Daniel, open your hand," said Hannah gently. "See this little mousie. He can't even see yet. He needs his mama to take care of him."

Daniel gazed at the mouse sadly. "I would take care of him. I can feed him milk."

"No, Daniel, he needs his mama. Frederick can take him back to where you found him."

While Hannah had no liking for mice, she hated how upset Daniel would be if she told Frederick to kill the mouse. She hoped he understood the look in her eyes when she told him to take the mouse back to its mama.

Rocking the weeping toddler in her arms, Hannah wished her

life still were so simple. Her mother and father had always fixed her problems when she was little and the problems got too big for her, but now it was up to her and Georg to work their problems out.

Margaret and Magdalena, who did everything together despite their three-year age difference, trotted off to see how the roast pig was coming along, and Hans took Daniel's hand.

"Come on, Daniel, let's go play with the chickens. They don't need to eat milk. I'll catch one, and you can hold it."

"Don't chase my laying hens," admonished Hannah. "You can catch a rooster and hold it so Daniel can pet it, but it's too hot to stir up my hens. They'll stop laying if you do."

Hans frowned, "Okay, Mama. I know about chickens." The boys ran off, and Hannah walked slowly back to the cabin. Her chores were done on time for once. It surely did help to have Georg home every day, but it seemed like they quarreled every day too. When she stopped to think about it, it seemed as if they were continually at odds with each other.

She wondered if this was normal for two people married for as many years as she and Georg had been. Somehow they needed to get back to those days when each could do no wrong in the other's eyes. Deep down, she suspected the source of their quarrels had to do with the stress over their finances, but it seemed to always come out in silly issues.

Now she could hear Samuel down the road shouting from around the curve of the dirt pathway.

"Papa, Papa, I see Reverend Claybaugh coming down the road again. Can he come to our picnic?"

That certainly was good timing. Hannah headed toward the road as well to welcome the circuit rider. She quickened her pace. Maybe he brought a letter from Emily. It had been a long time since she had heard from her sister, and a letter would make a bright spot in this up-and-down day.

Samuel was right. Off in the distance, she could make out a slowly plodding white mule and on his back, the unmistakable outline of

Reverend Claybaugh. He looked as if he was reading a book as he rode, and Hannah chuckled. Zaccheus was so slow, a person could read and not fall off his back. Reverend Claybaugh probably had the whole Bible memorized by now just from his travels. She waved, and he waved back. Zaccheus actually looked like he had picked up his pace. He probably remembered their tasty pasture grass and was looking forward for a chance to rest his weary bones.

Her amusement was stopped short by the loud report of a gun from somewhere nearby.

Now who would that be? Benjamin and Georg had already killed the pig. Benjamin took off running across the lane to where their new barn had been framed up. Georg was running right behind him, and Hannah didn't wait to hear the news but took off as well.

"I can't believe you took my gun!" Benjamin yelled.

As she came around the corner of the half-built barn, she saw Hans holding his right arm and weeping. Benjamin held his new rifle, and Georg glowered at Hans.

"Roll up your sleeve," Hannah ordered as she arrived.

Sure enough, a large purple bruise was already showing on his arm. Without wondering why Hans had Benjamin's gun in the first place, she knew he hadn't held the gun tight enough against his shoulder when he shot at whatever it was . . .

"Hans, what were you shooting at? I don't see any game around here, it's not your gun, no one ever showed you how to shoot it, and you've got a bruise from your shoulder to your elbow. You better explain yourself, young man."

"Hannah, I'll handle this," said Georg, irritated. "You always feel like you have to take control of things. You go welcome the preacher. Benjamin, stay here until I get to the bottom of this." As she trudged off, she heard Georg reprimand Hans for using precious ammunition that was only for emergencies.

Unwillingly, Hannah traipsed back across the lane. The children were all jumping up and down around Reverend Claybaugh, who was almost like a grandfather to them. Samuel was already leading Zaccheus away for a drink, so Hannah put her annoyance away for a time. It wouldn't do for the preacher to find them fighting again. He would start to wonder if they ever got along. She could hear Georg yelling behind the barn and decide to take the reverend indoors for a cup of coffee.

"Hannah, good to see you again." He smiled. "I brought mail for you. Guess who it is."

"Oh, I hope it's from Emily. No one's been past here with a letter for me in ever so long."

"Well, as soon as I get my saddlebag unpacked, you shall have your mail. I think there are two letters. Now, where is Georg? I thought he would be here to welcome me."

"He's just over there across the lane." She pointed. "He had a little discipline issue between Hans and Benjamin, but he'll be here soon. We have a pig roasting in the pit if you'll be here for supper. The children wanted to celebrate the Fourth of July, and we can't go to Fort Augusta even though all the children were hoping for a trip." She hoped that didn't sound too critical.

"My goodness." The reverend clapped a plump hand to his mouth. "I forgot it was the Fourth. I planned to stay anyway, but I would never turn down a pig roast and a celebration. I'll just make myself at home in your shed again and hunt up your mail."

A letter—no, two letters. Hannah could hardly wait.

It wasn't more than fifteen minutes before Georg, Hans, and Benjamin came back to the house. Hans's face was swollen from crying, he was holding his arm gingerly, and Hannah was pretty sure his backside would be sore too. Benjamin carried his rifle tenderly, as though it were a baby, and looked resentful.

Georg slumped into a chair and ran his big hands through his thick blond hair. "Of all the things to do," he growled. "We barely have enough ammunition as it is, and Hans has to go waste it on target shooting with a gun that's not even his."

"He's just a boy," Hannah remarked defensively.

"You are always protecting the children, Hannah. If Hans is big enough to use a gun without permission, he'd better be man enough to take the consequences."

Hans waited by the table for Hannah to get a cold rag to put on his arm. "I told you I'm sorry, Papa. I won't do it again."

"You're right about that. Now you go up to your room. I have half a mind not to let you join us on the picnic."

Hans burst out crying again. "Papa, haven't I been punished enough? I've been waiting and waiting for Independence Day."

"Perhaps you should have thought about that before you stole your brother's gun. Go upstairs so I can think, and maybe I'll change my mind after a bit."

Hannah sighed. What had happened to all their peaceful days together? Discord seemed to hang over their little cabin like a cloud.

Reverend Claybaugh banged on the door. "Mind if I come in? I can't seem to find that mail. Don't know if it fell out of my saddlebag when I stopped last. I could ride on back the way I came. I stopped at Penn's Tavern to give Zaccheus a rest, and I did get in my saddlebags. I know how important news is out here in the wilderness."

"No, that's all right," said Georg. "I'll send Benjamin. He's a good rider, and our horses are much faster than Zaccheus. He could be there and back again before that pig is done roasting. He'd probably enjoy that responsibility. He's growing into a man already."

Hannah felt a little pang of fear clutch her heart. She was not ready for these boys to turn into men, not yet. Benjamin was only thirteen, although he did have a birthday this month. "Are you sure he should go that far?" she questioned.

Georg just looked at her. "When I was his age, I worked my father's farm almost single-handedly, as he was ill. And when I was not more than a year older than Benjamin is now, I was sent here to fight in a war I had nothing to do with. Don't baby these boys, Hannah. They have to grow up fast to survive here."

He stood up, stretched his tall frame, and opened the door. "Benjamin," he called on his way out. "Saddle up Brown Betty. I have an errand that needs a fast rider." He turned then to the reverend. "I've got some chores yet. When you've got the road dust off, come on out and join me."

Hannah shook her head and got out her pewter mug for Reverend Claybaugh. "Would you like some coffee? We still have some."

"Sure, I would. So, Hannah, what is bothering you? You always meet me with a big smile. Today you seem preoccupied."

"Do you have time for a long list, Reverend?"

"I have until your pig is roasted, Hannah, and I am the only pastor you're likely to have for quite some time, so tell me your problems."

Hannah sat down with her own cup of cold water. She ran her finger around and around the edge and didn't look at the reverend while she gathered her thoughts.

"I got a letter several weeks back from Emily and one from my father. My mother contracted yellow fever, and then she died. I wanted desperately to go home and visit my father but Georg forbade it. I know it was unreasonable, but surely we could put aside practical things for an emergency. He said I can't be gone from the farm. Everyone needs me, but he can go away on trips, and I do some of his work and mine besides, so I don't think that's a valid reason.

"Then there's the fact that almost every day we have such silly quarrels. We fight over how to discipline the children, how to weed the garden, sometimes even how I make the meals. Georg always wants to make the choices. I love my husband, Reverend Claybaugh, but some days I almost can't stand to live with him. It seems he makes so many wrong decisions, or else he just makes choices and doesn't even ask what I think."

"I know I'm a woman and maybe shouldn't be concerned in his business, but we are working this farm together. My father always consulted Mother about his ideas. I wish Georg could talk to me like that." She looked up then, feeling bolder.

"I could go on and on, but that is the short version. I have wished so many times for an older woman to help me understand this. Maybe it is just how marriage is, but I don't know. Aren't you married, Reverend Claybaugh? I could talk to your wife better than you." She blushed then. "I'm sorry. I don't mean to insult you, but you obviously have a different viewpoint than a woman would."

The jolly circuit rider laughed heartily. "Hannah, I'm not laughing at you. Indeed, I am not a woman. But I think we need a serious talk. I was married once." His cheerful smile faded and his eyes took on a faraway look. "My wife died giving birth to our first baby. We had been married several years already. I lost my whole family in a few hours. After I worked through my anger and my grief, I decided to leave the church I was in and travel around to areas that had no church. So I know a little about married life. And maybe I can be of some assistance."

Hannah blinked. Until today, she had never thought of Reverend Claybaugh having a family. She was embarrassed at poking into his private life, even accidentally. "I'm—I—I don't know what to say," she stammered. "I never knew. I guess I never asked about you before."

Reverend Claybaugh smiled again. "Hannah, don't apologize. That was years ago. I miss my wife and the baby I never got to know, but I spend my time now working with other families, and I will see mine again one day. Now why don't you tell me what's *really* bothering you."

Hannah paced restlessly around the kitchen. "I feel frustrated all the time. I can't seem to communicate what I really need or want. I'm not even sure I *know* what I need some days. Georg is always so busy—and he does have a lot of weight on him to make this farm prosper. I don't know how he keeps on, either."

Hannah took a deep breath and thought maybe she was revealing too much of her life. "I must go see what all the children are up to. It's not good to leave them alone too long, but I do want to hear your advice."

"Fair enough. Now you go check on everyone, and I'll help Georg with his work—and just maybe he'll give me some insights to share with you."

Daniel suddenly entered Hannah's mind. Hans was supposed to be watching him, but Hans had borrowed the gun and shot it and then the reverend came . . . where was Daniel? She bolted from the cabin.

"Daniel, where's Mama's little fellow?" she called.

"Here, Mama," said Clara, coming around the corner. "I found him wandering around down by the pigpen. He's got all muddy, and I don't know where Hans went."

"I know where Hans went," said Samuel. "He got in trouble, and Papa sent him upstairs until he gets done being mad. Just like Hans to spoil a nice fun day."

"That's enough," said Hannah heatedly." It's my fault. I knew Papa was talking with Hans, I was thinking about other important things and forgot about Daniel." She was still thinking about her talk with the reverend. Had she said too much or maybe not enough? Perhaps he would be the one to help her wrestle through the issues she was facing. Or maybe he could help her see things more clearly, and they weren't such big issues. She just didn't know.

Suddenly a wave of dizziness swept over her. What now? She shook her head, and it passed before anyone noticed her. It was time to focus on July the Fourth and give her children a celebration to remember.

The rest of the day passed quickly in preparations, although Hannah was still chafing inside over their choice of activities. She determined to keep her dissatisfaction to herself, lest the children realize her lack of contentment.

Looking out the cabin door several hours later, Hannah finally saw Benjamin return just as Georg was digging the dirt off the roast pig.

He jumped off, put the horse in the barn for Samuel to feed and water, and went out to help his father.

Hannah slipped out of the cabin to ask how the roast pig was doing. Benjamin and Georg had their backs to her, looking at the pig.

"I got the letters," she heard Benjamin say. "Someone found them on the ground and left them at the tavern. One is for you. It looks like someone opened it."

"Just leave it in the saddlebags and tell Mama you couldn't find it. I'll read it later and then tell her whatever news we have after the party. If it's bad news, I don't want to spoil her day."

"You want me to lie to Mama?"

"Not really, but last time we got any news, it was bad. Just try to stay out of her way and maybe you won't have to lie."

"Why don't I just tell her I gave it to you?"

"Benjamin, you are right. There is no excuse for lying. If she asks, tell her I have it and we will read it later. Can you help me with this pig now? Everyone is getting hungry."

Hannah realized neither one had seen her and scuffed her feet, getting their attention. They both glanced up but acted as if she hadn't heard their conversation. It was just one more thing to ask Georg about in private.

7

PASTORAL ADVICE

Despite the previous day's celebrations, everyone but Daniel was up early. Chores rarely waited for tired children, and July fifth was no exception.

In an unusual turn, Georg offered to milk and let the children have a day off. They were still responsible for the other chores, so while everyone was outdoors, Hannah bustled about boiling water and preparing breakfast. It was next to the hearth that Reverend Claybaugh found her and reopened their conversation of the day before.

"Hannah, I spent much of last night thinking," he began, fingering the coffee mugs sitting on the table.

Hannah brought the pot and sat down across from him. "And did you find any good advice for me?"

"I believe so. How did you get here to this little valley anyway?"

"You mean Georg never told you?"

"Sure he did, but I wanted to hear your version of the story."

"Oh." Hannah poured chicory into her boiling water and stirred it. "Well, after we were married, Georg had his heart set on a piece of land where the children could grow and we could farm and live the way we wanted, not like some lord or king told us how to live. You do know how he got to our country, don't you?"

The reverend nodded. "Like many other Hessian soldiers, yes, he's told me that too."

"So when we found this piece for sale, we made every effort to purchase it and then loaded up all our worldly goods and the children into a wagon, and here we are. What does that have to do with anything?'

The reverend smiled. "You didn't have any hesitations about following him here?"

"Of course not. He was my husband, and I was going to go wherever he went."

"But you see, Hannah, you didn't pick out your ideal location for living the good life and find a man there, did you? No," he went on before she could comment, "you fell in love with Georg, and although you were living in a town, when his dream of a farm looked to be coming true, you didn't say, 'Well that's it, I can't be married to you anymore.'"

"That would be ridiculous."

"Exactly my point," said the preacher. "You fell in love, you married, even against your parent's wishes, and here you are. And your love is the constant. Life will always be changing. Your job is to stay beside your husband and help him."

"What if he won't let me help?" asked Hannah petulantly.

"That, my dear, is a conversation for another time, because here comes your husband now, carrying a heavy milk pail—and he is followed by a crowd of children all looking like they're starving."

Hannah laughed in spite of herself. She could see them out the open cabin door, and Georg did look something like the boss cow followed by the rest of the herd. She folded her feelings back up, locking them in a little space in her heart.

She waved at her family to hurry and began dishing out scrambled eggs onto the stack of plates on the table.

Georg chuckled as he lifted the milk pail onto the table for Hannah to strain. "Reverend Claybaugh, I should just get you your own plate to keep here."

"I won't complain. Hannah is a wonderful cook. No wonder I look the way I do. Even all the nights I spend out on the trail eating my own sorry cooking can't keep me slender."

The children clustered around the washbasin, laughing too, and then they gathered around the wooden table once again and awaited the reverend's blessing to begin.

As the children chattered and Hannah refilled their plates, Georg got up and began rummaging around the cabin. Finally Hannah couldn't wait any longer.

"What are you looking for?" she questioned. "Maybe I could help you find it."

"Benjamin brought that mail yesterday," he said shortly. "In all the excitement of the holiday, I can't remember where I put it."

"I know where it is, Papa." Benjamin jumped up from the table. "You put them in your saddlebag, remember?"

"Apparently not. Can you go get those letters for me?"

"Of course, Papa, I'll be right back." Benjamin slammed out the door in his eagerness to help, and Hannah just shook her head. Next they would have to build a new door. The children were so hard on the cabin sometimes.

It wasn't two minutes before he slammed back in, panting and flushed, and handed his father two letters. Georg looked at both as if he had never seen them before and then handed one to Hannah. "Not from Emily, this time," he remarked. "It's from Molly."

"Molly! She never writes. I hope it's not bad news." Hannah held the letter and looked at it.

Finally Hans said, "Mama, aren't you ever going to read that?"

"Sorry, I'm almost afraid to read what she has to say. I guess I'll never know if I never open it." She ripped the envelope and pulled the letter out. It was short, just a few lines on one piece of paper.

Dear Hannah,

Yes, it's me writing. I wanted to let you know you are an aunt again. We had another baby girl just last week, and we have named her after Mother. Emily has been staying here for a few weeks to help out, and she insisted I write and let you know.

If you ever make your way back to civilization, you will have to come visit all your little nieces and nephews. Between Betsy and I, there are seven now; and if we can convince William to marry Emily, you may have a few more.

We are doing well. David sends his love as well.

Love, Molly

"Well, that's Molly." Hannah laughed. "She hates to write, and she never could understand why I would leave New York to live in such a wild place as Pennsylvania. She ought to remember that Philadelphia is civilized. And it was good news. You children have another cousin.

"Georg, what's in the other letter?"

"Looks like business news," he said absently, reading.

Hannah glanced over his shoulder. "It's all in German. Who writes to you in German anymore? Is it from your family?"

Georg shook his head. "No, from a group of farmers back east. Someone has heard that the government may be introducing a new tax, and they plan to protest—didn't I mention this before to you?"

"Maybe I forgot," Hannah said defensively. Will this affect us? How do these farmers know you?"

"Perhaps I met them in Philadelphia."

"Perhaps?" Hannah's voice rose. "What's that supposed to mean? Either you did or you didn't."

"Hannah, you're all bristly again. Yes, I met them on my last trip. Every farmer is struggling to survive just like we are, and the government is rumored to be planning new taxes. Of course we would meet and discuss it. And it does affect us. These fellows want to know if I would stand with them. I would imagine they will get as many men involved as they can."

Hannah looked around the table and suddenly realized that every one of their children was watching their heated interchange with great interest. Not only that, but the reverend was sitting here too. Suddenly Hannah felt like a little girl again, everyone watching her while she did something she ought not to have done. She could feel her face getting hot.

"Come on, breakfast is over, let's clean up this mess."

I wish I could clean up my mess, she thought. Before the reverend left, she needed to talk with him alone again.

He didn't look like he was in any hurry. He patted his belly and stretched. "Georg, can I help do anything around here? I'd better start earning my keep, and I don't need to leave until tomorrow."

"I can always use a hand," answered Georg. "Come on out, and I'll find a hoe for you to use before the sun cooks us."

Hannah watched the men leave and then sat down and fanned herself. It was hot already. This was July, after all, and the humidity was building up.

It was time to make a plan for the day. The first two items on her agenda were to read the Bible and pen a short note to Emily. The Bible wasn't far away, so she picked it up first.

"Go on outside, children," she said to Margaret and Magdalena. "Take Daniel along. I'm going to read a little bit, and then I'll come out too."

She opened the heavy volume to Philippians Chapter 4. "Therefore, my brethren dearly beloved and longed for, my joy and crown, so stand fast in the Lord, my dearly beloved. . . . Stand fast"—some days that seemed to be such a hard thing to do—"Rejoice in the Lord always: and again I say, Rejoice."

Perhaps she had picked the wrong chapter to read. She felt she was seeing all her failures to stand fast and to be rejoicing.

"But in everything by prayer and supplication with thanksgiving let your requests be made known unto God. And the peace of God, which passeth all understanding, shall keep your hearts and minds through Christ Jesus. Finally, brethren, whatsoever things are true, whatsoever things are honest, whatsoever things are just, whatsoever things are pure, whatsoever things are lovely, whatsoever things are of good report; if there be any virtue, and if there be any praise, think on these things. Those things, which ye have both learned, and received, and heard, and seen in me, do: and the God of peace shall be with you. . . . for I have learned, in whatsoever state I am, therewith to be content."

Hannah sighed. Her first instinct was to hurl the Bible across the room, but years of respect for the volume kept her from damaging it. The words were too convicting. She was far from content in her state. She slipped to her knees beside her chair.

"God," she began, "this verse says to let my requests be known. I don't even know what my request would be, but I need some peace here today. Please help me get along with my husband and show him the proper love and respect. Mother used to say You hear my prayers, and today I especially need You to hear me."

Before she could think further, she heard the children and Reverend Claybaugh outside the cabin window. He was telling them a story, and she decided it was past time to go out and give everyone a job. If they didn't pay attention to the crops and animals every day, there would be no crops or animals.

She shut her Bible, laid it on the table, and grabbing her sunbonnet off its hook, she went outside to join her family and contemplate contentment.

As she walked up the hill toward the orchard, Hans and Johann followed her while the other children stayed to hear the end of the pastor's story. Hannah could see Georg in the orchard, studying the pear tree, and she headed toward him resolutely, deciding to apologize for her poor attitude.

"Georg," she began hesitantly.

He didn't turn around, but she felt he was listening. "I'm sorry I was upset about that letter. If you need to join in a protest, I'll try to keep things going here. I feel like sometimes you shut me out of your life because I'm a woman, and I want to be more a part of your decisions . . . and I can't remember the last time I said I love you."

Georg did turn then. "I love you too, Hannah," he said as he gathered her into a hug. He kissed her forehead. "You are just going to have to trust me on this. I don't tell you every little detail because you get upset."

He held her tighter. "I didn't want an argument with you. I just wanted to think over this request and decide in my own mind if I want to get involved or if I can afford to get involved or if I can afford not to get involved. Not only that, I've been married to you for so many years, I know how you think, so when I make a choice, I *am* including you."

Still wrapped in his arms, Hannah stiffened. That wasn't consulting her, it was actually insulting. Did he really think that? Her fists clenched.

"Georg Zartman, thinking about me does not count. I want you to ask me what I think." She wrenched herself from his embrace.

Georg looked puzzled. It was clear to Hannah that he did not understand. "Just forget it," she muttered. "Do what you want."

Georg smiled. "I will," he said in an infuriating tone. "I'll start by letting you know that I need to haul lumber again soon, and I don't know how long a trip this will be. Can you keep things going with the big boys? There's more farm work now than early in spring when I left before."

"I'll try" was Hannah's glum answer, and she left him to return to her chores and ponder how someone who loved her could believe that thinking for her was the same as letting her help make family decisions. By this time, Hannah had completely lost track of which jobs she wanted to accomplish in her day. She found Daniel and Margaret and took them with her on a walk around the farm to see what needed attention. Georg dealt with the bigger fields while she often found herself in charge of the smaller vegetable garden.

The beans looked dry, so she sent Margaret off to find Hans and Johann. They would take it in turns to fill the milk bucket with spring water and carry it to the garden, giving the thirsty plants new life. Watering everything took a good portion of the day, but it helped ensure food for the winter.

The air felt heavier by the moment, and Hannah hoped that meant a thunderstorm was on the way. She sometimes felt that every time they made the effort to water the garden, it rained by evening. On the other hand, whenever they were sure a storm was on the way and so *didn't* water, the clouds blew over and the plants had another dry day. Since the spring was running full, she would water everything and see what evening brought.

Before she had the whole garden watered with the help of her children, Frederick came running up, shouting, "Mama. Look at the big ol' clouds comin'."

Hannah hadn't noticed the clouds rapidly piling up behind her. It was getting darker by the minute, and the dull muttering of thunder rolled along the mountains. She must have been hearing it for some time but was so intent on her job that she had tuned it out.

"Daniel, Margaret, come in the cabin. Rain is coming." She knew the other children would come too, as soon as they finished whatever task they were on. She laughed as she spotted Reverend Claybaugh running up the path from the cornfield, waving his hoe and doing his very best to get in before the rain. Little splatters began to hit the dusty path all around him, and the children watched and cheered from the porch.

"Hurry up, Reverend," yelled Clara. "You'll get all wet."

Georg ran out of the forge, looked at the sky, and cheered. Rain was overdue in their little valley, and the whole family gathered on the porch to enjoy the storm. Before long, the children left their shelter and ran out into the shower, dancing in the rain and letting it wash their dusty faces. Even the plants seemed to be rejoicing in the downpour.

Half an hour passed before the storm rolled on its way to the next valley. The lightning had done its work as well. All the vegetables in the garden were greener, and the air was much fresher.

Samuel blurted out, "Mama, I forgot, we found ripe blackberries already. Can we go pick 'em now?"

"Don't you want to wait a day or so for this rain to plump them up?"

"No, there'll be more. Let's get all the ripe ones, and you can make blackberry pudding for the reverend."

"Was he with you when you found them? I bet he put you up to asking."

"Well . . ." Samuel stood on one foot and rubbed his leg with the toes of his other foot. "Yes, he did come along and mentioned how tasty your cherry pudding was and wouldn't blackberries be good? We just all agreed with him."

"Oh, very well. Get the bucket and go on with you. I'll make a pudding since he has to leave. The poor man can't go away hungry." Hannah laughed and went in. She hoped they had enough flour left, but if not, there was corn flour, and they still had honey. She could whip up something for Reverend Claybaugh's sweet tooth.

The unexpected rain had lifted her spirits considerably, and as she looked out the open door, she saw a rainbow sparkling above the field. Georg, who had been in the cabin looking for a tool, came up behind her and stole his arm around her waist. Hannah felt a desire to flinch away but resisted the urge. The two of them stood looking at the rainbow, fading even as they watched.

8

AT THE CREEK

July wound its way slowly along. It was hot. Uncommonly hot. The crops began to look withered, and Hannah began to fear the plants wouldn't provide enough at harvest time to sustain them. So she gave the children the bucket and sent them back and forth daily from the spring to the garden, but the spring was slowing down, and there was no way they could carry enough water for the corn field or the wheat field.

When she woke every morning, the humidity was a weight lying on her like a wool blanket. Thunderheads would gather in the northwest almost every afternoon, giving promise of rain; but time and again, the promise was false and the clouds moved away before supper. Tempers were short, and the fun they'd had on July fourth was long forgotten.

Hannah was sitting down for a moment on an old stump near the cabin, watching the children carry water up the hill from the spring to the garden. Little puffs of dust rose at each plop of a bare foot, and the gnats, out in full force today, buzzed around her face and forced her to cover her eyes and finally flee back into the cabin. It was only slightly cooler inside. They had all the shutters closed to keep the pesky gnats outside, but no breezes could make their way in either. The air smelled of dust inside and out, and it was difficult to imagine fall colors and cool air arriving in only two months. Magdalena was worried that it would be summer forever. Hannah's thoughts suddenly flitted back to the day in May she had prayed for a hot summer for the crops. She had certainly had that prayer answered.

The barn they had begun building back in April was going so slowly. It seemed it would never be finished, but Hannah was beginning to think there wouldn't be any extra hay to store. The first cutting had been excellent, but the dry summer would make a third cutting unlikely and the second cutting, just about ready now, was sparse and brown before it even left the stalk.

Georg had left again just two days ago with another load of lumber. "I'll be gone longer this time," he had told Hannah. "The animals can't travel very fast in this heat. We'll just take it easy and be safe. Now don't worry if we're later than usual."

Hannah had kissed him and all the children waved good-bye. She felt a secret relief that the discord in the cabin would diminish with Georg's absence. This was tempered by her equally guilty feeling that relief was the wrong emotion. She should miss her husband more.

Benjamin had asked to go along, but Hannah still relied heavily on him to help her with Georg's workload. The hope of financial improvement and the ensuing peace in the house helped her agree to her husband's taking another trip, but the secret she was holding made her question the wisdom of doing so much work.

She ought to have told him about the baby before he left, but then he might not have gone, and they still needed some sort of help to hold on to the farm.

Would he be doing more secret business dealings on this trip? The sweltering weather made her too torpid to be angry about it.

She decided to write another letter. Not much else would get done in this heat. Unable to decide which was worse, pesky gnats or the lonely dimness of the cabin, she carried her ink and paper outdoors.

July, 1798

Dear Emily,

I wonder if you will ever see this letter. We have heard no more news of yellow fever in New York. I pray that the absence of news means you and Father were spared, and no one else dear to us succumbed to that plague. Does New York seem empty with so many friends and loved ones missing from people's lives? I try to imagine how I would go on if I lost a child, but I cannot fathom that and am thankful that God has kept us all safe and healthy.

Life here remains uncertain. We are all healthy, but there is so much pressure that I sometimes wonder if either Georg or I or both shall become sick from trying to hold things together.

We fight like cats and dogs, and then we fall into each other's arms and ask forgiveness; and all the while we each are wondering how long we can go on this way. I would pack up and return home in a flash, but Georg is stubborn. "There must be another way," he says. Two days ago, he left again with more lumber to sell, and I left him go without sharing my joyful secret. We are going to have another little one in the early spring.

Do all married couples act like this? I can't remember Mother and Father quarreling, but Georg and I usually have our disagreements when the children are elsewhere, so perhaps this is normal.

Honestly, Emily, sometimes I feel trapped in this life. When Georg is gone, I must manage to hold things together; but when he's here, he acts like I'm just a woman—well, I am just a woman—but I'm his woman, and we used to share the decisions, or at least he would tell me of them before he made them.

The other day, Samuel caught a little sparrow and had it in a cage. I watched it fly and beat itself against the slats until it was exhausted, and then when he wasn't looking, I let it out because it reminded me of myself. Samuel thinks he forgot to close the cage when he fed it, and I don't have the heart to tell him his mama let it go.

I am such a tangle of emotions. I want to come home with Georg, I am fed up and want to come home without Georg, I can't live without my children but I am exhausted by my children, and I am expecting a baby, which always did make me act a little crazy.

Emily, pray for me and for all of us when you get this letter. Somewhere there are answers, and I am determined to find them. I love you, and as soon as someone passes by, I will send this along, finished or not.

Even writing seemed too much effort in the heat. Hannah put her letter back in the cabin, gazed around her kitchen at the dust everywhere, and decided to take everyone to the creek.

It was only half a mile by the path, and there wouldn't be any bears roaming around; it was too hot. Benjamin could bring his gun anyway, since he was getting to be quite a good shot. And wading in the shallow water would cool them all off.

It didn't take much to persuade the children that an outing would improve their spirits.

Samuel even offered to carry Daniel on his back and they set off in a better mood than Hannah had seen in a while. I may have to try this every day while this heat lasts, she thought. The tree leaves seemed curled in on themselves, and the grass was brownish as they trudged down the wagon path, sending little dust curlicues into the air.

"Look, Clara." Margaret suddenly pointed. "There's a big, big bird standing in the creek."

"That's a heron," Frederick interjected. "Papa told me. He's catching fish. Watch and be quiet."

Sure enough, the beautiful bird was stalking through the water. He stopped, stood very still, and suddenly plunged his beak into the shallows and brought out a large fish. The children cheered, startling him, and he took to the air with his fish.

"You scawed him," wailed Daniel. "Now he's all gone."

"Oh well," soothed Samuel. "He would have flown away anyway when we all put our feet in the water."

No one needed to remove shoes since they were all barefoot, and with the dry weather, the water was shallow enough for even Daniel. Hannah went in too, much to the amusement of her children.

"Hey, look at Mama," shouted Magdalena gleefully. "She's getting all wet."

"I guess you children don't think mamas get hot sometimes. Hannah stumbled a little on the rocky bottom and then found her footing as the pebbles underfoot changed to soft sand. "This is just what we all needed to cheer us up since Papa left again."

"Let's come every day," said Frederick. "Until it rains again and the creek gets too high."

"I'll tell you what," said Hannah. "We'll get up early in the morning and work in the cool while it's still dewy and foggy. Then when it gets too hot, and we feel miserable, I'll walk down here with you— but you have to know that suppers might be small and simple if we do that."

"It's okay, Mama," Clara spoke up for all of them. "It's too hot these days to cook much and eat supper anyway. We'll be fine. We'd rather play in the creek when it's hot than eat."

"Well, it's all settled then." Smiling, Hannah splashed Hans so he giggled. "As long as the chores get done first, we can come here and play until Papa gets back or we get a big rain. I hope the rain comes soon though."

The creek was shallow enough to see a few small fish scooting under the rocks. Since they didn't look big enough to eat, the boys began to amuse themselves by catching crayfish. The brown crustaceans looked scary, but Samuel had a plan for them.

"Mama, Papa said the Indians eat crayfish. Do you think we could try them?"

"No, Mama!" shouted Magdalena. "Those things look awful. Who would eat them?"

"Well," said Hannah thoughtfully, "I have tried them before. They take the right kind of cooking. What we need is something to carry them home in, and we need a lot or they won't be worth all the work."

"If I take the shortcut," offered Benjamin, "up over the hill and through the pasture, I could bring back a pail to collect them in. Please, Mama, it'll be fun."

"All right, now scoot so you get back soon and don't overheat on the way. Get a good long drink before you return."

It was surprising how much the cool water had revived them. Daniel was so short, the water almost reached his belly, but he splashed and chuckled and seemed fearless. Johann jumped up and then flopped into the water, and soon he and Margaret and Magdalena began a contest to see who could make the biggest splash. Clara, at ten, already had decided she should try to be more ladylike and waded sedately with her skirts held delicately in her hands as if she were at a ball.

Frederick glanced over at Clara and then at Hannah with mischief in his eyes. Holding up his finger, he warned his mother to

silence. Ever so quietly, he slid up behind his sister and then suddenly
bent and heaved a great wave of water all over her.

"Mama," she shrieked in surprise, but her natural tomboy nature
took over immediately. Soon everyone, even Hannah, was engaged
in a water battle. They only quit when Daniel, who was getting the
worst of it due to his small size, began wailing. They soon were lying
on the rocks in the middle of the creek, where the sun reached warm
fingers down through the hemlock trees, and awaiting Benjamin's
return with the pail.

I could live like this all the time, thought Hannah. Life seems easier somehow down here next to the stream. But I suppose we couldn't
eat crayfish all winter.

Benjamin was soon heard panting through the trees. "Hey, you're
so loud, you'll scare the crayfish," shouted Hans, equally loudly.

"Nah, they can't hear me. They're all underwater. Come on. We
have to work hard if we're going to get enough for Mama to cook."

The crayfish hunt was a splendid success. They must have been
multiplying under the rocks all summer, and there were many large
ones, including some longer than Hannah's index finger. The girls
weren't quite so eager to catch the creatures, but after Samuel and
Benjamin showed them how to sneak up and grab them behind the
head so they didn't get pinched, they began to enjoy the sport almost
as much as the boys did. They still weren't sure they wanted to eat
them, but Hannah assured them that she knew the proper way to
cook a crayfish. "You'll be surprised" was all she would say.

Finally the pail was almost full, and Daniel was drooping from
missing his nap.

"All right, children. Let's leave a few here to grow for another
time. It's time to go. We still have to milk and feed the animals, and
then we'll have a crayfish supper."

The walk back home was slow. Daniel had to be carried. When
he fell asleep in Benjamin's arms, Hannah thought he looked even

heavier than usual. Looking at his sweaty curls against Benjamin's shoulder made Hannah feel soft and tender. It wouldn't be long before they had another little one to cuddle. Daniel was growing so fast. She determined to tell Georg her good news as soon as he returned.

Once they were out of the little valley where the creek lay, the heat seemed to beat on them. It must be close to six in the evening, thought Hannah. She wondered how much longer this hot weather would last.

The children began bickering over whose turn it was to milk the cow even though the regular routine made it impossible to forget whose day it was.

"I traded with Hans," said Clara. "It's not my night."

"Well, I traded with Frederick," retorted Hans, "so it can't be my night either."

"Papa said I didn't have to milk when he was gone," asserted Frederick with his hands on his hips. "'Cause I'm just learning, and I need his help sometimes. So I'm not gonna milk even if I did trade."

"That's not fair," cried Clara angrily. "I always get stuck milking when we can't remember."

"Stop it, everyone," ordered Hannah sternly. "I'll decide who milks tonight, there will be no more quarreling, and then we'll use Benjamin's slate and write down everyone's turns so no one has an excuse. I know it's hot, but maybe you should think about poor Blossom, out in the sun all day, full of milk and waiting patiently for someone to come milk and feed her."

Slightly ashamed of their fight, the children all became silent until they came in sight of the house.

"Mama," said Benjamin in his new, almost manly voice, "I'll milk tonight and Samuel can help feed the other animals. These smaller children are too tired. I guess when we go again, we shouldn't stay so long."

Hannah gave Benjamin a hug even though he had told her he was too old for such affections.

"Benjamin, you are turning into a young man. Thanks for your offer. We'll get the crayfish washed while you two are taking care of the animals."

Twilight was approaching before the crayfish were all washed. Hannah had her iron kettle over the outdoor fire. When it was boiling vigorously, she called all the children to come watch. Carefully, so as not to get splashed, she dumped the bowl of wiggly squirmy brown crayfish into the water and covered it with the lid.

"Mama, they were still alive?" cried Magdalena. "That's mean."

"It's the only way to cook these fellows," said Hannah. She hadn't really thought about how her children would react to cooking something alive. "Now watch when I take the lid off. You'll see a surprise."

After waiting a few minutes until she was sure they were done, she grabbed the pothook and carefully lifted the boiling pot off the fire and set it on the ground. When she opened the lid, the crayfish were all bright red.

"What happened?" asked Margaret. "Why are they red?"

"Now they're ready to eat," said Hannah. "Let them cool off, and we'll have a feast."

Benjamin helped her dump off the boiling water, and they let the crustaceans cool a while.

"Now, get your plates," said Hannah, "and I'll show you how to eat them."

It didn't take long for the children to get the hang of opening up the crayfish, peeling off their shells and legs, and popping them into their mouths. It was one of the first foods Hannah had found that everyone liked on the first try.

"How come you never made these before, Mama?" asked Johann with his mouth full.

"Eat a little slower please," said Hannah automatically. "Your Papa doesn't like crayfish, so there never seemed to be a need to cook them." She stopped then and reflected on the fact that she had never made this treat. *Was that fair?* Possibly she should keep her thoughts from straying too far in that direction. "You also might have noticed it took us all afternoon to catch enough to eat. I surely can't skip all my work to catch critters. I ate crayfish when I was little. Your grandfather had eaten them somewhere on his travels, and he taught Grandmother how to cook and eat them, so all of us girls learned the trick too."

"I think they are excellent," remarked Frederick to a chorus of assent.

Daniel smiled. "Exlent, exlent." He giggled at his mastery of the English language.

The lighthearted supper made the past day seemed less hot and humid and Hannah allowed the children to sleep downstairs where it was much cooler. They spread their blankets out on the floor in front of the cold hearth and listened to the soft trickle of the spring running through the trough while Hannah read them stories from the Bible about Samson and Joshua and Moses until everyone was asleep.

It was still hot upstairs, so she spread a blanket out too and lay quietly, waiting for sleep and thinking about Georg. She wondered where he was by now and if it was any cooler out on the road. Thinking about Georg always led to thoughts of their relationship and what she could do better.

Georg's comments about making decisions still felt like a thorn in her thumb, painful only if she rubbed the spot. Hannah knew she had some insight into their life, but the longer Georg acted like her thoughts didn't matter, the more she began to doubt herself and her abilities.

The more she thought about marriage, her conviction grew that marriage was not about two people falling in love and then living happily ever after. Her life with Georg was changing her, growing her; and the process was painful, extremely painful at times.

She wondered who she would be when life was over, who God was making her into, and finally she let sleep overtake her.

9

THE BEST IDEA EVER

Hannah's nausea had abated somewhat, but still Georg hadn't returned from his latest trip. August was just around the corner.

The weather had continued hot and hotter still until the thought of snow seemed like a distant dream. Despite all the water Hannah and the children carried, the garden was so dry, it scarcely needed weeding, which suited the children just fine. The corn had all curled in on itself, and the plants were too short for a generous crop.

Some afternoons were spent at the creek and others doing school-work under the apple trees in the orchard. The cow wasn't giving much milk anymore, the pasture was getting sparse and dry, and with Georg's absence, no one had attempted to cut the hay a second time. The grass had all gone to seed, and what little green was left, the cows were nibbling.

The air smelled like dust, and locusts began to sing every morning and evening. The first day they began hatching, the children were intrigued with the brown bugs shedding their skins on the trees; but as day after day passed, the constant droning began to wear on Hannah's nerves. She had heard of seventeen-year locusts, but this was her first experience with them.

This morning had dawned hot, but there was the hint of something fresh in the air. Benjamin had walked down the road toward Fort Augusta early, before it was even light, on the lookout for deer or turkey, because their meat supply was low. It was too warm to butcher the hogs yet, so fresh venison would be welcome, and the deer didn't spoil as quickly.

Hannah kept thinking Benjamin was growing up too quickly. He did many of the jobs a man would do and was a thin, well-muscled brown from his summer of work. Georg kept assuring her that such work was good for him and not too excessive.

Every morning since Georg had left on his latest lumber delivery, Hannah had woken up and stared at the half-built barn across the wagon lane. The barn they were using now was rickety and barely kept out the winter wind and snow. Hannah always felt sorry for the animals in its drafty shelter. The new bank barn also would have much more storage space for hay and tools.

With the current state of their farm, and Georg always leaving to sell lumber, the barn was merely framed up—and that only partially. There would never be time to finish it before winter.

Staring absently at the barn now, waiting for the milk to be brought in, Hannah had a sudden inspiration. They could have a barn raising. There were no close neighbors, but she knew of some settlers farther away that would be willing to come. There were so few social gatherings out here that people would gather just for the food and fellowship—and a barn further along would be simply an added bonus.

If she came up with a date, Benjamin and Samuel could travel together and get in touch with everyone. The more she thought it over, the more excited she became.

If Georg didn't return in time, he would be surprised by all the progress, even delighted with her ingenuity. The possibility that she would irritate Georg by going ahead without consulting him flickered briefly through her mind, but she dismissed it just as quickly. *He will be too grateful for the help to be angry.*

Plans for meals for the day swirled through her head while she fried up several dozen eggs for her always-hungry brood of children. Chicken corn soup would be an easy meal, since they had some old hens and plenty of young roosters and the corn was almost ripe, small though the ears were with this dry spell. All the neighbors attending would bring a dish to share. She could hardly wait.

The hot day scarcely seemed hot anymore when she had such anticipation and planning to do. One by one the children trickled back into the house, having finished their morning chores, and sat around the table.

"I've had the best idea ever," Hannah announced cheerfully. "I wonder if I should tell you all or keep it a surprise."

She loved to see the children's responses to the promise of a surprise.

"Oh, Mama." Samuel plunked down his cup of water, sloshing it on the table. "I don't think you can keep a secret anyway. Please tell us."

"Supwize, supwize," shouted Daniel although he had no idea what a surprise was.

"Come on, Mama." Clara grabbed at a rag and instinctively mopped up her brother's mess. "You know you want to tell us. Don't keep us waiting."

"Oh, all right . . . I'm going to surprise Papa with a barn raising."

"Are you sure we can plan all that?" questioned Samuel. "That's a huge job."

"I have it all thought out," answered Hannah. "I heard Papa say before he left that all the timber was cut for the barn, he just didn't have any time to work on it. It's such a big project for one man and his sons to attempt.

"I also know you boys have been carving pegs for the beams. We'll have to make sure we have plenty. I want to figure out a day that we can do this, and you and Benjamin can go all over the county and tell everyone."

The children were every bit as excited as Hannah. Once breakfast was over and cleaned up, they gathered around the table, and she got out a piece of her precious paper to make a list of settlers near enough to invite to a work party.

Magdalena and Margaret soon tired of list making and took Daniel outside for a walk to see the new peeps that had recently hatched. It wasn't two minutes before they both began screaming, "The cows got out, the cows got out!"

"Oh, no," said Hannah. "Why do they always get out when Papa is gone? It's so hot to chase after cattle."

She didn't voice her other concern, the possible effects on a pregnant woman of chasing cattle, since she hadn't told the children this surprise yet.

"Quick, Clara, grab your sunbonnet. Magdalena, you watch Daniel. Margaret, stay with them. Keep in the house if you must. I don't want him getting lost or scaring the cattle once they head back here."

"Yes, Mama."

"Samuel, go get the bucket with grain in. I think there's a little left. They might follow you if you have food. Hans and Frederick, come with me, and Johann, you go see where they broke out. We might have to fix the fence, but look and see first if someone just forgot to shut the gate properly."

The loss of the cattle would be a serious blow, so all other considerations had to be put aside until they were recaptured. Hannah ran out the door on the heels of the boys to see where the cattle were headed.

"Blossom is the boss cow, Hans. If we get her to follow us, the rest will come too. Here comes Samuel with a bucket."

"Mama, there's hardly any feed left," Samuel said with a worried look.

"Well, we will just make them think we have plenty," answered Hannah. "Bang on the bucket and get their attention when we get close enough, but don't let anyone put his nose in there, or they'll catch on and we'll have a lot more trouble getting them back."

Sweat was already trickling down the back of her neck as she headed toward the creek, where the cattle tracks in the dust seemed to be going. No wonder. It was so hot, they probably wanted to stand in the water. Everyone big enough to chase followed along. Within ten minutes, they saw the first fugitive.

"Head them off," yelled Hannah. "Don't let them stand in the water."

Finally Blossom stopped to chew on a morsel of green grass growing under a shady tree. Samuel banged and called, and Blossom stopped grazing to see who was bothering to come after her.

"Come on, Blossom," coaxed Samuel. "Come get your grain."

At first Hannah wasn't sure she would come, as it wasn't her mealtime, but curiosity won her over and the cow began drifting toward Samuel and Hannah. It wasn't too long before the rest of the cattle noticed her change of direction, and since she was in charge, they turned to follow.

"Boys, get behind the last one," whispered Hannah cautiously. "Don't spook them."

With some reluctance, the rest of the cattle followed Blossom up the path toward their home pasture. Hannah couldn't really blame them for looking for a cooler spot.

The horse flies were out in full force this time of year and spent much of their short lives biting her cattle. Down by the creek, there were many fewer flies and gnats, and the mosquitos that were there didn't seem to bother the cattle.

By the time they got back to the cabin with the cows in line behind them, Johann was waving that the fence was fixed. Slowly the little procession made its way back into their pasture, and Hannah breathed a sigh of relief when the gate closed on them all.

Dusty and disheveled, she glanced toward the cabin. There was a man standing right in front of their snug little home, staring up at the windows. What could he want?

Flustered, Hannah bit her lip. Strangers were rare in these parts, and she didn't want this one to know that Georg was gone from home. Hopefully the children's normal shyness around strangers would keep them quiet.

Walking up to him, she brushed her hair back. "Can I help you with something?"

"Oh, no," the man replied, writing something down on a paper he pulled from his pocket. "I'm just counting your windowpanes. I'll be gone in a moment."

Hannah bristled. "My windowpanes aren't anyone's business. We bought them with cash."

"Oh, it's not anything to do with how you got your windows. That's your business," responded the stranger. "This has to do with the new federal direct tax. I guess you haven't heard about it yet."

"I don't know anything about a new tax, and I think it's time you left my property," Hannah said crossly. She had no intention of letting a stranger know that Georg had mentioned this already. Suppose he was really looking for dissenters?

Was this man here under false pretenses? She didn't know what to think.

"No fear, I'm done." The stranger retrieved his horse, which was grazing in the yard, and rode off swiftly, leaving Hannah staring after him. Should she try to send someone to warn Georg? If this man was telling the truth, when would another tax be due and how would they pay it? If he was not telling the truth, she wondered how many nights she should bolt the cabin door before she felt safe again.

Wiping her forehead with her apron, she noticed dark clouds beginning to pile up off to the northwest. Big storms often came from that direction in the summertime. Perhaps they would finally have rain.

"Come on, boys. Looks like we might get some rain. Let's make sure all the animals are ready for a storm and all the gates are latched. We surely don't want to chase a pig or cow in a thunderstorm. And we should stop a minute and pray for rain."

"I hope Benjamin gets back before it rains," said Clara with a worried look on her face.

"Oh, he knows how to find shelter," Samuel assured her. "C'mon, help me get things ready just in case."

The prospect of rain cheered everyone, and they were soon rushing around in the heat, sweating and clearing up. Thunderstorms always brought rough winds, so Hannah went all around their little home, closing the shutters and putting the cabin into an early twilight. Magdalena sat on the porch with Daniel, telling him stories and keeping him out of the way.

Margaret sat next to them, winding yarn onto balls. Yesterday Hannah had been trying to teach Magdalena how to knit, and Daniel had rolled the balls around the cabin floor and unwound the whole basket before anyone noticed him sitting under the table giggling.

Now the little girls had a mess to untangle. They didn't mind though, as it was breezy by now and sitting on the porch was cooler than running after chickens.

"I unwolled that," remarked Daniel sleepily.

"Yes, you did!" said Margaret. "Don't do it again. It's hard to get all these knots out."

"I sowwy," said Daniel, much too cheerfully.

The girls laughed and Magdalena gave him a big hug. "I guess we never told you not to unroll yarn balls." She smiled, and Hannah laughed too. Magdalena's attitude was such a nice change from the quarrels the children had been having with the humid weather. She reminded Hannah of her close relationship with Emily, how even when they argued, they were quick to forgive. Thinking of forgiveness rankled Hannah as well. She had such a hard time forgiving Georg when they had disagreements.

The clouds swirled closer and darker, and the wind increased. Dust was blowing everywhere and finally everyone scurried for the shelter of the cabin. Lighting flickered sporadically, and thunder grumbled in the distance.

"I think this is it," cheered Frederick. "Hooray for rain!"

Suddenly there was a loud thumping at the barred door, and they all jumped.

"Quick," said Hannah, "Samuel, see who that is."

With a bang, he wrenched the door open, and Benjamin, accompanied by dust and wind, almost fell in.

"I made it," he panted. "Sorry, Mama, I didn't see any game. I think they knew a storm was coming before we did, but it's awful dark out now. I had to run home. I just didn't want to be in the woods or the road with all that lightning."

"You made it." Her rapid heartbeat slowed even as she pressed her hand against her breast. She hardly knew she'd been frightened for him until he returned. "Come and sit with us. I think we're ready for this storm."

"I could see the rain in the distance, Mama. It looks like a good one. Except maybe there could be hail with it."

"We'll pray there's no hail, Benjamin. It would ruin the crops we do have left. Come on, everyone. Let me read something to you. Maybe it will make the storm less scary for the little ones."

By now the wind was whistling loudly all around the cabin. The shutters banged a little as the wind got between them and the windows, but they were sturdy and held fast. The air was much cooler than it had been for days, and rain began to beat on the roof.

Hannah lit the candles, thankful they had made new ones not so long ago. She really preferred bayberry candles, but the waxy dark green berries weren't ready to pick until November, so they would have to put up with the unpleasantly scented tallow candles made from beef and deer fat. It was only late afternoon but dark as evening already.

Hannah got out the one hymn book they owned and read some of her favorites.

"Ten thousand thousand precious gifts
My daily thanks employ;

     Nor is the last a cheerful heart
     That tastes those gifts with joy
     When worn with sickness, oft hast Thou
     With health renewed my face;
     And, when in sins and sorrows sunk,
     Revived my soul with grace.
     Through every period of my life
     Thy goodness I'll pursue
     And after death, in distant worlds,
     The glorious theme renew."

"Just think children, a man named Joseph Addison wrote those words almost ninety years ago, and we can sing them today and think about God's care for us. Let's remember always to be thankful and cheerful even when we are scared or sick or tired." And I am talking to myself also, she thought. God has been good to all of us.

A loud thunder crash sent everybody huddling close except Hans. He crept under the table.

"Whatever are you doing under there?" Frederick laughed. "It's not any safer there than out here with Mama."

"I don't care," said Hans. I just feel safer here. You can come under too."

"Never mind. I'll stay out here with everybody else."

The storm quieted and then renewed its fury. This time the hammering of hail could be heard. Hannah hated the sound of hail. It could mean the sudden ruin of everything. *God, do You remember we need these crops? Couldn't You have just sent rain?* Suddenly, all was still.

"Quick, run outside," urged Samuel. "You'll see all the ice on the ground.

Sure enough, hail lay everywhere. Most of it was small, though, and the plants seemed none the worse for the battering. The children ran barefoot through the ice, shrieking when their feet got too cold and reveling in the changed weather. Even the earthworms had come out to celebrate.

The ice soon melted, and Hannah joined the children outside, enjoying the cooler air. They roamed the farm, remarking at how quickly their wilted plants looked revived.

"Now if we can just have a few more rains without the hail, we might see a change in the crops," remarked Hannah, repenting of her angry thoughts about God. "One rain won't do it, but it's a start. Samuel, why don't you thank God for the rain and for protecting the crops from the hail before we have supper?"

The evening meal was cheerier than it had been for many days, and soon the smaller children were asking when Papa would be home.

"I don't know," sighed Hannah. "He said it might take longer than usual with the heat and all. I hope it's soon though. We'll just finish planning our barn raising, and tomorrow Benjamin and Samuel can begin telling the neighbors about it. It will be such fun to have company and we could make a great deal of progress on Papa's barn. Come on over here, everyone. Let's finish writing down what we need to do so we don't forget anything."

"Mama, Mama." It was Daniel, tugging on her skirt. "Mama, I tiwerd. Tuck me to bed?"

"Oh, Daniel, we forgot your nap again. Clara can tuck you to bed in my bed while we work down here. I'll be up soon. I'm tired too."

Obediently, Clara dried Daniel, washed his sticky face, and carried him upstairs while the rest of the family clustered around the table to finish plans for what would surely be the most exciting event in their summer.

When the initial plans were done, Hannah sent everyone else to bed. The air was much cooler after the storm, and a steady rain continued to fall for the thirsty plants to soak up.

Hannah's letter writing had been much neglected lately, and this was as good a time as any to catch Emily up on life in Pennsylvania.

Hopefully Georg had been able to pass along her last letter to someone going to New York, and this would begin yet another epistle in a
long line of correspondence. Now, where to begin?

August 1798

Dear Emily,

*Life is so changeable. I used to think once I
was married, I would live happily ever after. Not
so. I have suspected for some time that we are
going to add another little blessing to our family.
I have not told Georg yet. I haven't told the
children either.*

*I know you are saying, "Hannah, why would you
not tell your husband such a thing before he goes
on a trip?" The truth is, I thought he might not
go if he knew my condition. We need the money
desperately right now—or even if he could trade
for supplies—so he had to go, and I never have had
trouble in pregnancy. I am trying to have the boys do
as much as possible, but now that I no longer feel
sick, there's not much I can't handle. I will confess
too, to being annoyed. I thought after nine babies,
he would notice when I wasn't feeling well, but
he never even asked me any questions; so perhaps
I just felt spiteful. I certainly don't feel that
way now, and hope I don't regret not telling him.*

*In other news, I had the wonderful idea of a
barn raising today. The supplies are already here. I
am just hoping Georg can make it back beforehand,
but if not, he will be pleasantly surprised at his
newly completed barn when he does return.*

I also made the children promise not to tell if
Georg gets back before the work day. I want to
tell him myself and hear him say he's proud of me.

Now there is a soft steady rain falling. I
opened one window and all the ground smells of
earthworms. They come up when it rains, you
know. Don't wrinkle your nose. I am not a city
girl anymore and have learned to appreciate worms,
at least for fishing.

Benjamin is turning into a man. He has his own
gun now and has been doing a bit of hunting. We
hang the meat and dry it in the smokehouse for
winter. Even his voice is changing. He wants to
make his own decisions and in every way be a man.
I am not sure I am ready for such change in my
life. Perhaps it's good we're having another little
one. It will keep me from feeling old when I look
at the young men all around me that used to be
my babies.

Emily, I find myself tired sooner now in the
evenings, so I am going to say good night and
put my letter away. Tomorrow I'll pack some
lunches and send the boys on their journey of
invitation, and I can hardly wait for the fellowship.
I wish you were here. You always enjoy parties
so much. And you always have good ideas on how
to organize them. I will probably need your skills,
as I am not so accomplished in that area. Well, I
will think of you as I plan and cook and clean. As
always, I love you.

Your sister, Hannah

Once again, Hannah surveyed her tidy little cabin. Everything was cleaned up and put away for the night. Chores were done, and a cool breeze was wafting through the open shutters, and so she walked upstairs more cheerfully than she had for several weeks, looking forward to whatever tomorrow might hold. She climbed into her nightgown as her plans flitted through her mind, but added to them were niggling doubts about Georg's reaction to her wonderful idea. She brushed them aside. This would be the time that Georg was delighted at her ability to go ahead and help their situation.

10

WELCOME HOME

Plans for the barn raising sped along rapidly. Having picked a date and gotten a positive response from nearby neighbors, Hannah decided it was time to make one of her new dresses for the event. Eventually it would be an everyday work dress, but it would be new for the barn raising. She was glad Georg had gotten plenty of the gaily flowered calico, as it would have to be bigger than usual to leave room for a growing baby.

Now that the weather was cooler, it wasn't such a chore to spread out the fabric, cut it, and spend days with cloth draped all over while she sewed tiny stitches in the seams. Her mother always had complimented her on her tiny, even stitching, Hannah remembered. Now she wouldn't get to see this new dress or the new baby.

Thoughts of her mother always made Hannah melancholy, so she pushed them to the back of her mind and reviewed all her barn raising plans mentally once again.

Next week was the big day. They planned to gather early Wednesday morning. There were several families with older sons attending, so she was anticipating a lot of progress. She had also put the word around that if anyone saw the circuit rider, to let him know. He did so love a gathering of folks.

As Hannah sewed, she could hear the children up on the hill laughing and screaming. Daniel was napping, and they were playing tag under the apple trees. She considered going out and asking them to be quieter but decided quiet was for indoors. It was good for her to hear them so cheerful.

The barn raising idea had put everyone into a festive frame of mind. Most of the planning was done, and the meal preparation couldn't begin until next week anyway.

The screaming stopped abruptly, and then there was a cheer from the older children.

"Mother, I see a wagon," yelled Frederick.

"Oh, that must be Georg. I hope the children remember the barn raising is a secret," whispered Hannah. In her hurry to see who it was, she jabbed the needle into her thumb.

"Mother always told me to use a thimble," she scolded herself as, sucking on her thumb to stop the bleeding, she gathered up her skirts and ran out to join the children on the hill. There was a wagon, away down the road. There were two men in it, but it looked like Georg's wagon, and the slowly plodding team looked like his horses.

The children were all running down the hill, toward the road. Margaret had such short legs, she quit running and just jumped up and down, yelling, "Papa, Papa."

Hannah felt like running but thought that might be unseemly when there was someone else along. She saw the horses suddenly pick up speed. They both knew that home was near too.

The closer the wagon came, the more she felt she knew the passenger as well, and suddenly it dawned on her just who had come to visit.

"Father," she whispered, and then gathered her skirts and ran as heedlessly as the children to welcome the travelers home.

The weary men climbed out of the wagon to the smothering hugs of children and wife alike. The cheers of "Papa, Papa" were joined by "Grandfather's here. Mama, look, it's Grandfather."

Hannah wept with joy as she hugged her father tightly. It had been years since she had seen him. He was thinner than she remembered and grayer now, but still her own dear father, and since she couldn't go to him, he had come to her.

"Oh, I can't believe you are both here. Come in, Father. Come in and rest, and then we'll take you all over the farm and show you everything."

"Now, now, Hannah." Her father patted her awkwardly on the back. "Don't take on so. I'm here for a nice long visit. We'll have plenty of time to catch up on all the news—there *is* more news if I don't miss my guess."

Hannah frowned a little. Did it show already? "I was going to surprise everyone but I guess this is as good a time as any. Georg, children, Father, we are going to have another little Zartman in spring."

Georg stood completely still with his mouth hanging open. The children began jumping up and down all over again.

"A new baby? Hooray, hooray, Mama's having another baby! Daniel, you get to be a big brother."

Hannah put her hands on her waist and smoothed her apron, untied it and retied it, and finally looked around at her family. She hadn't meant to tell everyone quite this way, but her father did have a way of making her secrets spill out before she was ready to share them. She glanced over at Georg. He was standing still, looking at her in amazement. Finally he grabbed her and swung her around and around the yard.

"Hannah, I love you!" he shouted.

"Georg, the children will hear you."

"And so what if they do? It's the truth, and they should hear it from me."

All the children began spilling into the cabin, following Hannah and Georg. Hannah quickly folded up her partially-cut-out dress before little fingers could soil it, and she handed it to Clara.

"Clara, please just take this up and lay it on my bed until all this commotion settles down. Then come down quickly, and we can hear all about Papa's trip.

"Father, please come in. The boys can get your luggage for you. I will need a little time to fix up a place for you, but we are all so happy you came." Impulsively she kissed his cheek, and he in turn gave her another hug.

The excitement of their seldom-seen grandfather excited the children almost as much as their joy at Papa's finally returning. Hannah eventually went upstairs to take a pause from the noise. She opened her dresser drawer and looked at her latest letter.

"Oh, Emily, why didn't you come too?" she whispered.

A short rest restored her momentum, and she joined the rest of the family on the porch. Georg looked inquiringly at her when she came out but said nothing, and Hannah just smiled at him. He always did worry about their babies, and she was fine, just a little tired.

She was so glad he had returned home before the barn raising. He and Father would be proud of how she handled all the arrangements and would also be glad the barn could be completed, or almost completed, by next week.

Winter was still far enough off for the finishing touches to be done before the cold arrived, and the animals would have a much better winter in a new shelter. She clapped her hands together just thinking about it and then felt foolish when everyone looked at her.

"I'm just happy," she said, not ready to share another secret. "Girls, come and help me get supper on. Boys, go sweep out the shed and I'll get my other set of covers for Father. You can help bring his luggage in too so he can get settled."

Daniel seemed fascinated by the idea of a grandfather, and Hannah realized suddenly that her mother had never met her youngest son. The little boy had never actually met any grandparents of his. Father must seem an old, old man to him.

It was high time they got acquainted, she decided, and left Daniel following Father around the cabin and back and forth from the wagon to the shed as he got settled in.

Margaret and Magdalena had set the table already, and Clara was just pulling two squares of butter from the spring. Magdalena had made this butter all by herself and could hardly wait for her papa to come in to supper so he could eat some of her handiwork.

Yesterday Hannah had made soup out of the many fresh vegetables growing in the garden, and there was plenty left for tonight's meal. She pulled the pot off the hook where it had been slowly warming and stirred it lest it burn, but tonight everything was going smoothly. She would surely hate to burn the first meal her father ate with them after so many years of not seeing him.

She looked in the battered tin bread box too. There was enough bread left for supper, although tomorrow she would definitely have to bake. She had been enjoying the sourdough starter, and it had been used since Martin's kind gesture back in June. Hannah had heard of sourdough starter lasting for years. Every time she tended hers, she was thankful for the gift and resolved not to forget to feed it weekly.

It wasn't long before the whole family was gathered together again around the table. Hannah breathed a sigh of relief. They hadn't had any cross words yet, and then there was the added blessing of her father joining them. Her heart felt like it couldn't hold much more joy. Georg asked her father to say the blessing, and as they all joined hands, Hannah whispered her own little prayer of thanks. Surely God knew she couldn't have waited much longer to see the two men she loved most in the world.

While the children all talked at once, Hannah sat and watched Georg. He had aged on this trip. His shoulders seemed to droop, and his hair was grayer. Would life never even out so they could just enjoy a day at a time? *Shame on me! I have all my family here and healthy. I have nothing to complain about.*

"Father, I can hardly believe you are here, but why didn't Emily come with you? Is she in good health?"

"Of course, Hannah." He smiled at her. "Emily sent a letter, but I will tell you some of her news myself. After all these years of taking care of your mother and me, Emily has finally found herself a husband. She was so busy planning her wedding that she had no time to come. And I was only getting in her way, so I decided it was past time to come see you."

"Emily married?"

"Yes, and I do think it will be quite a joyful occasion, so why act so surprised?"

"Well, I'm so used to Emily at home with you. Where's my letter, Father? I can't wait any longer to read it."

Her father chuckled, went over to the nail on the wall where his coat was hanging, and pulled it out of his pocket. "I didn't think you would wait once I gave you that news."

Hannah grabbed the envelope, and oblivious to all the children around her, ripped open her precious letter.

Dear Hannah,

You will never believe my news. After almost despairing of finding the right man (perhaps I was too particular as some said), I am getting married. No, I can't say I was too particular because otherwise, I would be already married to William—which is its own tale—and never have met Jacob. It's a long story, and I will take time to write it all down for you; but Father has determined to come for a visit, and I want you to have this note when he arrives.

The wedding is set for early spring. I don't know if there will be any way you can come, but I do know that whether you are here or there, you will share my joy. I am so longing to be a mother and a wife, and I can see now that all my helping Mother and Father was simply training for my new role.

I feel I could ramble on and on extolling all the virtues of my man, but you would just laugh and perhaps reflect back on how you acted when Georg was courting you.

Remember how you would lie in bed at night and recount every little thing he had done when you were with him? And how about those many times you would sneak out to meet him at a dance, and I would make up tales so Mother and Father wouldn't guess?

My courtship has not been nearly as exciting as that, but I have no complaints. I'm just so in love. Write and tell me how excited you are and send it with Father whenever he returns.

Much love,
Emily

Hannah clasped the letter to her breast and smiled. Oh, Emily would be such a good wife, and she was happy for her. She did wonder what had happened to William, who had been in Emily's life for years and never seemed any closer to marrying her. Now Emily had found the right man. She was so happy, she felt silly. She had never been one to show much emotion, but this was such special news.

Georg smiled too, taking years off his looks.

"It's so good to be home," he said, and raised his eyebrows at Hannah when the children weren't looking at them.

Hannah giggled. She felt like she had years ago. All this talk of weddings must be affecting her.

"Let's clean up supper," she said to the children, "and then we'll sing. Your grandfather loves to sing, and I know he'd like to hear you join in."

The table clearing went smoothly with none of the usual bickering that the children had indulged in lately. As soon as everything was put away, they joined Georg and her father out on the porch. Georg had already brought out her rocking chair, and the children sat around on the floor.

Hannah smiled at eighteen pairs of dusty toes in many shapes and sizes peeking out from under skirts and pant legs grown too short as the children lustily sang one favorite hymn after another. At last, with much protest, they all made their way to bed. No one had even mentioned the barn raising, and Hannah looked forward to telling Georg about it by herself. He would be so pleased.

The evening was still, and the air was heavy now, with a smell of clover blossoms. It was probably time to cut hay again, Hannah thought. She wondered how much longer it could wait now that Georg was back. She rocked slowly, savoring her unexpected joy and listened absentmindedly to Georg and her father talk while she watched the fireflies flit around the yard and listened to the crickets sing cheerfully. Off in the distance, she could hear the bullfrogs down by the creek. Maybe she should have left the children up longer to catch the lightning bugs. No, this was nice, just rocking gently back and forth in a little peace and quiet.

Hannah had almost rocked herself to sleep when two thoughts popped into her mind.

She should tell Georg about the man in the yard. And she wanted to tell him about the barn raising while the children were sleeping.

"Father, there's something I'd like to tell you and Georg before there are any more interruptions," she began hesitantly.

Both men stopped talking and stared at her. "What interruptions?" asked Georg.

"Well, I meant the children running about and so much commotion. It's hard to just talk about all the things that happened with so much laughter and excitement."

"Well, it was a lively evening." Her father laughed. "No question about that."

"And it's going to be even more lively next week," blurted out Hannah, twisting her apron into a knot. "You see, I planned a barn raising."

"A what?" Georg's voice rose.

"You know, a barn raising. I invited all the neighbors and planned—"

"I know what a barn raising is," interrupted Georg, suddenly gruff. "I meant, that's the last thing we need."

"I thought you'd be happy." Tears welled up in her eyes. She brushed them away angrily. "You were gone again, and I was just helping out in the best way I could. Why can I never please you?"

"Oh, calm down," her father said quietly. "We can sort this out. Hannah, why did you think you needed a barn raising?"

"Well, if you didn't notice"—she sniffed—"there's a half-built barn across the road, and the one over here is ready to fall down, and we've been trying to get a place ready so the winters aren't so hard on the animals and we can store more hay, and I hate when I cry, but sometimes I just can't help it, and . . ."

She blew her nose loudly on the corner of her apron. "I was trying so hard to give you a wonderful surprise, Georg. How could I know you wouldn't want it?"

"All right," said her father firmly. "That's your side, and I already know Georg's side. But you need to hear it, Hannah."

"Come over here, Hannah." Georg held out his hand. "Sit right beside me, and I will try to explain myself. I am frustrated over our situation, I can't see my way out, and honestly, a barn raising is the last thing we need.

I had even thought about selling the lumber we already prepared, all those pegs the boys whittled—everything—there are plenty of new settlers around that would buy those supplies and save themselves time over doing it themselves. That money might tide us over until we have a better plan.

"You had no right to plan such a project while I was gone. Why do you need to control things?"

Hannah couldn't believe her ears. Control? He was the controlling one. She was only trying to help the family. She could not see how selling their supplies and depriving their animals of proper shelter was the wrong choice. "What exactly do you mean when you say you can't see your way out?" she replied irritably.

Without seeming to notice her annoyance, Georg went on, "I've been talking with your father about selling our farm, and part of the reason he came out here with me was to see just what we have here and help advise me.

"Hannah, when we got married, your family wasn't any too happy with me. Now fifteen years have come and gone, and we need to put that behind us. Your father is a businessman, and I think he can help figure out a solution."

"Oh, Georg, you can't sell our home!" Hannah felt her throat swell and swallowed hard. "This is your dream farm. Your own land. You have always wanted this. How can we sell it, and where would we go?"

"Well, as I see it, we have three choices. Stay here, move farther west where land is cheaper and some is free—but the work will be much harder—or move back east closer to your family and do something besides farming. We can't decide this overnight. It's going to take a lot of thought and prayer, and that's why a barn raising didn't excite me." He frowned again and Hannah tensed. "So explain to me again why you thought you could plan this without my knowledge."

She shook her head, exasperated. "You were gone. I want to help. What's so hard about that? If you had thought up the idea, would it be a good one?"

Now it was Georg's turn to shake his head and then look at Hannah.

"Actually, you might be right. I should have thought of it first. It's my place to solve this problem, and I am going to solve it."

Hannah gazed back in disbelief. "Did I really hear you say that?" She jumped up from her spot next to Georg and clenched her fists. "I am going to bed. Maybe Father can talk sense into you. He let his wife help him." Her voice shook with her anger. She turned her back and slammed the heavy wooden door.

She was only halfway across the room when she remembered the stranger. She would have to swallow her pride as well as her anger and go back outside. She could still hear her father and husband talking on the steps. Unwillingly, she retraced her steps and tugged open the door.

"Oh, Georg, there's something else I need to tell you." Hannah set aside her anger for a moment. "The other week, I was chasing the cows with the children, and when we got them back in, here was this fellow just standing, looking at our cabin. He said he was counting our windowpanes for a tax. I told him to leave. I didn't want him to figure out that you weren't home. But he said he was done anyway. I wasn't even sure he was telling the truth."

"Oh, yes, he was." Georg's jaw knotted, and Hannah recognized the signs of anger and frustration. "There was a new tax passed in July, and that's another problem. Windows aren't even a part of that tax, but some of the assessors are saying they will tax us based on the number of windowpanes we have. It's ridiculous, but the government says it can do it. I am going to be meeting with other farmers from some other counties to see what we can do."

A pang of fear clutched at Hannah. "Oh, Georg, this won't be the Whiskey Rebellion again, will it? The government won that fight— and why must we fight the government anyway? They are supposed to be working for us."

Georg sighed. "Hannah, it's much too late at night to explain this all. Let's sleep on it and figure it out in the morning. It's late, and we haven't seen each other in weeks."

Hannah's father chuckled. "Well, I know a hint when I hear one. I'm too old to stay up so late anyway. My bed is made, and that is where I am heading right now. Good night, you two."

Hannah followed Georg up the stairs. She knew he'd already forgotten his accusation of control. He wouldn't even know she was upset by the time they went to bed. How could a man live with a woman for fifteen years and still not understand her?

11

BARN RAISING

September and Barn Raising Day, as the children called it, arrived in the same week. Hannah was up long before daylight, making meal preparations that couldn't be done until the last minute. Every single one of her young roosters had gone into the pot, leaving only one old one to keep the hens happy.

Daniel was too excited even to eat breakfast and jumped down from breakfast immediately, saying, "Mama, can I be full yet?"

"No, silly," said Clara. "It's a long, long, long time before we get lunch. Eat your eggs."

"Don't wanna."

"Clara, leave him be. He's so excited, he probably won't even notice he's hungry," said Hannah. "If you girls have finished your chores, I have lots of things that need to be carried out to the tables your papa put up under the apple trees.

"It's so nice and cool today that we can keep most of the meals outdoors, and I don't see any signs of rain either. The men won't get too hot working, and we won't have to quit for a rainstorm. Why don't we stop a minute and thank God for this perfect weather? Frederick, you pray."

The children all joined hands around the table, and Frederick's young voice rang with sincerity. "Thank you God for the day that Mama ordered. Please keep everyone safe at the barn and all the little children safe while the ladies cook. Amen."

Hannah smiled at her son and sent everyone off on various chores. Georg and her father were already over at the barn, laying out the supplies that had been waiting so long to be used and making a last count of the whittled pegs that would be used for nails. Even though no one knew how long the family would remain here, the Zartmans were about to enjoy a new barn. Despite the controversy of the decision, Hannah was proud of herself. This had been the right choice.

Magdalena soon ran in, her curls bouncing around her face, and yelled, "Mama, there's a wagon coming up the road."

"So it's time," said Hannah. "I hope I'm ready."

Georg and Benjamin had set long tables made from rough planks and sawhorses in the orchard, and Hannah and the girls began carrying out every plate and bowl they owned. If the families coming to help didn't bring their own dishes, they would have to eat in shifts and wash up between groups. Not that Hannah minded; all the women would help, and while they worked together, they would get to know each other and catch up on each other's lives, and the day would fly past even though filled with hard work.

Once all the dishes were out, Hannah began a mental tally of all the food she had prepared, determined not to forget a thing. Her neighbors would remember this as the most organized workday they had ever been to.

One by one, wagons came up the dirt road; dust blowing around the horses' feet, women and children were let off at the cabin, and the men tied their sweaty horses up in the shade. Older girls were set to carrying buckets of water to each team, and the men and any boys big enough to handle a hammer were set to work by Georg, who had laid out many of the jobs ahead of time to keep them in the proper order.

Soon shouts for this board or those nails filled the air along with the ring of hammers, and Hannah, watching distractedly for a moment, gathered her thoughts and headed toward the cabin to organize the ladies.

Most of them would bring along sewing to occupy them until it was time to set out the noon meal. It looked like everyone had brought along a quilt to sit on under the trees. No one expected a settler to have enough chairs to seat a crowd of company. Benjamin and Samuel had hammered together long benches for the tables, but after the barn raising, the long tables and benches would be dismantled and the lumber used for other purposes.

It was still cool under the trees. Hannah brought out some baby clothes she had cut out earlier in the week and looked around for an empty spot to sit. There were already at least ten ladies visiting eagerly with each other. The word must have spread beyond the homes Benjamin had visited. She wasn't even sure she knew all these people.

"Okay, Hannah," she told herself sternly. "You be brave. You used to be the life of a party—remember? Now go and meet everyone. They've all come to help you and Georg."

"Welcome to our home," she told the first woman she came to. "I'm Hannah Zartman, and I really appreciate your family coming to help someone you've never met."

"Oh, my husband knows Georg from Fort Augusta," was the quick reply. "As for me, I couldn't wait to come. I hardly meet any new folks where we live either, and whenever Georg stops in, he talks on and on about his beautiful wife and all his fine children."

Hannah was flustered. When had Georg stopped at this family's home? Or had she just forgotten that he'd told her about it? Well, no matter. They had come to help, and she could get to know someone new. She hadn't realized this barn raising would become so intimidating. The woman brushed back her curly blond hair, which kept straggling out of her bun, and went on chattering, not even noticing Hannah's momentary discomfort.

"Now, over there, that's Betsy, and her husband is Matthew. They came with Esther and Andrew Dunkleberger. Neither one have children yet, they're both newlywed and new to the area, but we invited them to get to know their neighbors and lend a hand."

Hannah smiled as she thought of New York, where neighbors actually lived close enough to see each other's houses. Here, neighbors could be a two-hour wagon ride away and were still neighbors. Still, more and more people were moving into the area. Farmland was easily had if one worked hard, and towns were growing up nearby.

"I don't believe I know your name yet," Hannah said quickly to stem the flow of information for a moment so she could process all the names. This woman seemed to know everyone.

"Oh, I clean forgot to mention it. I'm Anna Maria Fenstermacher. My husband's name is Henry. We live close to Fort Augusta, north of Penn's Tavern but on the same road. That way we meet many travelers coming past. I just love meeting new folks. Why, if we didn't have five children to take care of, I believe I'd like to run an inn."

"I think you'd do quite well at it." Hannah smiled. "Maybe when your children are older, you can tackle that, and they can all help in the business."

"Now, there's a thought," said Anna Maria, waving her plump hands at this person and that while she named her five children to Hannah.

And so the morning went. Hannah bustled here and there, her sewing in her hand, but never seemed to get a moment to sit and sew. It didn't really matter though. She was meeting new friends and rediscovering old friends. Her loneliness and isolation of the summer had vanished for a time.

The barn raising was worth much more, she realized suddenly, than just free labor. It was fellowship and the joy of renewed acquaintance. Hannah had been so caught up in the struggle of their little world that she never bothered to think how others were getting along or what struggles they were facing. Today was a good day to bring her back to her senses.

Lunchtime came all too soon. The ladies carried dish after dish brought by the many families. There were cakes, all sorts of summer squash dishes, pickles of many kinds. It seemed anything that was preserved over the summer was available. In addition, there was the enormous pot of chicken corn soup that Hannah had prepared, knowing it was a traditional summer dish among the German settlers, which most of their neighbors seemed to be. The dishes that would spoil easier, they ate for lunch, saving others for the supper meal. The soup would keep, simmering gently over a small fire until the men were all hungry again.

Once the men were fed, the women washed up all the wooden plates and fed the children, and then finally they sat down to eat their fill.

"I've thought of one good thing about eating last," said Anna Maria. "We can pick which cake we want and save it. The men don't have any idea what kind of goodies are in here."

Everyone laughed, and they picked out a moist-looking chocolate cake to cut for their dessert. Hannah, taking a mental count, saw that there were plenty of leftovers for the evening meal. She called Clara and asked her to round up several older girls to carry buckets of their cool spring water across the road to the thirsty men.

The third round of dishes finished, the women returned to the shade of heavily laden apple trees to sew and gossip before hunger struck again. One or two ladies took it in turn to check on the smaller children, but having playmates was so new to most of the children that quarrels were few. Esther Dunkleberger, one of the newly wedded women, stopped near Hannah's quilt.

"Can I talk to you?" she asked quietly.

"Of course," said Hannah. "Sit down here by me."

"No, could we take a walk? Could I see your chickens?"

Slightly puzzled, Hannah jumped up. "They're back here behind our old barn. Come with me."

Once out of earshot of the other women, Esther confided, "I just didn't want to tell so many women what's on my mind, and back on the quilts someone would for sure hear me."

"So what's on your mind?"

"I think I'm expecting a baby." Esther clasped her hands nervously. Her brows drew together, giving her a worried expression. "I didn't tell Andrew yet because I wasn't sure, and I am so scared. I don't know anyone here well yet. When we got here and I saw all your children, I thought you could give me advice and maybe come stay with me when the time comes. My mother is a midwife, and I helped her many times, but it's not the same thing, and then I got married and we moved before I had any children . . ."

Hannah reached over and gave Esther's hand a squeeze. "Of course I'll help you. I'm no expert, but I will come be with you. And if I can be helpful beforehand, just send a message with your husband or someone passing by. Where do you live?"

"Oh, Hannah, we live the whole way up in Northumberland. That's over twenty miles. We only came today because we were visiting down in Fort Augusta, and I was so desperate to talk to other women. Andrew was working with Matthew, and I came along to see Betsy, and they brought us along. I shouldn't have asked you such a thing. It's too far."

"Don't worry about that," said Hannah. "I'll see if Georg can loan me the smaller wagon and a horse. I can drive, and there are enough people here to help with the children. By the time your little one is due to arrive, my baby will be plenty old enough to travel. We'll work something out."

The women walked slowly past the chicken coop and then back around the pigpen and arrived back at the ladies' gathering without anyone taking much note of their absence.

From beneath the trees where the women visited, the barn was clearly visible across the road. Already the rafters were up. Hannah could see men on top working on the roof and hear men in the back, building the walls that had been framed up previously. Thus far the only injuries had been a few of the older boys with hammered fingers and a bruise or two where a board had banged into a shin while moving lumber around.

Hannah breathed another prayer of thanksgiving for the safety of everyone this far into the day. The project was going smoothly, and it looked as if their animals would have better protection this winter after all.

Hannah had barely seen her father all day. For being a business man, he dove right into physical labor and worked as hard as anyone present. This visit must be good for him, Hannah thought, after losing his wife. Tonight, if she had any energy left, she was going to write to Emily and tell her how well Father was doing in this farm life he had jumped into.

"I believe it's my turn to check on the children," she spoke up suddenly. "It's been a little too quiet since the dishes were done. Will someone join me? I don't know how many children I should be checking on."

"I'll come." Anna Maria clambered to her feet. "Five of them are mine, you know, and I'm sure I know everyone else here, so we can figure it out."

"Come on, then." Hannah smiled. "We'll get to know each other better on the way."

They banged on the outhouse door, startling one little girl inside, and then made their way around the old barn. There was a large group of children inside playing hide-and-seek.

"All right, everyone come in a minute," called Hannah. "I need to see who all is here. Margaret, Magdalena, well, you two are always together. Who has Daniel?"

"Clara is watching him and Johann and some other little boys," volunteered a young girl Hannah didn't know. "They were playing by the side of the cabin with some marbles."

"Anna Maria, are all your children here, or have you seen them all?"

Anna Maria fluttered her hands, looked around quickly, counted heads, and replied, "Actually, no. Henry doesn't seem to be anywhere around. He's ten."

"And I don't see all of my children either, and I was pretty sure there were more children here earlier than I've counted. We'd better keep looking."

A second circle of the farm yard and barns brought the same results. Some of the children were not there.

"Do you think they went over to the barn?" asked Hannah. "I thought we gave strict instructions not to go over and keep out of the way, but you know how children are."

Esther joined them then, and Hannah asked her to check for the children at the barn.

"In the meantime, I have another idea where to look. Come on with me, Anna Maria. If they're where I think, there's going to be some explaining happening."

Without further explanation, she set off rapidly on the path through the woods and down to the creek, with Anna Maria following her at a trot. If only nothing had happened down there. Who ever heard of barn raising where children ran off and got hurt or fell in the creek? What kind of mother would all these families think her anyway, unable to keep track of her own or other's children?

Sure enough, as they headed down the hill through the briars that scratched at them in their hurry, they could hear the voices of a lot of children.

There they were. No one appeared in distress. Hannah breathed a sigh of relief as she stopped to catch her breath. Once the relief settled in, she prepared to scold her children for enticing everyone else into forbidden territory.

Hans and Frederick would be the two of hers down here, but there were at least ten children all splashing in the water. The girls had their skirts tied up, and the boys' pants legs were rolled up to their knees; but everyone looked wet anyway, and it wasn't nearly as hot as it had been two weeks ago.

"All right, everybody. Out of the water," yelled Hannah, startling the children.

Guilty looks covered their faces.

"Who gave you all permission to be down here? Hans and Frederick, why would you bring any children here without telling someone where you were going? No one asked permission to come here."

Hans spoke up immediately. "I'm sorry, Mama, I didn't think we should come, but I didn't want these boys all down here without anyone who lived here, and then some of the girls followed us. I should have told you, but they were all running down the path."

"I'm just relieved everyone is safe."

Anna Maria frowned at Hannah but said nothing as they herded the children back toward the cabin.

"I sure hope no one catches cold today" was all she finally said.

Hannah winced. A cold or pneumonia. Her neighbors would never return after this. And it was supposed to be such a perfect day. How many mothers had lost track of their children? And how many fathers were going to be upset at the incident?

Still, no one had gotten hurt. They had prayed for safety this morning, and it would have been all too easy for disaster to occur at a creek with a crowd of unsupervised children.

"Thank you, God," she whispered as they came up the last small hill and out of the woods.

The men were still hammering on as if they had no clue about missing children. "Come on everyone, inside. We'll find you clothes to change into and hang yours out close to the fire. They should be dry before supper, and absolutely no one is allowed to leave the farm yard unless your father or mother is with you!"

"Yes, ma'am," the children whispered meekly and were soon changed into dry apparel.

Clara helped the women hang the clothes to dry. None of the women whose children were involved seemed anxious to report their children's exploit to their husbands, so Hannah hoped it would simply end there.

The rest of the afternoon passed without incident. Having all survived their adventure, the children played quietly, skipping rope and shooting marbles. The women sewed and visited. Hannah introduced herself to several other women she hadn't met yet, including Elizabeth Dornsife, who appeared to be about her age.

She had two sons, Daniel aged eight and Henry aged four. They both looked to be lively boys, fitting in well with her sons. Elizabeth mentioned that her husband was Hessian and had stayed after the war to raise a family in this new country. Georg should get to know him, Hannah thought. They would have much in common. Elizabeth also mentioned they didn't live far away, which boded well for female friendship for Hannah.

As the sun began to sink into the west, the last of the chicken corn soup was served. More than one young child drooped over the bowls, and the men all seemed glad to spend a few minutes resting before they had to head back to their own farms. One of the men had brought a fiddle. There was some halfhearted singing, but everyone was exhausted from the successful day, and soon the yard was empty.

Hannah was weary herself and hoped she had remembered to thank every last person who had given of his time and energy to help Georg. The barn stood tall in the twilight across the road, and Hannah could see it wouldn't take much work to make it ready for winter shelter.

"Hannah, you are a success!" her father proclaimed proudly. "Georg surely got a good wife when he stole you away from me."

"Oh, Father, that's enough. I just wanted to help us survive here. If all our animals were to die from poor shelter this winter, I would have felt guilty—and how could we ever replace them? Now they will be warm and cozy. Even the children will get to milk in a warmer spot. They'll love that."

Georg turned from slapping a horse on his way and gave a weary smile. "Hannah, you do have a tender heart. Those animals have survived many winters, and they would have survived another. But it seems you knew we did need a new barn, and I have no doubt the children would rather milk in this new barn than in our old, drafty, tumbledown barn.

"I am planning on pulling it down tomorrow and using some of that bug-eaten wood for kindling. Anyone who wants to help me better get right to sleep."

It took no urging this night to get all the children into bed, and even though they were dirty and sticky, no one seemed to mind, and the house was soon completely quiet.

12

NEW NEIGHBORS

Late September was much cooler than August; a promise of crisp fall was in the air every morning, and all the myriad tasks of a farm were easier to accomplish with the drop in temperature.

From oldest to youngest, Hannah's children had thoroughly enjoyed getting to know their grandfather. Hannah spent a great deal of time with her offspring as well and acquired a new appreciation for her father as he interacted with his grandchildren.

When they tired him out, he spent time sitting in the cozy kitchen, watching Hannah work, or out in the new barn or the forge talking with Georg.

Father's presence had brought some much-needed peace, Hannah reflected one afternoon as she sat on the porch, sewing. Her father sat on the top step, trying to teach Daniel how to whistle with a blade of grass, but Daniel was much too small to master the art.

"You better wait a few years." Hannah laughed. "I don't think he'll get it before the grass is covered in snow."

"Oh, don't mention snow yet," replied her father. "I have to be on my way before the snow flies. Emily will need help, even from her father, before the wedding. If I got snowed in here, I'd be in trouble."

"Well, we don't get that much snow usually," put in Hans. "You could get out sooner or later. We don't want you to go anyway."

"Ahh, but your Aunt Emily will expect me to return, and if I don't, she will find a way to come get me."

"I shouldn't mind that," said Hannah. "Maybe we'll just hold you captive here until she finds her way to you. I hate to think of you leaving already."

"I do too, but I will soon have to make plans. In the meantime, let's just enjoy each other's company. Now who wants to make boats to sail in the creek?"

"I do," a chorus responded.

There was soon a circle of children watching as their grandfather whittled a little boat out of a branch. When each child had one, they set off toward the creek with Hannah and Georg following behind to watch the boat launch.

When they reached the creek, Georg was appointed the race starter. All the children stood in the water holding their boats still against the little currents. Grandfather held a branch across the prows until Georg shouted, "Go," and the boats were off.

Two capsized almost immediately in a whirlpool, but Samuel's and Margaret's soon took the lead, and with children screaming wildly, floated swiftly down the creek until they were out of sight.

"Looks like it's a tie," said their grandfather, grinning.

Hannah hadn't seen him look so cheerful for many years and realized suddenly that the death of her mother and its accompanying grief was finally leaving her father. He seemed to have a new lease on life. That realization cheered her, as she her family had been part of his change. So she had been a help to her father after all, even without joining him in New York. Impulsively, she gave him a hug.

"Now, what's that all about?" protested Georg. "Why don't you come and hug me?"

"You're standing in the water," answered Benjamin. "Mama pro'bly doesn't want to get all wet. Do you, Mama?"

"No, indeed! Those warm summer days are gone. I'm staying right where I am."

"Then I'll just have to come out and get my hug." He scooped Hannah up and hugged her in front of all the children and her father. The he replaced her gently on the ground, smiled at her embarrassment, and hugged all the children as well.

"That wasn't so bad, was it?" he asked Hannah.

"No, not so bad." Before the ray of happiness had a chance to fade on its own, there was a scuffle between Hans and Frederick.

"What's going on, boys?" asked Georg.

"Nothing, Papa," Hans blurted while Frederick elbowed him in the ribs.

"Frederick, answer me honestly, something's between you two."

"No, Papa," Frederick said innocently. "I was just reminding Hans of last time we were here and he kicked me and said, 'Be quiet, don't tell Papa.'"

Georg's brows drew together, and Hannah sensed an explosion about to mar their peaceful day. "Now it had better come out," he growled. "When were you here last, and what did you do?"

"Nothin', Papa. Only it was the barn raising, and Mama couldn't find a lot of children and . . ."

"What?"

Here it comes. "They were at the creek," she interjected. "I found them before anyone got hurt, so it didn't seem worthwhile to mention it."

"Well, you thought wrong. These children must learn to answer for their behavior, and *you* should have told me right then. How many children are laughing at us because they got away with misbehaving and no parents knew it? Hannah, you have to let me handle these things."

Hannah clenched her fists, but the words tumbled out before she could stop them.

"I guess you wanted me to interrupt all those men helping you to report missing children that were already found and safe. How helpful would that be?"

Clearly that was the wrong answer, and she knew it.

Georg wouldn't let it rest either. "Oh, and I guess I was the one who asked for all those men to come help me. I was doing just fine on my own with the boys to help before you got mixed up in it."

Hannah whirled around. She refused to answer these accusations. She wouldn't look at her father either. He would most likely take Georg's side. Now she looked foolish in front of her children once again. She shook her head and then called to her brood, "It's almost time for chores, we'd better go back."

There was a chorus of groans; but the frivolous mood was beyond repair, and they all followed her up the trail, cowed into silence by the spat they had witnessed. The older children passed her and began racing up the path, and she walked more slowly. Georg and her father were right behind her. Hannah made a point to keep walking without looking back at them. The smaller children trailed along, and Georg finally picked up Daniel, whose legs were still too short to keep up.

"Hannah, Georg and I have been talking," remarked her father in the quiet just before their cabin came into view. "I'm sure you don't want to hear this right now, but it's time for me to go home. I will need to leave tomorrow or the next day. I'm going to borrow one of your horses and send it back with someone heading this way from Philadelphia. My horse is there boarding at a livery stable. Anyway, I just wanted you to know my plans."

Hannah turned around then at looked at her father. He was acting like he hadn't even noticed their fight. Whose side was he on anyway? She took a deep breath, willing her frustration far away.

"I hate to see you go, but I am aware that snow is not far away. Could we plan a special day tomorrow, then, and you could leave the next day? The children won't see you again in ever so long." Hannah wondered why she found it much easier to forgive her father his lack of sympathy than Georg's lack of understanding.

"For sure! I would welcome a farewell party. Makes me feel important."

Georg grinned crookedly. "I'd better leave too, then, if that's what it takes to feel important."

Hannah bristled and then forced herself to relax. She didn't want to stir up anything else.

"Eggs for supper tonight, and tomorrow we'll make something special."

After chores were over and supper cleaned up, Hannah, Georg and her father all sat out on the porch. Since it was almost her father's last night, Hannah did not even suggest bedtime. There were still fireflies out even though it was late in the year for the cheerful insects, and the children chased them, screaming with silliness. Soon, tiring of firefly chasing, Benjamin organized a game of tag, and Hannah leaned back in her chair, trying to hold on to her feelings. Her stomach was tied in a knot, anger still bubbling below the surface, but she was too tired to deal with her emotion tonight.

Tomorrow her father would pack up, and all would change again. She truly did dislike change, and these days with family had been precious. One by one, the children came panting up to the porch and lay down on the rough wood. Daniel had already been carried away to sleep. Margaret and Magdalena both washed up without being reminded, and Clara helped them up to bed before returning to sit quietly with the bigger boys.

Finally Georg had to break the mood. "All right, everyone," he said. "Tomorrow is another day, and there is much to do. Time for a good night's sleep."

He kissed Clara, hugged the boys, and walked with Hannah's father down to the shed. They went off together every night and talked. Hannah had been bothered by it at first and then reflected that she and Georg had married and left her home on such negative terms with her family that this new closeness was a blessing. After today, however, she resented their camaraderie all over again. This was *her* father, after all.

She went indoors, checked to make sure all her children were properly covered in the cool fall air, and went to bed herself, only dimly hearing Georg come in an hour later.

Morning arrived with the barking of a dog somewhere far off. Hannah lay in bed and wondered which of the neighbors she had met at the barn raising owned a dog. Her thoughts skipped from dogs to what kind of special treat she could make for the farewell party. Bread pudding came to mind almost right away. Her father loved bread pudding. She had bread today. For once, it hadn't been eaten up as soon as it left the oven. There were also eggs, and of course, milk. She didn't have all the spices her father liked, but there were dried cherries she could use. Yes, that would be the special treat.

Hannah jumped up, ready to start her day.

"Hey, where are you going so fast?" asked Georg. "It's still early. Come back to bed awhile, and we'll get up together."

Hannah looked at him in disbelief. Had he forgotten they'd gone to bed angry with one another? "I have to get ready for father's farewell party," said Hannah abruptly, turning to brush out her long brown hair. Several practiced twists, and it was out of the way of dirt and dishwater, up on her head.

As she was pinning it, Georg stretched and remarked, "How about I help you this morning? You've been looking tired lately."

Hannah relented. Maybe they could discuss things rationally after Father left. "I never turn down help," she said slowly. "Come on, I'm going to make a big bread pudding. It's one of father's favorite desserts."

"Lead the way, ma'am. I am at your service."

Together they went downstairs, and Georg blew on the coals left from the night before to get the hearth properly warm for such a treat as bread pudding while Hannah bustled about, gathering the ingredients.

The children heard stirring downstairs and soon joined Georg and Hannah. Clara, in a rare mood of generosity, offered to milk Blossom for Benjamin, who in turn volunteered to cut more wood for the stove.

"I wonder how I could get the children always to be this cooperative," Hannah murmured.

"It won't last," Georg observed. They're just excited since you said you were planning a farewell party."

Samuel came running in not two minutes later. "Papa, Mama, there's a wagon coming up the road. Someone's comin'."

Hannah and Georg both ran out just as her father also came out of the shed. Shading her hands against the morning sunlight, Hannah watched as the wagon rolled slowly closer. She wasn't sure, but it looked like someone from the barn raising.

She knew that rumpled hat. It was just on the tip of her tongue to blurt it out, and then the pair was close enough to see. She had been correct. It was Esther and Andy Dunkleberger.

"Can they stay?" she asked Georg. Guests would be a welcome diversion.

"I surely don't mind. Let's find out why they are so far from home first."

As the wagon drew closer, Esther waved and Hannah waved back, excited for a female visit. Andrew pulled his team to a stop, and Samuel came over to talk to the horses and offer them a pail full of water.

"Can you stay awhile?" asked Hannah.

"As long as you want us to." Andrew grinned. "We're your new neighbors. We decided to buy a farm closer to Fort Halifax, since I'm often there on business, and when we had an offer on our place, we set about finding somewhere else before winter set in. That way we'll be all settled before spring.

Esther hugged Hannah. "Can we go in?" she asked.

"Come on, I have to look at my fire, and I'll get you something hot to drink." Hannah put her arm around Esther's waist, and the two women went indoors.

"Oh, Hannah." Esther began crying as soon as they were indoors. "I can't hold this in any longer. I wanted to see you for so long. I know we barely know each other, but I think we'll be friends. Remember I told you I was expecting a baby?"

"Sure, I do."

"Well, I had a miscarriage, and I needed someone. Andy was wonderful, but he is not another woman. I think he was worried about me, and that was part of why he wanted to move this way, but I don't mind. I'm looking forward to being neighbors."

"Oh, me too." Hannah put her arm around Esther. "This is good news for me. Not your loss, I mean." Hannah stumbled over her words. "I mean having a friend close by. Stay for the day if you can. My father is leaving today, and we're going to have a farewell party—but now it will be mixed with the joy of new neighbors."

The two women hugged again, Esther wiped her face, and then they set about planning the day. They would have games for the children and as much good food as they could get cooked on short notice, and the men could sit on the porch and discuss the state of their country and their farmlands while the children ran about and enjoyed a day off from the normal routine.

Hannah was relieved at the distraction in her day. She could keep busy now without seeming to avoid her husband.

Not much later, Hans found a cow staggering about, and when he called Georg, Andrew noticed a small wild cherry tree just within reach of the fence. He thought the cow might have eaten some of its leaves, which were poisonous to cattle. Georg frowned and put the cow in the barn to keep an eye on, remarking that perhaps the animal might not have eaten enough to do serious damage. Losing a cow was serious business. Once a cow was down, it almost always died; but this one was only lurching about, and Benjamin offered to come out and check on her hourly, which was about all they could do.

The three men set off together to cut down the offending tree before any other livestock decided to partake of it, and Esther and Hannah soon had the children shrieking as they ran races and had contests to see who could jump rope the longest.

The shadow of the departure of Hannah's father drew closer and closer as the sun passed over the roof of the cabin and began sinking slowly toward the west.

Hannah and Esther sat on the porch, husking some late corn and waiting for the pot to boil to throw it in. Corn on the cob was the only other treat Hannah had on hand, and since she had just churned butter in the morning, it promised to be a tasty farewell meal.

"Esther, do you ever miss your family?" asked Hannah, feeling the inevitability of her father's departure.

"When I lost the baby, I cried so for my mother. I wondered why God brought us way out here so far from home." Esther gazed at the silky cob in her hand as if she had never seen corn before, then she tossed it into the basin. Realizing what she had done, she picked the ear back up and stripped the silk off before finishing her thought. "Now, even though I miss her, I feel I need to pick myself up and carry on. Andrew was so sure that we were supposed to come west, and I think I can rest in his judgment. It's hard some days though. That's why I was so excited to move closer to your family. I think we can help each other in the hard times."

"Oh, I hope so." Hannah yanked the silk off the corn. "I need another woman around every now and then. Clara is too young to share all my thoughts with, and Georg is either too busy with farm work, off on a lumber expedition, or just doesn't understand the way I feel."

"I have my own horse," Esther offered. "I can ride over. You send one of the boys if Georg is gone and you need help or just company. I can come."

Hannah jumped up, hugged Esther impulsively, and then laughed. "I never used to hug anyone. Ever since Father arrived, I've been hugging lots of people." Esther looked startled, and Hannah returned to her seat. "I hope that didn't offend you."

"Oh, don't be silly. Friends don't offend that easily. I grew up in a family where hugging was a part of life. You hugged when you met, you hugged when you said good-bye—we just were not very formal with each other. Come on, the water's boiling. Let's cook this corn. I'm starving."

Both women, sharing a laugh, threw the corn into the pot, and Hannah rang the supper bell. "Come on, everyone. Corn is quick. Wash up."

Supper was eaten outside. Georg and Andrew carried out the benches, and some of the children sat on logs set in a circle. Daniel sat on the ground until he was overtaken by ants. Once every belly was filled with all the corn that it could hold, Hannah carried out the bread pudding.

Andrew groaned as he saw it. "Hannah, you should have warned me. I love bread pudding. Now I'm full of corn."

"I guess that's all the more for me then." Hannah's father chuckled. "It's my favorite too. Hand me that serving spoon, Hannah. I'll dish it up. That way I'll be sure to get enough."

Oh, how she would miss him when it was just her and Georg and the children again.

Frederick, who was standing close by, laughed. "Don't worry, Grandfather, we'll keep a close eye on you so we can all have some. Mama might not make any more for a long time."

"Clara, bring those bowls out," said Hannah, ignoring the banter. "This bread pudding is famous in Europe—it's been in my family for generations. At least Mother always said so. I guess it will now become famous in America."

"Three cheers for bread pudding," said Johann, and the children attacked their treat as if they hadn't just eaten their fill of corn on the cob.

Georg and Andrew watched for a moment while they awaited their servings and then attacked their portions with equal gusto.

"I see what I need to learn to cook next." Esther sighed. "All right, Hannah, let's see how it is."

By the time the bread pudding had been devoured, Andrew announced it was time to head home, and Hannah sent her children to get ready for bed.

It had been a bittersweet day, but night was here, and tomorrow would begin early with her father's departure. His visit had been satisfying, and Hannah, Georg, and her father had all agreed that it was past time to mend the rifts between them. He would leave in peace. Hannah closed her eyes, wondering the best way to mend her other rifts.

13

THE COLLAPSE OF THE WORLD

Hannah woke each morning wondering if today was the day she and Georg would tackle their ongoing disagreement. Georg's attempt at apology was to act as if nothing had passed between them. When she brought her distress out into the light of day, he always had an excuse: he was tired, he had to go tend the stock, crops needed attention. Something always prevented him from talking with her of anything deeper than surface concerns.

Hannah's mounting discontent with their relationship was carefully disguised between her attempts to goad Georg into a confrontation that would fix everything. Today she had the fleeting thought that maybe their discord was irreparable and she should give up. She stopped in her housekeeping chores to gaze out the window at the mountains again, thinking somehow she would receive inspiration for her problem.

The sumac had been deep red since late August. Now in the morning, the air was crisp and cold, and even though the days were still hot, they felt different somehow. Dryer and clearer, bluer too. Fall was clearly here now.

Hannah took another moment to thank God for the successful barn raising. Benjamin and Samuel had helped put some split-rail fence around the rear of the barn to keep the cattle in when the snow got deep, and the pigpen had been moved across the path into the cellar of the barn. There would be no cold animals this winter.

The leaves hadn't turned yet, but they would soon burst into all colors. There were plenty of sugar maples scattered throughout the mountains, in between the dark green pines, as well as hemlock and oak trees. Each day the children ran outside to see if the leaves heralding fall showed yet.

Hannah loved fall, but she was content to wait for it, since the turning of the leaves also heralded winter, with its dreary gray days and incessant cold. While the children looked forward to sledding and snowmen, Hannah knew how the wood pile shrank swiftly, and she sometimes feared the woodcutting days with potential for injuries among the older boys. Georg instructed them over and over about safety, but an ax could slip and cut even the most careful young man and a falling tree cause permanent damage.

Today there was no woodcutting in the plans. Georg had promised everyone who was big enough a hike through the woods and up the mountain. Yesterday had been spent making soap. This was a tiresome process at the best of times, but more so when stirring gave a backache to a pregnant lady. The older children had all taken turns stirring the large pot, while the younger ones kept Daniel out of trouble. Hannah still had most of the work, since she was the one who knew the soap-making process best.

Along the hike, the children planned to gather bayberries. Most of the berries wouldn't be ripe yet, but Hannah wanted to start in on making the fragrant green candles and knew there already would be some to be found. Once the children knew where they were, they could always return later as more and more got ripe. Benjamin and Georg planned to take their guns, since venison would be a welcome change, and squirrel hides were handy as linings on winter mittens and hats. Hannah was good at knitting, but at times yarn was in short supply, and rabbits or squirrels could serve as warm clothing as well as providing a tasty meal.

Hannah had decided to keep Clara home with her to watch Daniel. She planned to finish her second dress and start on some new baby clothes. There was also plenty of mending to be done, and Clara could do the housework.

Morning dishes done, the children scurried out to their chores while Hannah and Clara packed a knapsack with sandwiches stuck together with honey. A rare treat, but Georg had found two honey trees since he had been home, so Hannah was glad to give the children a special lunch on their hike. They also had fresh apples and boiled eggs. Water wasn't a problem. There were plenty of springs and streams on the mountain, so no one needed to carry along a water skin.

An uneasy peace had settled over their home, and Hannah took care to tread softly lest she be the one to break it.

"Georg, take care of the children," she whispered as she kissed his grizzled cheek.

He had announced last week that it was time to grow his winter beard, and so far it was just itchy for the children when he gave them whisker rubs as he wrestled them in the evenings. The little girls would shriek and run away, but the boys pretended his new whiskers didn't bother them,

Hannah thought Georg would look quite handsome in his winter beard—once it was properly grown out—and Benjamin had just announced that he was hoping to soon grow his own whiskers.

Georg kissed her forehead. "Of course. Their safety is always my first thought."

Hannah glimpsed him wink at the boys behind her. She knew she was much more protective than their father and suspected that not all the adventures that happened on outings with him were recounted to her.

Hannah put her suspicions aside. These were Georg's children too, and she would trust him to bring them home before the little ones were too exhausted. This was the first big hike that Margaret and Johann had been allowed to go on, and they couldn't wait to begin.

Georg herded everyone out the door. "I promise to walk slowly," he called over his shoulder. "There is no hurry."

Once the door closed, Hannah breathed a sigh of relief. "I am going to write a letter, Clara," she announced. "You and Daniel can play outside or read stories in here. I just need a few minutes to gather my thoughts. It's been a long time since I wrote your Aunt Emily."

"Go ahead, Mama," said Clara immediately. "I'm going to take Daniel on a little walk, since he couldn't go with the big children. We're going to walk down to the creek and back."

"I don't know," Hannah answered. "I don't mind you walking, but don't go near the water. Daniel's too small. If he fell in, you couldn't rescue him."

"I could," asserted Clara, "but I promise we won't even go close to the water. It's way too cold even if we had permission. I want to see if I can find a maple tree that's turned colors already."

"I trust you," Hannah replied with a quick hug and sent them on their way before turning to her welcome task of writing to Emily.

The air was so fresh that she left the cabin door hanging open. The blue outside was deeper and the clouds puffier and whiter than they had been most of the summer. Another sign of fall, she supposed. Well, she would enjoy it before the cold of winter brought the heaviness of spirit she always seemed to feel.

As she bent over to pick to retrieve her stash of paper, her protruding stomach reminded her of their new little one. Maybe with a baby on the way, she would feel anticipation this winter, and not her usual sadness.

Once her paper and ink were spread out on the table, Hannah couldn't think of where to begin.

Dear Emily,

My almanac says fall, but the trees are still green, except the sumac.

I am in no rush, since the thought of winter is heavy on my heart.

I still don't know how we are holding on to this farm. One part of me says sell everything and move home near my family; and the other part of me says Georg is the most important part of my family, and I must help him hold to his dream, and it will be worth the struggle when the children are older. I write this today, for we are getting along this week. When Father left, we were so hard on each other.

Emily, I am struggling so with my feelings about Georg. Sometimes it seems what I know is right and what I really want to do or say are at complete odds with each other.

And then I wonder, what happens if I lose control and spill everything out to him. He would be crushed. So I hold my tongue, but then I'm not being honest and feel like we have no real communication.

I'm in a tangle, and on top of that, the new baby is growing, and now I have one more little one to be responsible for. I'll love this new little one as much as all the rest, but my mind is weary of all my thinking, and I believe I still love Georg; perhaps that's why I'm so frustrated with him.

Well, enough of this. Emily, write and tell me all your wedding plans. I know you can afford a red dress—but will it be silk or satin

or something even more extravagant? I assume
Father will give you a big wedding like the other
girls, but he will need help planning a big feast
without Mother there.

Emily, you will love your new life—please don't
let my complaints discourage you. I wish could
be there to witness this event, and I wish too
that Mother could still be there with you helping
in all the planning. She was such an organizer.

I love you, Emily.

Hannah

Hannah folded her letter up and replaced it in the dresser. It was past time to get something accomplished. She had been in the sewing mood for days now, just awaiting an opportunity, and today looked to be the time.

First on the list was her second piece of fabric Georg had bought her last spring. The dress she had in mind could be taken in after the baby was born, so she could wear it much longer.

New fabric was so scarce that she was always thinking up new ways to stretch the family's clothing. The girls were easier, as hems could be lowered or a ruffle of another color added to the bottom. The boys seemed to wear everything out before they grew out of it, even as fast as they were growing. Today, however, was all about a winter dress for her and some baby clothes for the new arrival.

Hannah had her own dress cut out and neatly folded, and some leftover flannel laid out for baby clothing before Clara returned with Daniel. They had armfuls of furry brown cattails with them.

"Mama, look, aren't they pretty?" asked Clara. "We could put them in a vase and make the table look so nice."

"Well," said Hannah hesitantly, "they are nice and so soft, they feel like velvet. But they will burst open soon, and fuzz will fly everywhere."

"Oh, Mama, how about just a day or two? And then I'll take them out. I promise."

"All right." Hannah smiled. "They are lovely, at least for a few days. We could eat them, you know."

"Mama," shrieked Clara. "That is awful. Think of the fur in your mouth. Who would eat cattails?"

"Well, if we were really hungry, we would. But God has blessed us with plenty of tasty things to eat, so I won't make you try them. I was just teasing."

Clara gave her mother a hug and ran back out the door. "Come on, Daniel, let's go play with the kittens."

Hannah was still puzzled as to how a large mother cat had found its way to their cabin and then promptly had a litter of five kittens, but her girls were delighted; and even though Hannah was not a cat fancier, they were useful out in the barn. In the winter, many field mice made their way to the grain stored up, and cats would keep that problem under control.

She returned to her scissors and fabric while listening with half an ear to Daniel and Clara outside playing with the kittens. She had some woven wool left as well, which, when boiled, made wonderful swaddling, especially in the cold winter months.

An hour sped by and then two. Startled, Hannah suddenly realized the time. She couldn't hear either of the children any longer. What in the world was Clara doing anyway?

Then from far off, she thought she could hear Daniel. She dropped the scissors as she ran out the door. Where was he? Up past the garden and beyond the fruit trees—she could hear him calling, "Mama, Mama!"

"Daniel?" She tried not to sound frightened. "I'm here by the cabin. Come here."

"No, Mama, come to me," wailed the two-year-old. "Clara can't come."

What was this? Hannah grabbed her skirts and dashed up the hill. She was heavy and awkward already, but she could still run.

"I'm coming, Daniel, I'm coming."

"Mama, come, come!"

Oh, he must not hear her. Where was Clara? Fear seemed to help her run faster, up the hill and into the trees. Just before the trees grew thicker was the stone wall from all the rock picking. And then, suddenly, she knew and thought her heart would stop.

It had to be a snake. She grabbed a branch off the ground, and then she saw Clara lying on the ground crying and Daniel clutching Clara's apron and crying, "Mama, Mama. Come, Mama."

As she dropped to her knees by Clara, who lay so still, she forgot all about hitting snakes. Clara could barely move and hugged her mother weakly.

"What happened?" Hannah asked. "I can't help you if I don't know what happened."

"It was the snake," Clara whispered. "It was so big, and Daniel was going to grab it, and I tried to hit it, but it bit me first."

"What kind of snake, Clara?" Hannah tried to speak calmly. Not everyone died of snakebite, and Clara wasn't a tiny child. She had to keep her wits about her.

"I guess a rattlesnake, Mama. It shook its tail at Daniel, but he didn't listen."

"Clara, listen carefully. Where did the snake bite you?"

"Mama, look," said Daniel suddenly. "Clara's arm is all fat."

It was true. Clara's upper arm was almost purple and swollen. How had a snake bitten her way up there? A leg bite would have been so much less threatening.

Hannah gathered her daughter up in her arms.

"Mama, don't pick me up. I feel like throwing up."

"I have to get help, Clara. I have to do something."

"I'm sorry, Mama. I was trying to keep Daniel safe and . . ." She lay very still gasping for breath.

Hannah refused to believe what her eyes were telling her. She picked Clara up carefully. "Daniel, grab hold of my skirt and walk with me."

Slowly she got to her feet and began walking down the hill. All the way she said loudly, "Not everyone dies of snakebite, not everyone dies of snakebite," as if by saying so, she could keep Clara from what she knew deep inside would be the outcome of this day.

By the time she reached the cabin, she could scarcely stagger up the steps. Clara was so heavy, but she would not put her down.

"God, don't do this to me," she said. "Not now, please, God." She could already feel the tears building up but refused to let them out. She rocked back and forth, gently so she wouldn't disturb her daughter, and tried to think of something that would help.

When Georg and the other children came singing down the hill several hours later, Hannah was still huddled on the porch with Clara wrapped in her arms. Her numbed mind told that if she just held on, Clara would wake up.

Daniel was lying beside her, fast asleep, still gripping her skirt, his face red and swollen from crying although he could not understand what was wrong.

Hannah heard her children and realized with a jolt that she would have to repeat what had happened and that repeating would make it real. Her heart felt as if it had been punctured; she could scarcely breathe; and as Georg came closer, the look of question and then alarm moving over his features forced her to concentrate on how to explain this. What she really wanted to do was start the day all over and lock Clara in the cabin with her so none of this could have happened.

Georg ran to Hannah. He put his hand on Clara's head and then felt her pulse. Hannah watched the color drain from his face as he realized the worst of fears was true. Clara was no longer breathing.

By now Hannah's throat was swollen from holding back tears, and she could no longer talk. Georg shook her, gently. "Hannah, what happened?"

She shook her head mutely and held up Clara's limp arm, now bruised and swollen, so he could see the bite.

"Snakebite," he whispered and tried to pry Clara out of Hannah's grasp.

"Come, Hannah. Let me help you," he said firmly.

"No, don't take her. I'm going to get help," Hannah mumbled. "I'm just so tired. I'll get up and take her to the wagon. We can find someone to help."

By this time the other children were gathered around. No one seemed quite sure what had happened, but just looking at their mother was enough. Hannah looked up at the crowd of children surrounding them.

Margaret and Magdalena clung to each other; dirt streaked both their faces, and Magdalena was shaking all over. Benjamin's face was hard and angry. Samuel, Frederick, and Hans were all weeping unashamedly. Benjamin blew his nose loudly on his sleeve and turned suddenly, slamming the door of the cabin as he disappeared inside.

"Hannah, look at me," Georg pleaded. "We can't help Clara. She is beyond help. But you need help yourself now. Let me take Clara."

Hannah finally had to admit that all her weeping and pleading with God was to no avail. Clara had succumbed to the snakebite, and Hannah found herself at the edge of a cliff with no bottom in sight. One more step, and she would fall over and lie crushed at the bottom, down deep with all the joy Clara had brought her.

Daniel began to squirm awake. He rubbed his eyes, stared dazedly around him at his family, and brushed clumsily at the dirt on his face. His grimy thumb went into his mouth even though he had given up that habit months ago, and he tugged and tugged on Clara's apron.

"Wake up, Clara," he said. "Papa's back for supper."

Hannah wanted in the worst way to hug him to her breast, but she couldn't move.

Samuel grabbed him up in an anguished hug and kissed him even while he cried.

"Clara can't wake up," he said, his voice cracking with emotion. "She will never wake up. Mama, what happened?"

Hannah opened her mouth to explain, but the words were gone. How could a sentence or two explain her devastation or her anger—at herself and at God for letting this happen to her? Many of her neighbors had had to deal with the death of a child or even a spouse, but she had never felt this disaster would come near her. Now she had no choice but to face this grief; it lurked outside her door, a seductive serpent that beckoned to her, and she could not refuse its summons.

Benjamin opened the cabin door, softly this time. He squared his shoulders, took a deep breath, and was the first to hug Hannah. "Mama, can you tell us anything?" he asked gently.

Finally Hannah choked out what she knew. Daniel had called, and she had come running, but it was too late. If only she hadn't been so preoccupied by her sewing. She could never forgive herself for not noticing Daniel's cries soon enough.

Georg pried Clara from Hannah's unwilling arms, which were now cramped from holding so tightly. She rubbed her arms and stood watching Georg, who laid her in the cabin on the table, since there was nowhere else. She ran upstairs then and grabbed Clara's quilt.

"She'll be cold." Hannah covered her softly with her favorite blanket. She sat on the bench next to her still, still daughter and softly rubbed Clara's hands, willing her to wake up.

Benjamin had followed them into the cabin and stood beside Hannah, awkwardly patting her back. Georg turned to him then. "Benjamin," he said sternly. "I know you want to be here, but I need you to ride to Fort Augusta and get Reverend Claybaugh. I heard he was there last week, and he was holding meetings, so he will still be in the area.

"Your Mama is going to want to some comfort besides just me. Do you understand?"

Benjamin frowned. "Papa, I need to be here with Mama. She needs me. I always help her when the little children get hurt."

Georg, caressing Clara's soft blonde hair, raised his fist in frustration. "*I* need you, Benjamin. I need you to get the reverend. You have to understand. I can't go. I have to stay here."

"Yes sir, I understand." Tears welled in Benjamin's eyes, but he angrily wiped them away before turning toward the door.

"Take Brown Betty. She's the fastest horse. And switch horses in Fort Augusta if you need to. We can pick up the mare later. Also, get the reverend on a horse. That mule is too slow."

"Yes, sir." Benjamin ran out and Hannah followed, watching him from the doorway. She sat down on the porch steps then and covered her face with her apron. The other children, not knowing what else to do, sat down around Hannah. She knew they were there, and her mother's heart told her they needed comforting, but her grief had paralyzed her and she could not respond.

The air was growing chilly, and the sun had set. As twilight deepened, Georg picked Hannah up too and carried her back inside. He set her down in her rocker, where Hannah heard him banging her skillet and then smelled the aroma of eggs frying. *So, someone will feed my children.* Hannah was dimly grateful to Georg. She rocked and cried, and then without saying a word, got up and went slowly to her room. She curled up under the blankets and heard Georg come in. She hoped he would go away and not talk to her.

"Darling, I need you to talk to me," he said. "This wasn't your fault."

Hannah simply clung to him. She laid her head against him and felt closer to her husband than she had in many months. Eventually, exhausted, she fell asleep against his chest.

She was awakened by the sound of hooves outside. At first she couldn't remember why she was in bed, still clothed. Georg was gone now; and then she heard the creak of the steps and the squeak of her doorknob.

Benjamin put his head in the door. "Mama, I brought Reverend Claybaugh."

Reverend Claybaugh came in then, crossed over to Hannah's bed, and took her hand. Georg was right behind him.

"Ah, Hannah," the reverend said. "Your world is shaking. You must cling fast to God, your strength to get through this."

Hannah gazed up at him, her sleep-clouded mind making her feel stupid. Then the day's events flooded back over her with a rush. "I don't understand. Where was God? He could have kept that snake away. He could have spared my Clara. I can't understand this. I don't even want to understand."

"Hannah, you are not the first person to feel this way, and I am not going to preach at you, but I want you to think about a Scripture passage from Deuteronomy chapter 33, verse 27. It says that 'The Eternal God is our refuge and underneath are the everlasting arms.' When you can't go on, remember God's arms are around you."

"Go away." Hannah pulled the cover up to her chin. "I'm too tired. I can't think. I want to wake up tomorrow and find this was all a bad dream. Please leave me alone."

Reverend Claybaugh patted Hannah's shoulder. "I understand. I'll go out in the shed to sleep. I know where to find everything, and I'm going to stay here a few days and help you and Georg."

Hannah didn't answer. She turned her back to the two men and closed her eyes.

Tomorrow everything would turn around, and this day would be gone. She knew it.

14

LAST FAREWELL

Hannah woke to find frost on her small windowpane near the bed. The leaves might finally have turned if it was cold enough last night. She jumped up. She would wake up Clara; Clara loved to be the first one to see the leaves in fall. She grabbed the quilt, wrapped it around her, and then stopped dead. Georg wasn't even in bed—where could he be so early? And Clara, Clara was never going to enjoy the leaves again. Sleep had been merciful to Hannah last night, but now the previous day's events returned. She could see once again Clara lying on the hill and Daniel crying and crying for his mama. And she had not even heard him for how long? Perhaps if she had heard him sooner, Clara could have been helped.

"Clara," moaned Hannah. How could she bear losing a child? The house was so quiet. What were the other children doing? Last night seemed so fuzzy. Had anyone fed them supper? She couldn't remember anything beyond carrying Clara to the cabin.

Georg had been so kind last night, but what grief was he holding in so she could weep? Hannah wiped her eyes, changed out of the filthy dress she had slept in, and climbed slowly downstairs. Her unborn child felt so heavy. She suddenly realized all she had done the day before and wondered at the fact that the baby still kicked and rolled. He must be all right even though she had carried Clara down the hill.

All her children were sitting around the table. Reverend Claybaugh was at the head, and they each had a bowl of cornmeal mush.

"Good morning, Hannah," he said, his weather-beaten face creased with worry. "You probably don't feel like eating, but I made you breakfast anyway. You'll need it."

"Where's Georg?" wondered Hannah.

Samuel spoke quietly as if he might disturb her. "He went to dig a grave." He turned around suddenly, wiped at his face, and turned back. "Benjamin and I offered to help, but he said he had to be alone."

Hannah put her hands over her face and then pushed back her uncombed hair. "He needs me," she said. "I'll come back. Where did he go?"

"I don't know," answered Samuel again, slowly spooning mush into his mouth. His hands shook. "He said something about a sugar maple."

Hannah knew where he was. Just the other side of the stone wall was one of Clara's favorite trees. Autumn almost always turned it into a flaming orange, and Clara never failed to drag the family out to see it on every clear fall morning when the sun, rising over the hills, shone on her tree.

She set out slowly. Her legs ached and her back ached and her mind felt so cloudy. Life was such a struggle here. She did not know how to go on, but Georg must feel the same way. She would just go stand near him so he knew she was thinking of him too.

As she walked through the orchard, she could see him. His back was to her, he was on his knees, and his shoulders were shaking. He never had been one to show sorrow around the family. She hesitated a moment, uncertain if she should interrupt. But he should know she was thinking of him, and so she went on.

Each tree and blade of grass seemed to etch itself on her mind as she passed. This day and the one before it would be forever in her memory even though she longed to blot them out. Finally she stood next to Georg. He was weeping as if his heart would never mend. Even when they had gotten news from Germany of family members of his who had died, he had not wept. Now it seemed to her as though all his stored-up tears had escaped, and she could not stop the flow. Tears welled up in her own eyes even though she thought she had cried them out yesterday. How much weeping could a person endure?

"Oh, Hannah, I left Clara behind so she could help you. She would still be here if I had let her go along, and Daniel would have just played indoors with you. I don't know if I should say this is my fault or yours."

Hannah's face turned white. How could he say those things to her? She was suffering as much as he. Perhaps more. She had carried this little girl under her heart for months and known of her before anyone else. Their firstborn daughter. Hannah had wondered yesterday if Clara's death was her fault, but that Georg should think so was more than she could bear.

Her desire to share this time with her husband fled along with his cruel words, and she turned and walked dejectedly back down the hill. Let him dig a grave alone, then. She would dress Clara in her best dress, and Reverend Claybaugh would preach his best funeral message. Then when Clara lay still under her favorite tree, they would try to pick up the pieces of life. But she could not and would not stay to comfort her husband.

How she got through the rest of the day, Hannah could not say. She did dress Clara in her best dress, and the reverend did preach a brave message about Christ, the Resurrection and the Life. They sang "Rock of Ages" and read Psalm 23. When they came to the part about the shadow of death, Hannah knew she was in that valley.

The Scriptures and hymns were a rope pulling her up out of the valley, but as the day wore on, she thought the rope was stretching thinner and thinner and would soon tear.

The children stood in a cluster around the raw earth. They were all holding hands and weeping. Daniel certainly did not understand what was happening.

"Mama, why is Papa putting Clara down in that hole? Can't she come out wif us?"

Each of his questions tore at her heart, and she simply could not find the words to answer him. Margaret and Magdalena surely didn't understand either. They just held hands while tears flowed down their cheeks. Benjamin and Samuel were obviously trying to be grown up and not cry, and Georg was not weeping anymore. His face was set and still, and Hannah felt her heart grow cold when she glanced over at him.

Hannah barely heard a word anyone said. She began to believe this was her fault after all. And God was punishing her for her neglect yesterday. Her sadness and her anger at God and Georg were settling themselves into a hard knot somewhere deep inside her. She had the uneasy feeling that if left to fester there, they would grow and infect her like a poison. Today, though, she must simply leave them be and hope she would have courage to deal with them later.

The rest of the day was a blur. None of their neighbors were close enough to have heard of the tragedy. Reverend Claybaugh would spread the word when he left, but he had decided this family needed him right now and planned to stay as long as seemed needful. Somehow the children managed to take care of the animals, but the rest of the daily chores went undone.

Hannah had gone back to rocking in her chair; she held Clara's unfinished quilt to her face and tried her best not to weep again. A quarrel between Johan and Margaret finally brought Hannah back to herself. She hated to hear her children fighting.

Looking around, she could see the devastation in her cabin. Her floor hadn't been swept, her few pans were piled in her washing basin, and it looked as if every dish she owned was dirty. Life couldn't go on like this. Hannah made the decision to bury her emotions, like so many other times, and gathered her oldest children around her.

"Benjamin and Samuel," she said, with a hand on each, "we need to be brave for the other little ones here. I am not saying don't weep. Men can weep, but the younger ones don't understand what really happened here yesterday. Daniel keeps asking when I'm going to get Clara back. Papa is feeling angry, but I think that is how he shows his sadness. I need you boys to help me keep things going."

And if I don't keep busy, I will fall apart, she thought but couldn't say so to her sons.

"I understand, Mama," said Samuel, while Benjamin merely nodded and wiped his eyes with his sleeve. "Come on, Benjamin, the kindling box is almost empty, and we'll need a fire tonight. Why don't we go cut some wood? Hans and Frederick can carry it in and stack it in the wood box."

Both boys left the cabin, Samuel grabbing the ax on his way out, and Hannah turned her thoughts toward the smaller children.

"Magdalena, go and get me some fresh candles, please. These have almost burned away, and it will be getting dark earlier and earlier. And Johann, could you please sweep up the floor for Mama?"

So the afternoon went. Hannah found task after task for the children, all the while pretending nothing had changed in life. Georg wandered into the kitchen and out again without speaking. She noticed that whenever he went out, he headed for the shed where the reverend was staying. She hoped he was finding some relief in talking with the minister. His face had aged overnight, and his shoulders slumped as if he hadn't the energy to carry them and face life. She and Georg had not said one word to each other since his comments on the hill, and Hannah was not sure if she should open a conversation or just leave him to himself.

Finally, needing desperately to share her troubles with someone who would understand, Hannah retrieved her ongoing letter to

Emily. Who would take these sad tidings to her father? She started a
new page.

> Dear Father and Emily too,
>   Yesterday a tragedy struck us. I do not know
> if I can even explain it without dripping tears on
> my paper, but I will try. I must admit that I
> was so caught up in my sewing that I had quite
> lost track of the children. I could hear Daniel
> far off, crying for me. A snake had bitten Clara.
> When Georg came home, Clara was dead, and I
> cannot erase from my mind the picture of her
> lying on the grass and Daniel weeping and my world
> crumbling about me. As soon as I close my eyes,
> it all comes back again.
>   I don't know when you will read this, but you
> must pray for us because I don't know if we can
> pray. I don't know if I am angry at God or myself
> or how I can resolve the many, many questions
> swirling in my mind.

She folded the piece of paper and got another one. This one she
addressed to Emily alone.

> Dear Emily,
>   I think my heart has broken. Georg is so angry
> at me. He said if he had only taken Clara along
> with him, this never would have happened. How can
> I argue with that? I already thought that perhaps
> somehow this was my fault, although the children
> all have spent time alone playing, and anyone could
> have run into a snake; but to have him accuse me

of being at fault is too much. I think he only said it out of anguish and pain, but I cannot forget that it was said, and we haven't spoken to each other all day. I couldn't write this to Father but I must tell someone, and you are the only one I trust with my deepest thoughts. Write and tell me you love me even if this was my fault.

    Hannah.

Twilight was already creeping over the hills as Hannah tied on her apron and went outside to see if the reverend would join them for a meal. She hadn't felt like cooking anything at all. But the children needed to eat so she had managed to stir together a pan of biscuits, and there was plenty of cornmeal mush left from last night's supper. She sliced up the cold, gelatinous mass and fried the pieces in lard in their cast-iron skillet. If they poured honey over it, at least their bellies would be filled.

She sighed and choked down the tears that threatened to overflow again. Everything reminded her of Clara. All the little jobs Clara did without being asked, her cheerful singing in the middle of the day, even the way her eyes twinkled when she knew her brothers were teasing her and planned a secret revenge. All those things were gone. The sounds of Daniel outside her window with Margaret broke into her thoughts. She had been so caught up in her own devastation that she had not even thought of her own children except to make sure they were fed. Maybe she should find out how her children were dealing with this.

Hannah, you need to be a better mother, she told herself sternly. Put yourself aside and reach out to your children now before something else happens. Then she turned around, and there were the cattails. Was it only yesterday she had told Clara they didn't belong in the house? Clara had pled for them to be kept in the house just a day or two. Already a bit of fluff was showing. Hannah thought maybe she would keep them forever.

The reverend was walking toward her with Georg and Samuel beside him. Right behind them were Daniel and Margaret. She rang the bell for the rest of the children, and everyone trooped silently into the cabin. Clearly, no one felt like talking. It might prove harder than she thought to figure out how each of her children was handling this rip in their family fabric.

"Come on, everybody," she said bravely. "Supper's ready. Reverend Claybaugh, you can sit here next to Georg."

"Mama, that's Clara's chair," said Magdalena. "No one can sit there."

"Yes, children, we have to go on with life. Clara cannot come back to us, although we all want her ever so much. This spot is Clara's, but if we have guests, I will let someone else sit here. Now sit down, all of you, please."

Georg had remained silent ever since he came into her kitchen, but now he spoke up.

"Reverend, please say the blessing." His voice caught and broke, his shoulders slumped even further, and he finally admitted, "I'm not sure any of us feel like praying."

"I will," said the reverend in his deep voice. "Be sure God knows how you all feel. Maybe you're angry or hurt so deeply that you can't even express it, but God knows, and any of you can talk to Him about it when you are ready. He won't judge you for having those feelings. We are all human, after all. I miss Clara too. So let's take hands and pray."

Holding hands was the last thing Hannah felt like doing right now. But glancing at each other several times, they did join hands in a circle around the table and waited for the reverend to offer a blessing.

"Our gracious heavenly Father," he began. "You see us down here with grief and feelings we've never felt before. You see these little children who have lost their sister and these parents who have lost their first daughter, and You hurt with them. Father, comfort us in the ways we need to be comforted, and we thank You too for this food you have blessed us with. In the days to come, help each of us to seek You for understanding and for healing. Amen."

Hannah didn't know how she should respond to such a prayer and mutely began passing the biscuits and then the fried mush. Their meal was a quiet affair, with each person wrapped in a cloak of silence.

With supper finished, the dishes were cleared, and then Hannah asked the children to head off to their beds. Despite her resolution, she wasn't quite ready to hear all their feelings. Suppose they all blamed her for Clara's death? Since no one else seemed to want to talk either, bedtime was silent. Only last week it had involved tickling and laughter when Papa was home. Only Daniel, clad in his nightshirt, stopped to say, "I luf you, Mama and Papa," before he climbed up into the loft and into bed with Johann.

"Reverend, I'll walk you out to the shed," said Georg. "I need to check the animals anyway and make sure they all got fed. I hope you don't mind us being so quiet."

"Not at all," said the reverend. "You forget that I lost my wife before I was a traveling preacher. I have been through grief too."

As the two men went out the door, Hannah retreated to her bed. Undressing, she gave in to the tears that had threatened her all day. She didn't have to be strong for anyone here in her own bed.

While her tears traveled down her cheeks, Hannah thought over and over of hearing Daniel call her name yesterday. She remembered the awful feeling of her heart turning inside out when she saw Clara on the ground, and again when she finally grasped that Clara was dead. She tried to shut out the pictures flitting through her mind, but it seemed impossible.

Cried out, finally, she wondered when Georg would come back in. The animals should have been taken care of by now. She heard the clock chime for the second time. Her wedding clock. Now it was chiming the end of her happiness. She wondered if perhaps Georg had bedded down with the reverend. That would be a first for their married life, but so was losing a child.

She crept out of bed, and pulling her shawl over her shoulders against the chill, Hannah looked out the window into the darkness. *These silly glass windows.* She had been so upset over taxes on her glass, and now she couldn't care less if her whole house burned up. She only wanted Clara back in her arms. She could see light at the shed, so she knew the men were still up.

I'm always the one to say I'm sorry. I did not deserve those angry words, and Georg is going to have to be the one to tell me he is sorry. He is going to have to speak first for once.

She was surprised by how rebellious and angry she suddenly felt, but she was in the right, and she was justified in her angry thoughts. Deep down stirred a little thought that her attitude was wrong, but Hannah could not listen to it tonight.

She climbed into bed again and tried to sleep. After tossing and turning and listening to the chiming of her clock for what seemed like hours, she got up again to look for the sunrise. It was still pitch black, and even the dim light under the shed door was no longer shining. Georg must be sleeping out there tonight.

Hannah sighed, got back in bed, and hoped that by morning, Georg would be ready to apologize. Perhaps the reverend could help him see the wrong in his hasty words.

Tomorrow she would take stock of what was left. God had still given them much, and living in the wilderness as she did, she should have been prepared for such an event. She would just pull herself back up to the top of the cliff from which she had fallen yesterday. Right now she couldn't think why, but it seemed the right thing to try. Shove all this down somewhere and go on. At last, completely exhausted, despite these thoughts swirling round and round her brain, she thought she could finally fall asleep.

15

CIDER AND SAUCE

Two weeks passed in much the same way as the first days after Clara's sudden death. Hannah tried to keep the children busy, and each day was a little easier to bear, although the heavy weight of grief still clung to the family. Georg and Hannah talked when they had need, but it was a strained relationship at best.

Autumn was at its glorious climax now. Reds, oranges, and vibrant yellows shone over the mountain behind the cabin, and the air was so fresh, it often caught in Hannah's throat early in the morning. Many of the birds had headed south already.

The corn crop was sparser than usual due to the dry summer, so Hannah had sent off the children almost every day to find acorns in the woods. It was cool enough now that snakes were not a worry. Each child carried a large basket or the wooden bucket or any kind of container that could hold acorns.

When they returned with everything filled, Hannah and the two oldest boys would convert the acorns into flour by first drying them out in the sun, then pounding them and sifting off the shells. Once they were in small pieces, Hannah would soak them in water and change the water several times a day until the acorns no longer had a bitter taste.

After that, the result was a sort of acorn mush, which they spread out and dried until it resembled flour. It was a long, tiring process but in the middle of winter, acorn flour would be a welcome addition if the corn flour ran out.

When everyone was fed up with pounding and pouring water and drying, they would store the remaining acorns in empty casks. The flour would be used first, and more flour could be made later if necessary. The children all hoped it would not be necessary as they much preferred corn bread.

It was also cool enough to butcher the piglets. The smokehouse was full of hams hanging, and the scent of apple wood and hickory wood filled the air for days. Hannah was kept busy making *panhaus*—a tasty dish consisting of meat scraps, cornmeal, salt, and lard. The whole concoction was boiled in the iron kettle over a fire and involved a lot of stirring to prevent burning.

Once it was the proper thickness, it was poured into pans to cool. Then the pans were dumped out, and each gray, square, sticky mass was wrapped in greased paper. It was easily sliced and eaten fried with maple syrup or honey or just plain with salt and pepper and fried eggs alongside. The children loved it for breakfast. Since panhaus didn't keep long, it was a special treat around butchering day. Once the panhaus was out of the kettle, the fat had to be slowly melted for lard. The fire was kept low, and as the meat scraps floated to the top, they were skimmed off until all that was left was a kettle full of pure white lard. As it cooled, it too could be wrapped and stored in the crocks in the ground cellar and would last for a long time for frying food or baking pie crusts or even making soap.

It looked like there would be plenty of meat for the winter months. Georg had also brought in several deer, which they dried, and following the Indians' example, made the meat into pemmican using lard, dried meat, and berries. It wasn't very tasty but would sustain them in the event of a shortage of other food.

Hannah went through these needful tasks in a fog. Many times, she would put down her spoon or big wooden stirring paddle and sigh and look off into the distance.

"Mama," said Johann one afternoon, "I asked you three times now if it was time to make supper, and you didn't hear me."

"Oh, Johann, I am sorry. This autumn weather keeps reminding me of Clara. She loved the colors so." Her eyes unexpectedly filled with tears.

"Well, we're getting hungry," responded Johann grumpily. "I miss Clara too."

"All right, I'm going to cook." Hannah wiped her hands on her apron. "I feel like all I've been doing for days is cook for the winter, and you children are always hungry. Come on, let's see what we can make. You can be my helper."

"Mama, boys don't cook," Johann said. "I probably should help Papa with something."

"Oh, yes, boys do cook," Hannah said. "How do you think the mountain men stay alive on the trails when they go trap beaver? Or the Indian braves out on the warpath? Of course men cook. Now come along with me, and let's make supper."

Once assured that cooking could be a man's job also, Johann proved to be a good kitchen helper and a quick learner. He seemed to enjoy working along with Hannah, and she unexpectedly enjoyed his company.

I don't know my younger boys well enough, she thought. She needed to get them all involved inside the cabin for a while.

The next day provided ample opportunity. The apples were ripe, and applesauce as well as apple cider were anticipated every year. Hannah made only small amounts of applesauce, since it was hard to keep for long; but they pressed many gallons of cider every year, and Georg sealed it up in crockery jugs that he saved from year to year and stored it in their large ground cellar. By spring, whatever had not been drunk had turned into vinegar, and they used it to make pickles of many kinds.

From Georg's German friends, Hannah had learned to make *snitz*, which was simply apples sliced thin and then spread to dry. Once dried, they could be strung together and hung up in the kitchen and used all winter. They also had enough crocks left this fall to make apple butter, another iron kettle task.

This job required all the older children. Benjamin and Samuel would start a fire and fill the kettle with apple cider and applesauce. Hannah had a carefully hoarded store of cinnamon, her secret ingredient, which Georg brought home for her every now and then. She also added a quart or two of last year's vinegar. This mixture was cooked and stirred for hours over a slow burning fire. As it thickened, it had to be stirred constantly, so the older children took turns. Even a few moments of untended apples could ruin the whole kettle. Sometimes the butter took more than a day. Then the family would stay up all night, stirring and telling tales. Finally the apple butter was thick and dark brown and ready to eat. The sweet taste and the smell of cooking apple butter made the tricky task well worth the effort.

All this effort to stay alive during the winter kept Hannah from focusing on her loss of Clara. She felt an ache in her heart, but there was not much time to reflect on what this change would do to their family. She tried to keep her mind on the days ahead, preparing for winter and preparing for a new baby. When evening came, and memories crowded thick around her, she would pull out her Bible and look through it for words of comfort. Georg's method of dealing with grief seemed to be to lock it up inside, and Hannah found herself talking more and more to the children about their memories and not to her husband.

One evening Hannah sat rocking in the kitchen, watching Magdalena, Johann, and Hans wash dishes. The older children had been cutting wood all day and so were excused from cleanup this evening.

Since the advent of cool weather, most of their cooking was done over the hearth indoors, so the cabin still had a delicious smell of stew. Georg had been out hunting and brought home a bear. Then the children learned that a thrifty settler could make bear ham. Two hams had gone into the smokehouse, and they would join the pork shoulders already hanging up once they had smoked long enough. A bear also brought bear grease, which, Georg assured Hannah, would make much tastier pemmican than they were used to. Hannah was just glad the bear was gone, as it had probably been the one that scared them so earlier in the summer.

The wind was picking up outside. A storm was moving in. They'd had several thunderstorms in the last two weeks, although it was late in the year for thunder. The storms seemed to move in at evening, blowing leaves from many of the trees, and then by morning, the day was clear and bright.

Hannah had taken to reading her hymnbook and her Bible more and more often, seeking comfort. Reverend Claybaugh had written a short list of passages for her to look up, and she would often take a few moments in the evening to do so. Her letter writing had come to a halt. She simply didn't know what to say to Emily. Everything she wrote sounded as if she was complaining about life, yet she knew that even with the loss of a child, their family was still blessed. She just didn't *feel* blessed, so her paper and pens stayed in the drawer, and her supply of homemade ink dried up.

The quiet of the evening was interrupted by the thunder of hoofbeats up the path. Georg jumped up almost as if he had been listening for someone and went out, slamming the door behind him. Hannah fought off the urge to follow him out. He would only scold her and send her back in. She could hear voices outside the door. They rose and fell in turn and then got louder as the discussion got more heated. They weren't quite loud enough for her to decipher, though, and then it sounded as if the men moved off the porch.

Her curiosity roused, Hannah beckoned to Samuel. "Go outside and ask Papa if he and his guest would like a cup of coffee. I've been saving a little bit, and maybe we should use it now."

Samuel gave her a knowing grin and jumped to his feet. "I'm tired of this arithmetic anyway," he said as he threw down his pencil. "I'll see who's here."

The other children giggled. They all knew Hannah had a boundless curiosity when it came to Georg's business doings. They had overheard plenty of discussions between the two, when Hannah pled for Georg to fill her in on his dealings.

Her son pulled open the heavy wooden door with more noise than usual, probably to warn the men of his approach. Samuel could be crafty, and he recognized that his papa wouldn't want to feel like someone was sneaking up on him.

He returned quickly. "It's Martin Reitz," he said. "Remember the man who brought us home in his wagon when we went canoeing? Anyway, Papa said to go ahead and make coffee, but they won't come in for a little while. They're talking about business."

Hannah resisted her desire to ask if Samuel had heard any of the discussion and busied herself with clearing the table of the schoolwork the children had been pretending to work on.

"Magdalena, go wash my other two pewter cups," she said. "I think they're still sitting in the sink. Hans, you and Frederick go put all these books and papers away, and Johann, you can sweep the floor."

"Mama, we just cleaned up from supper," protested Johann. "Isn't it clean enough?"

"Just get busy," said Hannah. "One should take extra care when a guest is here."

The water was boiling in the tin coffeepot already, so she wrapped her apron around her hand and pulled it off the fire. When she added the coffee, she also poured in some cold water to settle the grounds and set the pot on the table to cool a little before the men came in.

Hannah loved the smell of coffee, day or night. It brought memories of her mother making breakfast in their cheery New York home and other memories of her first married years and her own little kitchen before they had traveled as far west as this small corner of Pennsylvania. Someday her children would spread out, and when they made coffee, they would think back to this little cabin with its cozy hearth and a spring running through the kitchen.

The sound of the door opening yet again brought her back to today. Georg and Martin came in quietly compared to the loud voices she had heard outside just a few minutes ago. At the moment, nothing seemed wrong between them. They were conversing quite calmly about each other's readiness for winter, and Georg was remarking on how much apple butter Hannah and the children had made this year.

"Welcome again, Martin." Hannah smiled. "Last time I saw you, you were returning my half-drowned family."

Georg glanced sharply at her. Then she remembered she had never told him that Benjamin had shared the whole story. Well, compared to the last couple weeks, a ducking in the creek was nothing she was upset about anymore.

"I'm afraid I don't come under such welcome circumstances this time," remarked Martin, running a hand through his shaggy hair. "Georg can explain it to you later though. Someone told me there was coffee to be had here."

"Yes, indeed. Please sit down," said Hannah, flustered and more curious than ever. She opened a small crock of their fresh apple butter and set a plate of bread next to Martin. "Are you hungry, or did you have supper already?"

"I did eat, but this looks delicious. I'll just have to dig in again. Womenfolk's cooking is much more to my liking than my own poor attempts when I travel. Thank you."

He smeared apple butter generously over his bread. "Back where I come from, you need cottage cheese for apple butter. I guess you can't make that out here in the wilderness."

Georg laughed and grabbed his own bread. "You must be from somewhere close to my home. I thought only we retired soldiers and other German folk ate cottage cheese with apple butter."

"What kind of name do you think Reitz is anyway?" answered Martin. "My brother and I were both brought over for the fighting and decided never to return. This is the land of opportunity."

"For most folks, anyway," said Georg mysteriously, but he would say no more. There were too many children present, listening in, Hannah guessed.

The evening passed quickly. Fall had already brought an early dark. Georg offered Martin the use of the shed again, and the two men soon went out to build a fire in the little stove out there. Hannah shooed the children off to bed and sat again rocking, waiting for Georg to return so they could talk.

She didn't have long to wait. "Georg, can you sit down and talk to me just for a little?"

"Sure," he answered slowly. "What's on your mind?"

"Oh, Georg, how can you ask that? You have gotten letters you won't discuss, brought my father in for consultation, and now I hear you outside my door arguing with this Martin Reitz. How is he concerned with us anyway? And I think I have a right to know what is going on if it concerns me."

"Yes, Hannah, you do have a right to know what's going on." Georg ran his hands through his hair and then rubbed his beard. "I don't quite know how to explain everything, and you have been so caught up in Clara's death that sometimes I think you are not here at all. Just your body, going through the motions of our life, but my wife is not here." He ran his hands restlessly through his hair again.

"That's not fair." Hannah clenched her fists. Was she somewhere else all the time? Thinking back, she had been rather preoccupied. "It's only been a couple weeks, Georg. Can I forget so quickly?"

"No one wants you to forget." He came over and pulled her to her feet. "Now, look at me." He put his arms around her and held her close. "We are all dealing with grief in different ways. No one is forgetting Clara. But Hannah, we have eight other children who need us desperately. They are grieving too, in their own ways, and you have another little one to think about. If you don't come back here to reality, I'm afraid something will happen to the baby, and there will be even more grief. You can't take too much more, Hannah."

Hannah stiffened and pulled away. "Don't decide for me what I can take. Things are going on around here that I need to know about. I'm sorry I've been distant, but I'm not so far away that someone couldn't find me if he cared."

"That's unfair, Hannah. You know I love you. I'm not always the best at showing it, but you can't deny that I love you."

"No, I can't." Hannah stared straight into his eyes, really seeing him for the first time in days. Her heart twisted. "I know you love me, but I am overwhelmed. There are financial things I don't understand, and you aren't telling me everything in some silly attempt to spare me, and there is all this work before winter, and I am expecting a baby, and we just lost a daughter, and I don't even understand myself right now."

"Hannah, Hannah, you are saying two things." Georg reached out again to embrace her. "You're overwhelmed, and yet you don't want me to spare you information that might make you *more* overwhelmed. I won't be the cause of you breaking down."

Hannah still refused to return to Georg's embrace. Instead, she plopped down at the table, put her head in her hands, and stared at her coffee mug. Suddenly she burst out weeping.

"I'm just so afraid. I feel like life's falling apart, and why can't you be afraid with me? I'm the only one, and it's too lonely in here, fearing everything. Why can't life just go back to where we were all happy and on this adventure of farming and everything you always dreamed of? Were those dreams wrong? Is God punishing us? Can He even see that my heart is breaking?"

Georg stared at her. "Hannah, I've never seen you this way before. Life threw things at us, and you could always handle them with grace. I've never known you to be fearful."

"Maybe I just need sleep," she said finally. "Maybe no one can understand this. Maybe it's just in my head."

She untied her apron, threw it on the table, and made her way upstairs without even looking back to see if Georg would join her.

She stopped to look at all the children, but they were all sleeping soundly, so she crawled into bed and curled up in a ball without even taking time to change into her nightgown.

16

STOMPING TIME

As October faded into November, so too did Hannah's worries seem to fade. To be sure, they were still under the surface of her life, but not bubbling over as they had the day Martin Reitz had visited. Her heart seemed a little less bruised than it had several weeks ago, although it was by no means near healed. She and Georg had an unspoken truce as they both worked to prepare for the coming winter. Neither one spoke of the rifts between them, but they worked together as much for the children watching them as anything.

The fall tasks were completed one by one. The latest job had been gathering all the grapes, both the wild ones and the ones she and Georg had planted. The wild turkeys were eager to plunder all the low-lying vines they could find, so the children spent a few days gathering the rich purple fruit for the making of raisins. Every vine and tendril seemed to get ripe at once. And the days were long to ensure that nothing was wasted by getting overripe. Hannah loved the smell of grapes. Her kitchen overflowed with the large dark purple ones they had planted and the smaller reddish wild grapes. The children stripped the fruits from their stems and when they had a full basket of greenish brown empty stems, they were given to the two pigs still remaining in the pen, Peaches and one of her babies.

The grapes themselves were spread out to dry in the sun, which, although weaker now at the end of the year, was still warm enough to shrivel them, preserving their sugary insides and turning them into raisins, which would keep far longer than their original form. Hannah baked several sour-cream-and-raisin pies as a treat and would bake more for their upcoming Thanksgiving feast.

"Mama," said Frederick as they pulled grapes off still more stems, "aren't the turkeys sad when we try and get all their food?"

"Oh, don't be silly," said Benjamin. "Why should they care?"

"Well," began Hannah, "the woods are full of grapevines. We just picked the ones close to us. I think the turkeys will find plenty more."

"And if they don't," Samuel said eagerly, waving his purple fingers in the air at his invisible prey, "Papa will shoot them for us to eat, and they won't have to worry about all the grapes being gone."

"And we get Thanksgiving dinner," cheered Margaret, while Magdalena added, "We can't wait. We haven't had a big feast since the barn raising."

"Hooo-way, a feast!" Daniel banged on the table with a wooden spoon. "Mama, what's a feast?"

The children all laughed, and Hannah sat down and pulled Daniel onto her lap.

"Thanksgiving is a feast. It's a big, special meal where we remember all the things we are thankful for and all the blessings God has given us and the good year just past and . . ." Thoughts of Clara helping her bake last year suddenly flooded her mind. "Run and play, Daniel. We must finish with these grapes before the fruit flies eat them all."

"What are fruit flies?" asked Daniel as he slid down off Hannah's lap.

"Look here, Daniel," said Johann. "See these little flying bugs? They gather in the autumn all around the ripe fruit. Papa calls them sour flies. If we don't soon get this fruit stored somewhere, our cabin will be full of sour flies."

"Ewww," said Daniel. "I can help."

"You go play with the little girls," said Hannah. "We'll be fine."

Daniel jumped up and down and ran out the door. "Magdawena, come play," he yelled, and everyone laughed again.

"Who wants to guess the next big job?" asked Hans. "I heard Papa talking to Benjamin, so I already know."

"Soap?" asked Johann. "We have lard, and Papa made a lot of potash, so we can have lye."

"Nope." Hans smiled in his pleasure of knowing a secret. "We still have lots of soap. Someone else guess."

"Candles—we saw lots more ripe bayberries just yesterday."

"Nope. Guess again."

"I know I know!" Magdalena had run back in. "Papa said the cabbage is ripe. We're going to have a sauerkraut stomping day."

"Hoo-way," shouted Daniel, who had followed his sister back indoors. "Sawukwaut is the bestest food. Can I help?"

"Yes, Daniel, that is one job you can help with, and we will need everyone's help," Hannah answered. "Your Papa even bought a new barrel to put it in, so it can age down in the cellar. "We'll start picking the cabbage tomorrow before we get too many hard frosts on the plants."

Up to now, the frosts had been light, but the cabbages had large heads and were threatening to crack open. The colder turn in the weather meant it was definitely sauerkraut time.

After everyone was tucked in, Hannah sat rocking and sewing yet more baby things. Once the baby arrived in early spring, she knew there would be no sewing time.

Georg came in from checking the animals and dug out his harmonica. He sat playing a hymn softly and glancing at Hannah.

"Something is on your mind," said Hannah. "You only play your harmonica when there's something you haven't made up your mind to tell me yet. What is it?"

"Maybe you know me too well," said Georg, taking a pause from the hymn. "I do have something on my mind. We're almost finished with the fall work, and I think you need a break. Perhaps all our quarreling is a sign we need to do something different. A change of scenery will be good for you."

"Oh, and just where are you planning to find a change of scenery?" asked Hannah. "We don't live in New York or Philadelphia or anywhere with change. Every day here is the same"—though the day they'd lost their child hadn't been the same at all—"almost."

Georg smiled slowly and stretched before he answered. "Well, I heard of a ball coming up in Fort Augusta, and I have made up my mind to take you there. We'll go halfway and stay at Penn's Tavern, and—"

"I can't go away," said Hannah, suddenly alarmed. "Who will take care of the chores and the children?"

Georg was in an oddly good mood and went on explaining as if she hadn't interrupted him to question his plans.

"I am going to talk to Esther and Andrew Dunkleberger. If they can come, she can cook and watch the little ones. Benjamin and Samuel can do the chores, and we'll have adults here to look after things. You and I are going to go away and enjoy ourselves and take some time to talk about where our life is heading. Penn's Tavern is not very expensive—we can almost cut firewood to pay our way there. They use so much, and I can haul it.

"Then the fellow that has the inn in Fort Augusta owes me some money—we could probably arrange a trade—a stay for his debt. Or Martin has moved to Fort Augusta, and I'm sure he'd put us up. His wife wanted to meet you, and he's stayed here with us enough."

Hannah was quiet. She did want to go, badly. She just wasn't sure she was ready to leave. However, it had been years since she had been anywhere except this farm. Maybe a change was the medicine she needed.

"All right, I'll go!" she declared. "When is this ball? There will be a million things to get ready and to tell the children so everything goes smoothly while we are gone."

Her mind buzzing with ideas, Hannah put her sewing aside and headed toward their room. "I'd better go straight to bed so I can get an early start making plans."

Georg laughed. "Now that's what I like to see. A little enthusiasm. You won't be able to sleep. Your head will be full of plans before your eyes shut. And I never even told you when the ball is."

"It doesn't matter if it's a while off. I have to have a lot of time to get ready."

"Well, not too much time. It's next week, and I'm riding to the Dunkelbergers' tomorrow to see if they can come over."

Hannah felt suddenly light with joy. Maybe she could even fly. She ran back over to Georg, hugged him, and planted a kiss on his lips.

"Well now, that's more like it," said her husband. "I should plan to take you away more often."

"Oh, hush," said Hannah, feeling her face already growing hot. "The children will hear you." But she smiled too and felt better than she had in many days. The ball would be before Thanksgiving. She hoped she would have enough time to prepare for that holiday. However, the children would be expecting a special day despite the change in their life, and Hannah hoped she was ready to give it to them. "We'd better get to bed. Tomorrow is sauerkraut day."

"The children and I will deal with the cabbage." Georg stood up and prepared to follow her up to the loft. His voice was unexpectedly tender. "You rest up and make your plans."

As Georg had predicted, Hannah had a difficult time sleeping. She tossed and turned and got up several times to write down things she needed to remember.

"Go to sleep," groaned her husband. "Now I wish I'd never told you and just surprised you instead." He rolled over and draped his heavy arm over her as he had done when they were first married.

Hannah was surprised at this sudden change in her husband. Had he forgotten all that lay between them in the past months? She wished she could be so forgetful and then wondered how soon their struggles would surface again.

At long last Hannah fell asleep and dreamed of the new dress she had just completed, wondering if it was fashionable enough to wear to a ball.

She slept late and woke to the sounds of giggling in the kitchen. What were they up to now? Oh, it was sauerkraut day. She jumped out of bed.

She could smell baking. The smell wasn't familiar though, and then it struck her. Georg was making pretzels. He loved to bake pretzels, although he hardly ever had time anymore, and they didn't have a lot of flour—surely he knew that.

She went slowly downstairs, prepared to find her precious flour supply used in spontaneous baking.

"Morning, Mama," said several voices at once.

"Papa is making acorn-flour pretzels for breakfast," said Magdalena. "Come and see them."

Sure enough, there was already a small pile of pretzels on the table, and it looked as if the children were eating them as fast as Georg slid them out of the hearth.

"Hmmm," she said then. "I see you are having a healthy breakfast after all."

"It's a we-ward," piped up Daniel. "Papa said if we picked all the cabbagwes wifout you hearing us, he could make us sumpin' special."

"All right, then." Now Hannah had to smile. "I guess you picked all the cabbage."

"We did, we did, and now we can eat pwetzels."

"Come on, Mama, you hafta try them. They're made out of acorn flour but are pretty good anyway."

Georg laughed then. "Well, I hated to use up the last of the real flour. We might want it around Thanksgiving time."

Hannah silently reprimanded herself for thinking Georg would use her flour. Yet it was unusual for him to be that responsive to her wishes. Perhaps he *was* changing.

"You're right." Hannah felt a sudden urge to hug Georg for his thoughtfulness. "We need pumpkin pies in a couple weeks. Save the real flour."

Everyone gathered around to watch Hannah eat her pretzel.

"They're pretty good," she admitted. "I'll have to use all my acorn flour this way."

"Now then, madam," said Georg in his politest voice. "You must leave the kitchen and take the morning off. We will chop and stomp the cabbage, and then we may need you to help clean up, so rest up. Make your lists or something."

"All right, I'm going," said Hannah. "It's such a lovely day, I think I'll grab my shawl and go make lists outside."

The day sped by. Sitting on the porch, Hannah could guess, by the noise inside, exactly what part of the process they were in. Georg had brought in a large wooden barrel. The children would chop several heads of cabbage into slivers and dump them into a big wooden bowl. Then Georg would sprinkle salt from the barrel over the cabbage and mix it well with his hands. They would let the cabbage sit several minutes while a new chopper began on the next several heads of cabbage.

It wasn't long before the cabbage in the bowl got juicy, and then one of the big boys would dump it into the large barrel. Then, taking up a huge wooden pole that Georg had carved into a giant round paddle shape, the children would take turns "stomping" the cabbage, going round and round the barrel until all the cabbage was bruised and letting out its juices.

The whole process was repeated over and over until all the cabbage was stomped sufficiently. Then the big boys and Georg maneuvered the full, heavy barrel outdoors—a tricky process that required much manpower—and into the ground cellar.

Finally, Georg covered the whole works with a clean white piece of linen that Hannah had saved and put a large rock over that to hold the cabbage underwater, where it could ferment properly. In about six weeks, they would have a year's worth of sauerkraut.

Hannah walked back into the kitchen and was met by pieces of cabbage everywhere. Before she could say a word, the children assured her that they were already cleaning it up. The whole house smelled of cabbage, there was salt all over the floor, and no one was hungry because everyone had been nibbling on cabbage all day long; but every child in her house loved sauerkraut, and it would serve as a handy vegetable all winter long.

Hannah had heard the dish was good for scurvy as well, so she never minded the mess. Her family had never suffered with that ailment, and she planned to keep it that way.

"All right, Mama," said Georg, coming up behind her. "It's been a long day, but I have one more errand. I'm riding over to the Dunklebergers' to see if they can help us out, and Samuel is riding with me. We may do a little hunting before dusk. The rest of the children will help you finish cleaning up. I know you won't sit still and watch them do it if I leave."

"You're right." Hannah smiled. It had been a relaxing day, but she was more than ready to help get the cabbage remnants out of her kitchen and begin preparing for going away next week.

Once the cabin was under control, Hannah decided it was past time for the children to have a bath night. This was almost as much work as laundry day, so she tried to limit it to once a week, but sauerkraut was messy business.

"Benjamin, stir up the fire, will you, please? We need to give everybody a bath tonight."

"Oh, Mama, really? Benjamin had dismay written all over his face. Tonight?"

"Yes, tonight. Otherwise I'll have to wash all the sheets tomorrow. And you don't want little pieces of cabbage stuck in your quilt, do you?"

Benjamin's face cleared, and he laughed. "I guess not. We'll carry in more wood and get things going."

Hannah got out her metal washtub and set in the middle of the freshly swept floor. She filled her largest indoor pot with water and hung it on a hook over the fire that Benjamin was blowing on to make hotter. Frederick poured several buckets of cold water into the tub, and once the water boiled, she poured that in as well, making a warm enough bath. The rule was the cleanest children washed first, and that way they could reuse some of the water until it got too dirty.

"Come on, Daniel. You're first," said Magdalena.

"Send the gwils away," said Daniel, copying his older brothers from previous bath nights. "No gwils in the kitchen. Except Clara, she helps me."

"Oh, Daniel, I know you can't understand." Hannah felt as if someone had thrust a fist into her middle. "Clara can't help you anymore. I will help you.

"Girls, go upstairs awhile and work on your sums in your room. It's not nearly dark yet. You should be able to see up there."

"All right, Mama," said Margaret as she climbed up the stairs with Magdalena close behind.

Hannah swiftly lathered Daniel. They used the same plain soap for everything. There was nothing fancy like she had used at home as a little girl. If they wanted soap, they made it themselves, and everyone used it for every kind of washing.

Daniel was so little and hadn't helped much. He was quickly cleaned up, and then Margaret and Magdalena got their baths while the boys were banished to the upstairs.

I should have Georg make me a way to hang a curtain in the kitchen, thought Hannah, not for the first time. Then everyone wouldn't have to leave.

Once again, the girls switched places. It was growing dark now, so they sat on their beds and told Daniel stories until all the boys had been cleaned. By the time everyone was done, the floor was wet enough for Hannah to get out the mop; Johann cheerfully sloshed water everywhere, collecting the last little hidden bits of cabbage, and finally Hannah took the mop and finished the job.

As she replaced the mop on its hook, her eyes fell on the Bible lying on the shelf. "It's been a long time since I read the Bible with you children," she remarked. "Everyone come in and sit down. We'll read some before bed. If Papa gets back soon enough, I may have a surprise to tell you about."

Benjamin gathered everyone, and Hannah carried the Bible to her chair and opened it but couldn't decide where to read.

"Benjamin, you pick a spot. Read to us, and I'm going to work on my spinning while you read."

Benjamin handled the big Bible reverently and began paging through it while Hannah brought her spinning wheel over close to the fire. She loved to spin. It was relaxing, and by the middle of winter, she would have plenty of yarn to knit mittens. Magdalena could start knitting, she thought, and then realized she was not even paying attention. Benjamin was waiting for her so he could read.

The passage he had chosen was from Isaiah, and he read it out clearly in his new deeper voice. "Does the clay say to the potter, 'What are you making?'"

Before he could read further, Hannah felt pierced in her heart.

"Stop right there," she said, remembering how many times since Clara's death she had questioned God. "Can't you pick a psalm or something?"

Puzzlement all over his face, Benjamin shrugged and flipped through the pages again.

"How about this, Mama? It's in Psalms."

Hannah sat in silence and listened to Benjamin read again.

"As the deer pants for streams of water, so my soul pants for you, O God."

Surely this was how she felt these days, but she could hardly stand to hear her son read the Bible. Oh, what was wrong with her? Maybe Georg was right. A change of pace, a trip somewhere exciting when she had been cooped up here for years, was just the antidote for the hardness of heart she was feeling. She stood up abruptly, knocking her spinning to the floor.

"Bedtime, everybody."

There were a few groans, but most everybody was tired from the day of cabbage stomping. No one pointed out that it was early yet for bed, and Georg hadn't returned to tell the surprise. It was as though the children could sense Hannah's mood change.

Benjamin looked thoughtfully at his mother; while she saw his look, she felt unable to explain to her son what was in her heart.

"Benjamin, if you want to stay up awhile and read, it's okay, but everyone else needs to go to bed."

Moments after all the children were quiet in bed and the spinning put back in order, she heard Georg's horse clopping outside. He soon came in, although without Samuel. To Hannah's questioning look, he simply said, "The Dunklebergers will be glad to come. I left Samuel to help them this week, and he will return with them next week. I thought if we helped them, it would repay somewhat their willingness to come help us."

"Of course," said Hannah. "He's a big help. I am going to miss him though—a whole week away."

"*They* are trying to get all their fall work done too"—Georg's voice cooled suddenly—"and they only have a hired hand and no children. It just seemed the right thing to do. So, Hannah, it seems you'll get your trip, but you'll have to do without a son for a few days."

Benjamin had been listening all the time and now spoke up. "What trip, Papa?"

"Didn't your Mama tell anyone? I'm surprised it stayed a secret." Georg shrugged tiredly.

"I thought we'd better know first if it was going to happen," said Hannah in defense.

"I am taking your mother with me to Fort Augusta next week," said Georg. "And to a ball. It's time she got out of her cabin and spent some time with me."

"I think that's a great idea," replied Benjamin. "We can all help around here, and no one will miss you. Well, I mean, we will miss you, but we can do the work all right."

Georg laughed. "I knew what you meant. Now off to bed. I'm exhausted and I'd better help with your mother's plans, or we might not get everything ready."

Hannah climbed up to her bed with her thoughts in a whirl. First she was excited, and then thoughts of Clara plunged her spirit down. She remembered last year's sauerkraut day. Clara had been determined to stomp more cabbage than anyone else, and her competitive spirit had led to a contest with her two older brothers. Hannah sighed, remembering the cheering and wild laughter of her children.

The contrast of last year's joy and this year's grieving felt like a dark wave rushing to engulf her, so she deliberately pushed those thoughts aside and tried to focus on her anticipation of a trip off the farm and several days with Georg all to herself. She pictured their first days together when all was rosy and decided that's how this trip would be. She would revel in the company of her beloved and do nothing to break their truce.

17

FORT AUGUSTA

The day Hannah and Georg were to set out to Fort Augusta, the Dunklebergers arrived before sunrise in a wagon pulled by their two work horses, with a cow tied on behind. Samuel was with them, a big smile on his face.

"Hi, Mama." He gave her an exuberant hug. "We had to bring the cow 'cause no one will be there to take care of her."

"That's fine." Hannah returned his hug. She had missed her young man, and now they were going to leave him in a few minutes. "Put her out in the pasture with Blossom. If you get too much milk, the pigs will enjoy the extra. It will put some fat on them before winter. Otherwise, maybe Esther will get the girls to churn more butter or make some special pudding."

After some final instructions, Hannah and Georg were ready to leave. One last hug for each child, and a special thank-you to the Dunklebergers, and they were on their way. Georg's big roan horse pulled their wagon easily. A buggy would have been quicker for traveling, but Hannah had carefully counted their cash and brought some along. They both hoped to stock up on some last-minute supplies before winter shut them in on the farm.

The air was cold and crisp. A light fog drifted in the low-lying spots along the creek. After following the road for several miles, Georg pulled the horse to a halt.

"Hannah, we are turning right here, but look down the other way, off to your left. See that building down there? It used to be a trading post."

"You mean down by Samuel Wieser's stone house?"

"Yep, it was a trading post back before the war. I wonder sometimes if I could start a trading post instead of farming. Some of my relatives back in Germany were merchants for generations, and most of them were quite successful. Perhaps if we opened a store, we could stay on the farm and have other income."

Hannah sighed a little inside but refused to say what she really thought—ten children, a farm, and a store. That seemed a lot to handle, but if it could keep Georg and all the children here instead of moving, maybe it would be worth the effort. However, today was not the day for such thoughts, nor was it a day she intended to argue with her husband. This was a holiday.

Georg clicked to his horse, and they started off again, each full of their own thoughts. The leaves had all turned brown now, and most of the trees were bare; but even so, the drive to Penn's Tavern was scenic, and just the change of view kept Hannah's mood from darkening too much.

The miles sped by. Although the horse moved at a walking pace to save his energy, it seemed to Hannah, who walked everywhere, that they were flying. By lunchtime, they were in sight of Penn's Tavern, built right along the Susquehanna River. It had been there for ninety-five years now, serving travelers and occasionally Indians.

As they drove up, the ferry, run by a gentleman named Adam Fisher, was unloading its passengers from the western side of the river. Two men and their dusty horses disembarked first, followed by an older, neatly dressed gentleman. Three passengers was a normal load for the middle of the day, and Hannah and Georg followed them into the tavern for their noon meal.

The fare was simple: rye bread, fresh cheese, and apple cider. As a special treat, Georg ordered them each a slice of roasted ham. The jolly innkeeper laughed and said it was a good thing he had just emptied his smokehouse.

Most trips, Hannah would have packed a meal for the two of them, but Georg insisted this was a special outing. When the innkeeper explained that he owed Georg for some firewood bought that summer, Hannah relaxed, scolded herself for always thinking of money, and enjoyed her meal.

There were no other women present, so she sat quietly and listened as Georg talked of politics with the other men and kept her opinions to herself when they brought up the subject of the new taxation laws, which most of the local farmers felt were unfair. They especially protested the part of the law that required them to pay in gold or silver, which was scarce for everyone. More than one farmer felt this made the tax even higher than just the unfair methods of valuing property, such as the window-counting appraiser Hannah had met.

After a rest of several hours—for the horse, Georg said, although Hannah felt it was more to discuss politics—they harnessed up and were off again. Hannah had not been to Fort Augusta since the first year they had settled here. Typically Georg went by himself if they were in need of supplies so Hannah could keep an eye on their farm.

As they neared the settlement, they began to pass other travelers going and coming on the road, and Hannah began to feel nervous. Finally she put her arm through Georg's as he held the reins.

"What's the matter?" he teased. "You aren't scared, are you?"

"Yes," she admitted. "I don't know any of these people here. They will just think I'm a backward hausfrau."

"Well, you are a housewife, but I think you will be the best-looking woman at the ball."

Hannah blushed and smiled. "I appreciate the flattery, Georg, but we both know it's not true. I don't even want to be the best-looking woman there—but neither do I want to be the worst."

"Well, since you're so honest," said her husband, "I'll be honest too. To me you look beautiful, and I think you are the best wife a man could have."

Although Hannah was pleased at his compliments, she felt guilty as well. She had been struggling so with feeling like her love was ebbing away—and here was Georg, professing his undying love to her. She wasn't as wonderful a wife as he thought, if there were days she had to struggle to find love in her heart.

She kept her doubts to herself, and finally the fort itself was in view. The sun was almost below the horizon by now, and the whole settlement was tinted red, orange, and gold.

Last March, the area had been renamed Sunbury after an English village, and the actual fort had been dismantled four years ago, but most of the inhabitants still called it Fort Augusta.

Just north of Fort Augusta and across the river was the town of Northumberland, recently resettled since its evacuation during the war.

Hannah had forgotten the bustle of a town after her long absence in the wilderness. Everyone seemed to be busy, children running here and there, women with market baskets on their arms, men riding through the streets all intent on their own business and no one paying attention to others. She felt timid here among all these strangers, and yet she herself had grown up in New York, which was much busier than this town.

"Georg, I don't know," she said. "Perhaps I'm too old for so much change. I've gotten used to only seeing a few people every day."

"Don't be silly. You know Martin. You'll love his wife. She is much like you, and I think you'll get along well. We are almost to their home now. You will feel better once you know somebody, and there may very well be folks who were at the barn raising as well, coming for the ball tomorrow night. Now relax. This is supposed to be a fun time for you. Remember all the dances your father took you and Emily to. I'll bet you didn't know everybody many times back then."

"That's true, but I'm sure I had eyes only for you anyway, so it didn't matter."

"And who are you planning on having eyes for now, if not just for me?"

Hannah glanced at her husband, but his face was wreathed in a teasing smile.

"Oh, Georg, you know I didn't mean that. You always have to tease me so."

He laughed and hugged her to his side. "Hannah, it's just good to hear you laugh again. I miss the cheery side of you."

She put her arm through his. "I'll do my best. Now, lead on to this wife I must meet."

"Her name is Martha," said Georg drily. "And their home is just down this little lane."

The tired horse seemed grateful for the spacious barn he was led into, and as Georg was unharnessing him, Martin came out to greet them both.

"Now I can welcome you to my home," he said to Hannah. "Martha has been anxious to meet you."

It crossed Hannah's mind to wonder how Martin knew they were coming when she had heard of this plan only a week or so ago, but Georg had always enjoyed surprising her. He must have had this in mind for some time now. Thinking about it made Hannah feel loved in a way she hadn't experienced recently—as well as sorry for the list of grievances she had built up in her mind against Georg. She felt a stab of regret and determined to forget their past disagreements.

They followed Martin across the yard between the barn and the large brick house. Hannah guessed he must be wealthier than she'd thought.

"Welcome, welcome." She heard Martha before she came around the corner from the kitchen. Then before her eyes was a smiling, plump, red-haired woman who looked about her age and also looked very glad to see them. "You two must be exhausted. Come in, I'll show you your room, and you can wash up. Dinner is almost ready."

Hannah smiled back, feeling relieved already. Here was someone she could relate to and make friends with, she was sure. Georg was so kind to think of this.

Their room was enormous compared to her little cabin. There were huge windows along one side of it, looking out into a yard that was probably full of flowers in summer. Now the stems and dry leaves were only brown reminders of past glory and promise of next summer's enjoyment. A four-poster stood on the wall without windows, and close to it a bureau with a porcelain pitcher and basin for washing up. Martha also had beautifully embroidered linen towels waiting for them, and there was a fire burning in the fireplace, since the air was chilly already.

A rocking chair also fit into the room, and Hannah sank down gratefully. It was a welcome change from the bouncing wagon, and her back hurt. She wondered if pregnant women could tolerate much wagon travel. She hadn't sat more than ten minutes when she bounced up again.

"Georg, I can't sit here and do nothing. I should go and ask Martha if I can help."

"Not if I can help it," he replied from where he lounged full length on the bed with his boots hanging off the side to keep from soiling the bedspread. "Martha has two girls that come in and help her. They need to make an income, and Martha has help. You just rest, and she'll call when dinner is ready. She's a good cook too," he added.

"How come I never knew you and Martin were such good friends or that you had stayed here? Georg, you shouldn't be so mysterious with me. I'm your wife."

Georg just smiled at her rebuke. "Well, the first time I met him was the night he brought us home last spring. You do remember that?"

"Of course."

"I've met him here and there since then. He is working with other German farmers in the area to protest these new tax laws. He knows quite a bit about our legal system even though it's a new one, and I have had to ask his advice more than once on ideas I have had for our farm. I stay here whenever I am in the area now."

Before the discussion could go further, a knock at their door announced the evening meal, and Georg took Hannah by the arm and led her downstairs and into a sumptuous dining room. The Reitzes had five children, all seated at the table. They appeared to be used to company, as none of them stared and all made Hannah feel at home and miss her brood at the same time.

I will have to tell them all about my children, she thought.

Georg sat at Martin's right hand, and Hannah found herself next to Martha. They were served a delicious meal of pork, sauerkraut, and mashed potatoes, one of Georg's favorites. Hannah wondered if Martha knew that already or if it was also a favorite of Martin. For dessert, two fragrant apple pies made their appearance, and despite the fact that she was full of pork, Hannah dug in energetically. One of the little boys laughed suddenly, and Hannah blushed.

"I guess I didn't realize how hungry I was," she said apologetically. "This is delicious."

"I helped Mama make it," said Maria, a young lady of about thirteen. "She's teaching me how to bake."

"Clara was my little baker," said Hannah. Her eyes filled with tears. "I'm sorry," she said, wiping them with her handkerchief. "I can't talk about Clara without crying."

"What happened to Clara?" asked Maria.

"Shhh," said Martha, with a sympathetic glance at Hannah, "You children ask too many questions."

"No, it's all right," replied Hannah. "I have to talk about it some-time. This fall she was bitten by a rattlesnake. She was trying to protect her little brother Daniel. I didn't even hear him crying until a while later, and it was just too late to help her. It was my fault." Her eyes filled again. "Georg brought me out for a change of scenery and to help me think through all this."

"I'm sorry I upset you," said Maria. She stared at the tablecloth instead of at Hannah and traced a circle on the fabric with her finger. "I'm sorry," she said again with a quiver in her voice.

"Maria, it's fine. I am not upset at you." Hannah blew her nose, dabbed at her eyes again, and took a deep breath. "I just am quite emotional still."

The children were dismissed then. Martin and Georg went off into the study to discuss whatever men discuss at such times, and Martha and Hannah spent a while getting acquainted.

When Georg returned and said, "Hannah if you don't soon come to bed, you'll be too tired to dance tomorrow night," she glanced at the clock and could hardly believe two hours had passed.

"Oh, I lost track of time. Martha and I are going to visit some shops tomorrow morning, so I better go to bed." She leaned over and gave Martha a hug. "It's so nice to have female companionship. Thank you for opening your home."

As had happened so seldom since Clara's death, Hannah fell fast asleep no more than five minutes after her head touched the pillow, and she woke refreshed the next morning.

The day dawned foggy and cold, but before Martha and Hannah were ready to leave on their morning of shopping, the sun showed signs of steaming away the fog, and the evening of the ball looked promising for fair weather. Both women were warmly dressed and full of anticipation.

Georg had promised Hannah she could get a fine new bonnet to match her dress. They planned to look for a millinery shop, a shoemaker, and perhaps an apothecary. There was no need for a carriage, as none of the shops were far apart, and Hannah felt more than ready for some walking after a day in the jouncing wagon.

They met many other women out doing errands on the street: women buying bread—Hannah could scarcely imagine not baking all your own bread; women with children looking in shop windows; women who were clearly servants shopping for their mistresses, looking for a plump duck or savory piece of sausage for a special meal.

"Do your servant girls shop for you too?" asked Hannah.

"They would if I let them." Martha laughed. "But I like to do my own purchasing unless I'm in a hurry. That way I know exactly what I'm getting before it comes home to me—and I like to bargain. I think my serving girls are afraid to be assertive. They just pay the asking price."

"So you save money going yourself."

"Well, I think so." Martha smiled again, and her face lit up. "I also enjoy getting out, especially on a nice day like today. Let's stop in here"—she pointed to a chandler's shop—"I want to buy some more candles. My supply is getting low."

The candle purchase completed, Hannah stepped out of the shop and next door discovered a stationer's. She turned in excitement to Martha, a smile lighting her face.

"Oh, Martha, can we go in here?"

"Of course, this is your day for enjoyment."

Hannah clasped her hands in anticipation. "I write letters to my sister Emily, home in New York, and I would so love to buy some nice linen paper and a good pen and some real ink to write to her. It would make my next letter special. She'll know I was thinking of her on my trip."

"What a thoughtful sister you are. Come on. Let's buy the best paper we can find."

"I can't be too extravagant." Hannah hesitated. "Georg promised me I could buy a hat. I'm torn between accepting his offer and saving my money for a rainy day, but maybe we'll find a bargain."

"Just leave it to me," Martha assured her. "I'm known all over Sunbury as a shrewd bargainer."

Both women laughed, Martha extended her elbow, and after a minute, Hannah linked arms with her and marched into the stationer's. Hannah forgot to feel awkward in the midst of such a selection of pens, ink, and paper. Martha truly was a bargainer, and when they were finished with their purchases, she assured Hannah there still would be plenty left for a beautiful bonnet.

The next stop was the milliner's, where they spent a great deal of time admiring the latest styles and finally settled on a broad, flat-brimmed straw hat bordered by ribbons that closely matched Hannah's dress. She also purchased a new mobcap. At home on the farm, she never bothered with such conventions; but here in town, she didn't want to look out of place.

"Georg will love your hat," said Martha. "Let's stop for a cup of tea, and then we'd better go home and let you rest before tonight."

"As much as I work on my feet all day at home, I *am* feeling a little weary," admitted Hannah. The cup of tea refreshed her, and they walked quickly home.

Georg gave her a hug when they arrived and insisted on admiring her purchases immediately. "Now go upstairs and take a nap," he ordered. "You want to be fresh for the evening."

Several hours' rest did refresh Hannah, and as evening fell, she and Georg began dressing for the ball.

The ball was to be held at Colonel Hunter's mansion. There would be a group of musicians playing as opposed to the one or two fiddlers that Hannah had been used to as a girl. Martha had assured her that she would know the steps, although there was a new dance in vogue known as the waltz.

There were carriages drawing up from both directions as Georg, Hannah, Martha, and Martin walked up. The night was warm for November, and the Reitzes didn't live far from the colonel's home, so the men had decided walking was a better choice than negotiating all the traffic as couples were dropped at the entrance to the mansion. The music floating out of the doors reminded Hannah that she used to love to dance. This might be her last opportunity for years, and she planned to make the most of it.

As she took Georg's arm, she thought of Clara, who would have been old enough for such events in a few years. Was it wrong to enjoy this time when her daughter never could? She wasn't quite sure how she should feel. As if he sensed her thoughts, Georg tightened his arm about her and urged her on.

Inside, the entrance hallway was gaily decorated, and through the double doors to her right, Hannah could see dancers swirling about in a graceful dance underneath ornate chandeliers. The white walls had gilt paint trim, giving a regal feeling to this country mansion. She must be watching that new waltz, she decided. The rhythm was different than she was used to, but even as she watched, the dance came to a close, and the musicians took up an older familiar tune.

"Come on, Georg," she teased. "It's time to dance."

Georg had been eyeing some men gathered in a corner of the entryway, having some sort of spirited discussion. She was too far to hear the topic, but clearly Georg had an idea of what they were saying, for he looked ready to stride over and add his voice. She tugged his arm again.

"We came to dance, remember?" she reminded him, hoping to distract his mind from politics.

He sighed and patted her hand on his arm. "Yes we did, darling, and so we shall. But there are some men here I must speak to tonight."

"Then wait until I need some time to catch my breath. I'm sure I won't be able to dance all night in my condition."

"Fair enough." Georg looked down at her with a tender smile in his eyes. "Lead on to the dance."

As they joined the swirling mass of men and women, Hannah felt like she had stepped back in time to her adventurous courting days.

Most of the men she had seen Georg eyeing also joined the dance with their partners. Noticing them, Hannah felt a little thrill to be part of this world after so long. Her fear of not fitting in drained away; she relaxed and let the music move her and Georg as one.

He hadn't lost his dancing abilities either, and after several country dances and another minuet, they took on the challenge of learning the waltz. She could see why Martha had said this was a dance that many thought should be forbidden. She and Georg actually touched in dancing the waltz, unlike the minuet and the country dances she was used to.

It seemed very modern for such a small frontier town as Sunbury, and she wondered how it had arrived here. Such a dance couldn't be forbidden for married couples, although it did seem rather daring to hold Georg's hand and have his arm around her out in public while they danced.

"Just make sure you don't try the waltz with anyone else," Georg whispered in her ear.

When she looked at him, she could see he was only half joking. She grinned, unexpectedly joyful, and assured him that she didn't plan to dance with anyone else anyway.

Finally she was tired and asked Georg to find her some punch. He led her to several seats at the side of the room and brought her a cup of cider. Martha soon joined them, and Georg excused himself, saying he would return before too long.

Hannah knew she would find him in a study or a library somewhere, discussing the financial state of affairs or politics in general. She turned her attention back to Martha, who seemed to enjoy dancing as much as she did but had also been abandoned by her husband.

"Never mind, Hannah," she was saying. "We can find them when we want to. I've been here before, and I know exactly where those men go to talk business."

"I would hate to interrupt them though," replied Hannah. Secretly, she would love to interrupt men talking business, but Martha was too new a friend to express that rebellious desire to. Not only that, but she had promised herself to avoid quarrels on this trip. "Suppose it was very important?"

"Nonsense. They brought us here to dance, and they wouldn't want us to dance without them, so we'll just find them when we're both rested."

Both women sat for a while, simply watching the dancers. Hannah didn't regret sitting. Her pregnancy was making her more tired than usual. Finally Martha was ready to dance again, but Hannah shook her head.

"You go ahead. Find Martin, and I'll sit here a little longer. I really don't mind. If Georg asks, tell him to come find me in fifteen minutes or so."

Fifteen minutes stretched on and on. By the time an hour had passed, Hannah was slightly annoyed, but finally Georg reappeared. He looked angry, but she was sure this wasn't the place to ask the cause, especially since it didn't involve her. She would ask later.

I always tell myself I'll ask later, Hannah thought, *and sometimes I never do.* She wished Georg would feel freer to explain things to her. This was her world too, and whatever he got involved in would always involve her and their family.

She sighed but smiled at Georg, and they returned to the dance floor with renewed energy. Georg didn't only look angry; he danced as if he were angry. He was not nearly as light on his feet as earlier in the evening. Finally he stopped and led Hannah off the dance floor.

"Let's go back to the Reitzes'," he said abruptly. "I'm exhausted."

"I thought I was the one to get exhausted," quipped Hannah, hoping to get an explanation out of him.

As they left the mansion, he said quietly, "I'm not tired of dancing, Hannah. I'm tired of debating right and wrong on this new tax. No one here can afford such a tax, but everyone is afraid of speaking up. Since these other laws were passed this summer, no one wants to be branded an enemy of the government. Yet they are supposed to represent us, not oppress us. This is why our country became a country. This is why I stayed here after the war. I was tired of oppression, and many here from England were tired of the unfair taxations. Now the congress is passing its own unfair taxation laws. I am going to have to speak up even if I'm the only one."

Hannah didn't fully understand Georg's fears of the government, but she was unfamiliar with the new tax laws, since he had never completely explained them to her. They walked quietly the rest of the way back to the Reitzes' home and had been back only long enough to brew themselves some tea when Martin and Martha arrived. Martin looked equally disgusted.

Georg was the first to speak. "Martin, we do have to return home tomorrow or next day at the latest, but we have got to do something."

"I agree. Completely!" Martin's brows drew together and he frowned. "Let me sleep on this tonight, and tomorrow morning we'll make a plan."

The tea finished, both couples retired to their rooms. Georg's goodnight kiss was perfunctory rather than romantic, but Hannah was too tired to care.

Morning came late for Hannah. Georg had already left the room when she awakened. She supposed it was to further his discussion with Martin. She slowly got out of bed, washed at the basin, and after dressing in her traveling dress, went downstairs in search of Martha or breakfast or both.

Martha was in the kitchen making tea again. When Hannah looked at her questioningly, she laughed.

"I know the girls could do this, but I am particular about my tea. I always do it myself. I guess it's the English part of me still making tea properly although I've been married to a Dutchman for years. Would you like tea or coffee?"

"I'd love coffee. We've run out and have been drinking chicory for a month or more now. Georg did promise to get some more while we're in town. I'd better remind him."

The two women sipped in companionable silence, and finally

Martha said, "You know, Martin and Georg went out a while ago. They're trying to organize a meeting of some sort. Georg said he expects to leave first thing tomorrow, so we can spend one more day together. Would you like to make plans or just relax here today?"

"I'm not sure. I'd like a write a letter to my sister. I could mail it here before we leave. Then I'll let you know."

"All right," said Martha. "There are always chores to keep me busy here, but when you're done writing, wander about and find me, and we'll plan something fun. I feel like this is my week off too."

Hannah returned to her room, gathered up her new writing supplies, and made her way to the bright dining room. It had windows on both sides of the room and was filled with morning sunlight. She sat in the biggest puddle of sun she could find and pulled out a fresh sheet of fine linen paper.

Dear Emily,

You would never guess that I spent last night dancing away my frustrations and sorrows, but I did just that. I learned a new and scandalous dance called a waltz. It was very exciting to dance with Georg. After your wedding, you'll have to learn it yourself.

Georg worries me. I hope he doesn't get on the wrong side of these new laws, trying to prove they are wrong. Whatever would I do then?

I can go more than one day at a time now without crying—I wonder if that is good or bad. Everything reminds me of Clara. I never thought I would lose a child, and so I was not prepared. I guess I just assumed God would protect me from such a tragedy, and now I have to rethink why I had those assumptions.

Emily, do you think God is angry when we have questions? I have so many for Him. I wish there were someone around here who could help me find these answers. Here in Sunbury, there is a church; but we will not be here on Sunday, and I would feel odd asking my questions to a clergyman I didn't even know.

So, Emily, I am going to close my letter. I wrote it all at once—that is rare indeed, and it's not as long as I often write, but I want to be sociable with Martha, whose home I am staying at—you would like her, and she is going to show me where to send this on its way to you when Georg and I leave for the farm tomorrow.

Do you like my new paper? I bought it specially for you.

As I say every time I write, Emily, I love you. I miss you too.

Your sister,

Hannah

She folded her paper, put it in a crisp new envelope, sealed it up, and went quickly down the stairs to help Martha plan the rest of the day and find out what time they must be ready to leave tomorrow. It had been a relaxing few days, but she needed to see her children again and make sure they were safe.

18

THANKSGIVING

All the long-laid plans finally had come to fruition. Thanksgiving was at hand, and Hannah actually felt ready to give thanks. She still had days of despair, and yet deep down, she sensed God was there. This particular holiday always had been one of her favorites. It was a day to remember God's goodness throughout the past year.

Georg and the children knew her fondness for this celebration, and all of them had determined to make it as special as possible. Benjamin and Georg had been out hunting and had bagged not just one but two big turkeys. Benjamin was getting to be quite a good shot with his new gun. The hams were all finished, so Hannah put one turkey to hang in the smokehouse and roasted the other one and a large ham. What they didn't eat today would be devoured in the next couple of days.

They had invited Esther and Andrew Dunkleberger to share the day, as they had no family of their own close by and no children either to share their thankfulness.

This morning, Georg triumphantly presented a bag of pecans to Hannah with a flourish.

"Will you bake me a pie, Hannah?" he asked. "There's still some molasses in the barrel."

"Oh, of course I will." Hannah hugged the precious bag of nuts. "However did you find pecans way out here in the wilderness?"

"That's my secret." Her husband smiled. "Samuel, go build up the fire. Mama needs to bake some pies."

Magdalena and Margaret both helped with the pie crust, cutting the lard into the flour with two forks and taking great care in rolling out the dough with Hannah's old wooden rolling pin.

In addition to turkey, ham, and pie, there would be sweet potatoes, recently gathered from the garden and stored carefully in the root cellar until today. Dried corn had been soaking on the back of the stove since last night, and Frederick and Samuel had gone out early this morning and dug a few more red beets out of the garden. They were the last vegetable to come in this fall. Georg had spread straw over the row, and they would have red beets for several more weeks before the ground got too frozen.

Esther had promised to bring freshly baked bread so Hannah could use her oven for the meats and pies, and she had promised to bring a surprise also. The Dunkelbergers weren't expected for several hours yet. Hannah was free to clean and cook and enjoy her family all gathered together for the morning. Georg sat in her rocker looking peaceful while she bustled about. He had the big family Bible on his lap.

"I can't bring you all to a church," he said, "so I'm going to preach a Thanksgiving Day message for us."

"You, Papa?" asked Margaret in surprise. "Can you preach if you're not a preacher?"

"Of course I can, darling." Georg smiled at her question. "Just go ask your Mama."

"Can he, Mama?"

"Yes, indeed. Your Papa can preach without anybody's permission." Hannah thought of all the times she had been preached at by her husband. "Now let him get ready. I do so long to hear someone read the Scriptures to me and perhaps explain the parts I don't understand."

"Whoa, I'm not a studied-up preacher like Reverend Claybaugh. I just am going to share my thoughts."

The children looked at their father in some amazement.

"I guess Papa can still surprise you," laughed Hannah. "There are more things about him you don't know, I bet." And things I don't know either, she thought, watching her children's awe at Georg's impromptu sermon and feeling a stirring in her own spirit at his heartfelt faith.

The celebration atmosphere kept things moving along. Children swept and washed dishes and helped in countless small ways without quarreling, and before they realized how late it was, Daniel announced loudly, "I heared someone coming."

"It's the Dunklebergers," cried Samuel. He had enjoyed his time with them several weeks ago, and it had been his idea to invite them today for dinner.

Everyone ran outside to welcome the guests and invite them into the cozy kitchen. Everything not necessary for a meal had been moved along one wall, and Georg had brought in another small table to make enough room for the crowd and the food. Hannah owned one long lace tablecloth, which she had brought along when they moved, and it served nicely to cover both tables. The girls had gathered some of the few colorful leaves left on the ground, and Hannah laid them along the center of the table and put three bayberry candles in her three brass holders among the leaves. The room smelled more of turkey than ham, but the rich smell of molasses and roasted nuts was the first thing she noticed when she came back in with their guests.

"Hannah, this is beautiful and smells just like home when I was little," said Esther. "I have always loved Thanksgiving, and it seemed so strange to celebrate it with just two of us. You were so thoughtful to include us."

"I needed some feminine company too," said Hannah. "The women-folk are outnumbered here."

It took only a few minutes to set out the food, and the children proclaimed that they were starving and sat up at the table as soon as Hannah announced, "Dinner's ready."

Andrew offered a blessing on their meal and their fellowship, and Georg carved the turkey. The room soon fell silent as the whole group attacked the feast in front of them.

"Hannah, you are a wonderful cook," proclaimed Andrew. "Maybe you can teach Esther how you make your sweet potatoes."

Esther blushed and then laughed. "He's got good reason for asking that," she said. "The last ones I made, I roasted in the oven like regular potatoes, and then I forgot them and they burned. Even the pigs didn't want them."

Hans and Johann both laughed too. "Mama burns lots of stuff," Hans revealed with a few giggles.

Johan added, "She gives it to the chickens so it don't get wasted."

"Doesn't get wasted," Hannah said automatically. "Well, I guess we all have room for improvement."

"If you don't mind," said Andrew, "do you think we could eat dessert later? The men are going outside to shoot targets for a while, and we're much too full to give dessert its proper attention just now."

"Go right ahead," said Hannah, wondering why Georg, so angry at their son for wasting ammunition a few months ago, was in support of this. "But shouldn't we save our ammunition in case the winter is bad and we can't get out for more?"

"Don't worry, Hannah," Andrew answered. "Georg knew I had a bow and arrow collection. I've had it since I was a little boy, and when we moved, I just couldn't leave it behind. I think we'll have sons someday, and I'll need it then. Anyway, I brought along all my bows today for these boys to try out. Unless we lose arrows, ammunition won't be any problem. Why don't you ladies come out and watch us?"

"Just until we get cold," said Esther, wrapping her arms around herself. "I much prefer a warm fire to standing in a cold yard watching men shoot bows."

"Hannah does too," said Georg. "Come in whenever you like, but we'll show off for you a little first."

Samuel and Benjamin ran across the path to the barn, and each brought back a hay bale. Georg had saved some old brown wrapping paper from his last trip to town, and he drew a large circle on it using ashes and vinegar. This would serve as a target for the contestants.

Hannah and Esther stood outside, shawls wrapped about themselves, and watched for a while. The little boys were allowed to go first. Andrew had brought two small bows with him.

Since neither Hans nor Johann had ever shot a bow before, they missed the target on most tries, although Johann showed some good progress. Frederick was able to hit the target, but not close enough that he would have killed an animal with his efforts.

Daniel watched too and howled because he wanted to try, but even the smallest bow was much too big for him. Hannah picked him up a bit awkwardly, because the baby was beginning to protrude, and tried to comfort him. But he refused her attempts.

"I'm a big boy," he sobbed.

Finally Georg came over, knelt down, and helped him release an arrow from the smallest bow. It wobbled a bit and then fell to the grass, but Daniel was appeased and jumped up and down, yelling, "I did it, I did it," while the adults laughed.

Margaret and Magdalena watched for a while but soon went inside to work on their quilt patches. Ben and Samuel wanted to compete with the men, and since the targets were barely used, the four decided to start in teams: Benjamin and Georg against Samuel and Andrew. The women watched for a time and then headed indoors to make a cup of tea and warm up.

Esther had brought her quilting basket, so Daniel was put on the floor to play with his tops while four females sat busily stitching, drinking tea laced with honey, and catching up on the news of each other's families.

It wasn't long before the men came in, slapping their hands against their sides and laughing.

"Andrew and Samuel won, Mama," said Frederick.

"I guess I did have an advantage," said Andrew, "since they were my bows and I've used all of them before, but Samuel's a good shot. And Georg and Benjamin almost beat us."

"And now," said Samuel, "we're hungry again."

"Boys!" Hannah sighed. "Esther, when you have children, plan ahead. Boys are always hungry. As soon as I clean up one meal, they want another."

"Oh, just dessert, Mama," said Benjamin. "Mrs. Dunkleberger promised to bring a surprise, and you made pies this morning."

"All right. I give in. Dessert it is. Give us time to clean up our sewing, and I must put some more water on to heat."

Within ten minutes, the table was set again, water was boiling merrily in the pot hanging over the fire, and juicy pecan pies were displayed on the table. Esther went out to her wagon and returned bearing two large plates of ginger cookies. The children all cheered lustily when they saw the treat, for Hannah seldom made gingerbread. The spice was hard to come by, and the cookies disappeared so quickly that she always declared it wasn't worth the effort of baking them.

Esther laughed as the children set upon the cookies as if they were starving. When Hannah began to scold them, she laughed again.

"Oh, let them eat. It's my treat, and that is all the more pie you and I can eat."

"True," replied Hannah, "but I do wish they at least pretended to have manners. Besides, I'm running out of room for pie or anything else. This baby just keeps growing and growing and leaving no room for me."

"Hannah, you better be careful," broke in Georg, who had been listening to the two women. "You have a long time to go yet."

"I'm beyond the halfway mark." Hannah smiled. "I'm looking forward to spring and a new little Zartman."

She got up and began cutting up the pies. Despite their recent enjoyment of the ginger cookies, every child clamored for a piece of pie.

"While you eat that," Georg announced, "take some time and give serious thought to what you are thankful for today. We are going to have church right here after dessert."

"Wifout Wevewend Claybaugh?" wondered Daniel.

"Yes, wifout," said his papa kindly. "God is here whether the reverend is or not."

"Okay, Papa, I will think hard," said Daniel seriously, even though his siblings were trying hard not to giggle.

It was soon quiet again while the pie disappeared, and then Margaret and Magdalena carried all the dishes to the sink while the boys arranged the chairs in a half circle around the fireplace.

"Leave the dishes," said Georg. "We'll do them later or tomorrow."

"Tomorrow, please," said Magdalena.

"Well, maybe just this once." Georg smiled at Magdalena's wish. "Now, let's gather here for a bit."

The cozy room felt a little too cozy to Hannah, but she knew she was hotter than everyone else because of her pregnancy. Everyone joined in singing her favorite hymn, "Rock of Ages," which brought tears to her eyes as she recalled Clara's funeral service.

They soon moved on to Esther's favorite, a German hymn that Georg translated for the children, who had not grown up speaking German, "Now Thank We all Our God." This was a new one for Hannah, who was not German but she listened through the first verse and then joined in.

Nun danket alle Gott mit Herzen, Mund und Händen.
Der große Dinge tut an uns und allen Enden,
Der uns von Mutterleib und Kindesbeinen an
Unzählig viel zu gut bis hierher hat getan.

Now thank we all our God, with heart and hands and voices,
Who wondrous things has done, in Whom this world rejoices;
Who from our mothers' arms has blessed us on our way
With countless gifts of love, and still is ours today.

O may this bounteous God through all our life be near us,
With ever joyful hearts and blessed peace to cheer us;
And keep us in His grace, and guide us when perplexed;
And free us from all ills, in this world and the next!

All praise and thanks to God the Father now be given;
The Son and Him Who reigns with Them in highest Heaven;
The one eternal God, whom earth and Heaven adore;
For thus it was, is now, and shall be evermore.

Hannah especially felt she could embrace the verse talking about God guiding her when she was perplexed. She surely did feel perplexed these days. One day she was excited about the new little one, the next minute she was in tears over thoughts of Clara or angry at her husband for the financial situation they now found themselves in. She couldn't see her way to the end of the tunnel, but the song reminded her that God was still there and He could see the end.

After another hymn, the children were so wiggly that she knew Georg had better get started before their church plans were sabotaged by children. She caught his gaze and directed his attention toward the little ones. He nodded his understanding.

"All right, everybody," he said. "I am going to start with Andrew, then Esther, and then each of you can share something you are thankful for today."

As each child shared, Hannah felt her heart breaking with love. These little children that she had shared this hard life with all had something to rejoice about. She felt torn in two. They were rejoicing when she could focus on only the hard things in their life. Something must be wrong with her.

Even Daniel, her little baby boy, said seriously, "I'm fankful for my mama 'cause she takes good cawe of us and she wuvs us. Papa wuvs us too, but Mama cooks all the time fow us, and I luf her."

He jumped up and ran over and hugged Hannah, who suddenly burst out crying.

"I'm so sorry," she hiccupped, wiping her eyes with her handkerchief. "It's not that I'm not thankful either, but I can hardly listen anymore. I'm glad you are all so cheerful, and I am sorry I'm so miserable." She jumped up, and even as she noticed everyone staring at the floor in embarrassed silence, she fled upstairs to her room as quickly as her ungainly body allowed, leaving the guests and her own family behind.

It wasn't long before she heard pots clanking and dishes rattling in the kitchen, and then Georg came in and gave her a hug.

"This has been a long day for you," he said with compassion. "Esther and Andrew understand. You have been through a lot, and I want you to rest. The Dunklebergers are helping us clean up the last of the feast, and then they are heading home."

"I feel so ridiculous." Hannah sniffed loudly and wiped her nose with her handkerchief. "I . . . I'm afraid I'm not a very good hostess."

"Nonsense. Any woman would feel like you—I think." Georg smiled again at Hannah and patted her back awkwardly before heading toward the door.

"Georg," Hannah asked as he turned to leave the room, "could you ask Esther to come up here before she leaves? I want to say goodbye and ask her forgiveness."

"I'm sure you have nothing to apologize for, but I will ask her to come up."

Georg was true to his word, and Esther soon joined Hannah up in the little bedroom. The two women hugged silently, and Esther refused to let Hannah ask her pardon.

"If I had lost a daughter and had as much responsibility as you, I would be in far worse shape, I'm sure. I told your husband to come over and get me if I can be of help to you. You have a lot of children here but no other women to share things with. I am not that far away, and I can ride a horse. There's not even a need to hitch a wagon for me."

Hannah hugged her friend again fiercely. Suddenly knowing what she was thankful for, she blurted out, "Esther, I thank God that He sent me a friend like you, and I will send one of the boys if I have need of you."

"I'll just tell you again, I am young and childless as yet, but my mother was a midwife, and when I was old enough, I went on many deliveries with her, so don't be afraid to call me this spring either." Esther turned then and left the room, closing the door gently.

Hannah soon heard the sound of the horses clopping down the road. Her thoughts churned and turned, and she rolled on her side to ponder the events of the day and perhaps fall asleep. She knew Georg would help the children off to bed tonight before he took the big boys out to do the chores and then came in and put his arms around her.

If she could only get a grasp on what God was trying to teach her, perhaps the last several months would make sense.

19

GIFTED HANDS

With December just beginning, winter was not officially here yet, but there was no doubt it was on the way. Each morning the ground was covered with thick white hoar- frost and often with a dusting of snowflakes. There had been no real snowfall yet, but the air was certainly cold enough, and the ground was well frozen and hard.

Every morning, one of the boys would have to scurry out from under the warm covers and run downstairs to throw wood into the fire, which had been banked up for the night, before the coals went completely out. Hannah knew that Georg got up almost every night and put wood on the fire, but the boys seemed unaware of that fact and often grumbled as if they were the only ones who had responsi- bility for keeping the house warm. Georg's response was to smile and send them outside to chop more kindling. He called it wearing off the grumbles; and even if it didn't have that desired effect, it did keep the kindling box well supplied.

On this December morning, he had promised the children that he would take them out to find the perfect tree for their upcoming holiday celebration. The atmosphere in the house was festive as Hannah fried eggs and Daniel jumped up and down so no one could dress him. This year he was to go along, and even though all the older children knew they wouldn't go very far and their papa would make a game of finding just the right tree so that it took all morning and froze everyone's fingers, Daniel had no idea and was looking forward to the adventure.

Watching everyone get dressed reminded Hannah that new mittens were needed. They had dug out last year's from a chest, but many were too small, and most had holes from wear and the occasional mouse. While everyone was outside would be the perfect chance to knit further on the mittens she had been hiding and trying to complete before Christmas.

The children were used to getting mittens every year as a Christmas gift, but Hannah loved the fact that they never saw her make them and thus it was a surprise.

When they were in Fort August—now Sunbury—Georg had bought her several skeins of yarn for this project and proclaimed at the same time that he was buying some sheep when spring arrived, so they could shear their own and spin. Hannah was good at spinning; she had spun all the wool they had on hand already, so she too was excited at the prospect of one more thing they could do for themselves.

Thinking of mittens took Hannah's mind back to her trip with Georg and her new bonnet. Now she wondered if that was a wise purchase. When would she wear it again, and if her children saw her in it, would they wonder where their store-bought gifts were?

These thoughts in turn reminded her of their precarious financial position that she had been trying to forget about and the turmoil of the past months. Hannah shook her head to clear away her anxious thoughts and brought her attention back to the task at hand.

Hannah helped everyone get dressed and sent them off up the hill to where the perfect pine tree grew just waiting for one of them to discover it. Georg was bringing in a tree much earlier than usual, but Hannah had a feeling he was trying to cheer her up. She climbed heavily up the stairs. It seemed she was gaining weight more quickly with this baby, or perhaps she was just older, but it had never seemed she felt tired this soon in other pregnancies. She thought she had at least three months yet until the baby's arrival.

Picking up her yarn from its hiding place, she saw, with a guilty feeling, her latest letter to Emily, started at least two weeks ago and still not completed. She would work awhile on the mittens, and then if the children were not home yet, finish her letter. Emily would be wondering why she seldom wrote. Hannah frowned a little. She hated writing all her gloomy thoughts when her sister was at such an exciting time in her life, and yet she had always shared everything with Emily—good or bad.

Rocking quietly and enjoying the unusual peace in the house, Hannah knitted and thought about baby names. She did hope they would have a girl. Another girl would never replace Clara, but she so enjoyed her little daughters, and as they grew, teaching them all the skills they would need as they became wives and mothers. She had taught the boys many things as well, but it wasn't the same.

Time flew past. Hannah made herself lunch, and the children still hadn't returned. It must not be too cold out, or they would have been back. Her clock chimed again, and then she heard laughing and screaming off in the distance. That would be her family, and after a day of quiet, she missed them all.

She went out on the porch and saw Benjamin and Samuel running down the hill in a flat-out race to be the first back home. Behind them she saw Frederick and Hans dragging a tree, and Georg with Daniel on his shoulders—he must have gotten tired, poor little soul. Johann was carrying the saw, and Margaret and Magdalena were close behind him, holding hands and skipping down the hill until Margaret lost her footing and they both tripped and fell. Hans stopped and ran back to help them both up, but no one appeared injured and everyone was laughing. A minute more, and they all saw her watching and began waving.

"Mama, Mama, we got the best tree ever," said Benjamin, who had reached the porch first. "You'll love it. It's a blue spruce, and Papa says it will smell like Christmas for days and days. Come see it."

"I'll see it in a minute, dear. The boys are bringing it right to me." She laughed. Their enthusiasm was infectious. As the tree reached the porch, she saw that it was huge.

"Georg, how will that thing ever stand up in our cabin? There's no room."

"I have a plan," he said cheerfully. "It's early anyway. We are going to stand it up out here on the porch and string it with popcorn. When it's closer to Christmas, I'll cut the top off so it fits, and we'll bring it in. It was too pretty to pass up, and next year it will be way too big."

"All right, Papa, you know best." Hannah laughed again and went inside to finish making supper. The trip to Fort Augusta had lightened the tension between them, and despite Hannah's sad Thanksgiving evening, the last weeks had been more cheerful in the cabin.

Chicken corn soup was on the menu. Frederick had brought in several elderly hens and cleaned them for her last night. They'd simmered all day, and by afternoon, the meat was falling off the bones. Potatoes and onions from the ground cellar and dried corn that she had soaked all day completed the soup, and as usual, there was fresh bread.

Margaret had become quite adept at churning butter, and with a stir of the soup pot, Hannah saw that everything was ready. She was sure the children were starved, having missed the noon meal on their outing.

Sure enough, they lined up around the table immediately, and once again Georg clasped her hand as they gave thanks for the meal and the day that was almost over.

The soup was devoured in no time and almost silently, the children were so hungry.

After the dishes were cleared away, Hannah brought out her small cast-iron kettle and poured popcorn seeds into it, along with some lard from butchering day, and soon there was a merry popping over the hearth fire. They had to make several kettles full, as some of the children ate as much popcorn as they strung on the tree, but finally it was covered to everyone's satisfaction.

Georg laughed. "I never thought," he said. "The birds will come tomorrow and eat the popcorn. By Christmas, we'll have to start again."

"Oh, it's all right, Papa," said Magdalena. "I don't mind feeding the birds. The cardinals always look so hungry in winter. Can't we share some corn with them?"

"Yes, indeed we can." Georg picked Magdalena up and twirled her around. "We didn't have a huge crop, but I think we can share. Now everybody, it's been a long day. Off to bed."

Benjamin and Samuel had already pulled the bricks out of the oven with a metal shovel and wrapped them up to warm the beds. This was their job all winter, and by bedtime, the chill was out of the sheets.

There were no groans over bedtime tonight. Daniel had already fallen asleep on the rug, and the rest of the crowd was drooping over the last of the popcorn.

"Wood chopping day tomorrow," said Georg cheerfully. "I saw several trees lying down since the last storm. We could pull them in with the horses and cut them up before any real snow flies."

"Hooray," said Frederick, reviving somewhat.

For some reason none of the other children could understand, he loved cutting wood. He was just getting big enough to help handle the crosscut saw, and axes had always held a fascination for him. He also loved the smell of sawdust.

"I'm going right to bed so I'm rested up," he said and picked Daniel up to carry him to bed as well.

The other children all trooped up after him, and the house was soon still, leaving only Hannah and Georg by the fire.

Hannah rocked quietly for a while and watched Georg's strong hands as he whittled. Gradually a horse took shape under his knife. "I like that," she said. "I really like that. I never knew you were an artist."

"I'm not. I just thought I'd carve a toy or two for Daniel for Christmas."

"Oh, that reminds me—I could knit on the mittens. You came back before I had a chance to put them away. I had to hide them in the other kettle."

She crossed the room, pulled her smallest Dutch oven out from beside the fireplace, and retrieved the mittens she had been working on from under the cover.

The rocker creaked and squeaked, Hannah's fingers flew from row to row as brightly colored stripes took shape under her deft hands, and Georg whittled away. The evening was so peaceful that she wished it could go on forever.

When their wedding clock struck eleven, Hannah stood up and looked at Georg's woodcarving. "Georg, you *are* an artist," she said. "I never realized you could carve wood like this." She had a sudden vision of a woodcarving shop next to the barn and then pulled her thoughts back to listen to Georg.

"I haven't carved much since the war," he admitted. "Quite a few men in my family were wood-carvers back in Germany, and when I was imprisoned here, I carved to keep my hands occupied. But when I got out I thought I never wanted to carve a piece of wood again."

"Does that you mean you feel imprisoned here?" she asked lightly, hoping it wasn't the truth.

"Not at all. I suddenly missed the feel of wood and the look of something special being uncovered from a block of wood."

"I think you should teach the boys. Not so many men can carve like you. What a wonderful gift your hands have."

"Daniel will enjoy the toys anyway. I don't know about too much carving. It brings back some memories I thought I had forgotten forever."

"Georg, you never talk about the war. Doesn't that ever bother you? Don't you ever need to talk about it? I mean even after all these years?"

"No." His voice changed suddenly. "No, I won't talk about all the terrible things I had to be part of, and men I knew and respected suddenly facing death and imprisonment when we were forced to come here in the first place. I love this country. I will never return to Germany, but I will not discuss the war either. Please don't ask me again."

Surprised at his reaction so many years after the war, Hannah dropped the subject.

"I'm going up to bed," she said instead. "Are you coming?"

"Yes, I just want to finish this part before I lose my vision for what is here. I'll be up then."

Hannah went to bed but lay for a long while waiting for Georg and wondering why he'd reacted so strongly, what was taking him so long, and trying to find a comfortable position in which to sleep.

Finally, after hearing the clock chime several times, she had tossed and turned then got up and crept down the stairs. Halfway down, she could see Georg. His back was to her, and he was hunched over with his arms on his knees. From the shaking of his shoulders, she knew he was weeping.

Torn between wanting to know his trouble and share it and the niggling thought that she should just leave him alone and act as if she hadn't seen him, Hannah stood quietly.

She thought she would sneak back upstairs but suddenly changed her mind. This was her husband. They were supposed to share everything, good and bad; and on top of all that, she was terribly curious. Brushing aside the thought that curiosity had gotten her in trouble before, she coughed so Georg wouldn't think she was creeping up on him and walked the rest of the way downstairs.

As she put her hand on his shoulder, he jumped.

"Hannah, I thought you went to bed," he said gruffly.

"I couldn't sleep. I didn't know where you were."

"Leave me alone, Hannah."

"Georg, what is troubling you? I could help you."

"No, no one can help me. It's my past . . . and my present, and I can't see my way to the future. I've tried so hard to make a home for you here and give the children a good life. It's not the way I wanted it. And I hadn't thought about the war for so long, but now all these memories have come back to me. I don't know how everything fits together, and then there is Clara. I miss her so. I wish you'd go back to bed. I never meant you to know I was crying."

"Oh, Georg, you've seen me cry many times. I'm not ashamed of that. The children didn't see you, and I'm your wife. I supposed to share things with you."

"Well, you cannot share this. Now please go back to your bed."

Hannah did as she was told but lay for a long time, shivering between the sheets. Georg didn't come up, and after a while she heard the cabin door open. Wrapping the quilt around her, she slid out of bed again. She could see him in the moonlight, walking to the shed, and after a bit, she saw smoke rising out of the chimney. So he wasn't coming to bed tonight. She sighed and got into bed for the last time that evening. Time to let him alone, she supposed, although she wouldn't know how to look at him tomorrow. She turned on her side and longed for a deep sleep.

Morning arrived before she had slept enough, but chores never waited, so she crept out of the blankets. The fire was nothing but ash; Georg had slept out in the shed with his memories, so no one had added wood in the middle of the night.

Hannah thought about calling the boys but decided to let them sleep a little. She broke kindling into smaller pieces yet and made a neat pile in the center of the hearth. Poking around, she discovered a few hot coals and blew gently to get them to light her kindling.

Once her kindling was burning cheerfully, she gradually added larger and larger sticks of wood until the fire was blazing once again.

"Mama, why are you starting the fire?" Benjamin asked.

She jumped. "Oh, you scared me!" She hadn't even heard him coming down the stairs.

"Well, where's Papa?" He cocked his head to one side.

"He's outside. I do know how to start a fire, you know."

"I can see that, Mama. It's a very nice fire, but that's no job for my Mama. If Papa was busy, you should have called me."

Hannah smiled and patted his cheek even though she knew Benjamin hated that gesture. It made her feel like he was still her little baby boy.

"I guess I thought you boys needed a rest. You can chop some more kindling. I used most of this up getting the fire going."

"Just wait until I tell everyone that Mama started the fire," Benjamin said as he ran up the stairs. "They will be so impressed."

"I'm counting on that," Hannah said under her breath.

"Come on everyone," she called. "Papa is planning on cutting a lot of wood today."

She could hear thumps, mumbles, and sleepy groans from upstairs, so she turned her attention to a hot breakfast for her hungry family.

By the time the children had fed their allotted animals and milked Blossom, Hannah had bacon and eggs ready. Georg had also come in after helping the boys with their chores. He acted like nothing had happened the night before and he hadn't spent the night alone in the shed, reliving old memories. Hannah was perplexed by his behavior but could say nothing about it in front of their children.

Once breakfast was over, the boys began gathering their warm clothes while Georg sharpened the axes out in the barn. He harnessed both horses, and Hannah knew the downed trees must be fairly large if they required two horses to drag them home. That was good. No one wanted to run out of firewood before spring.

With the boys gone, Hannah cleared up the breakfast dishes, gave Magdalena sums to work at the table, and asked Margaret to play marbles with Daniel. She set herself to sorting through the winter clothing, patching holes, taking in boys' clothing to hand down to the next smallest boy, and noticing again how quickly they wore holes in their knees and elbows.

As she worked, her thoughts flitted every which way. From her discovery that Georg was carrying hurts so deep they kept him from a craft he loved, to the lack of money to pay their obligations, to new tax laws, and back to Georg again. There must surely be an answer to their troubles somewhere, if she only thought long and hard enough. By the time two hours had passed, and her head was aching, she could hear the shouts outside and knew they had brought back at least one tree to saw up. Hannah wished she could speak freely to her husband of her thoughts, but once again there would be children stomping into the cabin, announcing they were starving.

"Those children remind me of hungry baby birds," she said to Magdalena as she put her project away and grabbed her shawl to run outdoors and properly admire the find of wood before she began preparing yet another meal for her hungry brood.

20

CHRISTMAS

Christmas week arrived quickly, much to the children's joy. Hannah thought to herself that the older one got, the swifter time went by. She had gotten all her mittens knitted, one pair for each child—and even a new pair for Georg, which was harder, since he was usually in the house when she knit late at night. She also had sewn him a new shirt, which was easier to manage, since she could sew during the day, and the children had promised secrecy.

This morning, Georg and the older boys had removed what was left of the popcorn strings from the tree and brought it inside. The cutting off of the top hadn't gone so well, and the tree was looking a little lopsided, but no one minded.

Earlier, Hannah had gone up in her room and rummaged through her trunk. Down at the very bottom was a box of brightly colored wooden beads. They came in three sizes; some were round and some oblong. The wood was worn smooth and soft from years of play. Hannah had had them since she was a young girl, and they were one of the few things she had brought along when she moved to the wilderness with Georg.

Now she took out her box and called all the children to the table. Everyone but Daniel knew this tradition and ran over eagerly. Hannah had saved one skein of yarn, and each child got a single long piece on which to string beads. When all the beads were strung, they would tie them together and hang them around and around the tree. While they worked, everyone got a turn to pick a Christmas carol.

As the children worked, Hannah pretended to string beads, watched her children, and thought about Georg carving wood. She had never realized his hands that worked so hard cutting trees, milking cows, handling the plow and other tools, and throwing firewood could carve such beautiful things as he had made these last winter evenings when the children were in bed.

It was a gift he had hidden for years, and suddenly it had crept out of hiding. She wondered what other things about her husband she had never known or appreciated before. This Christmas, she decided, she would look for more hidden gifts.

Georg had told her that after Christmas, when the children had all gotten their gifts, if any of the boys were interested in carving, he would begin to teach them what he knew.

After the beads were hung, everyone was treated to a cup of hot tea, a rare treat that Hannah saved for very special occasions.

"Only three more days to Christmas, Mama," said Margaret eagerly. "I can hardly wait. And just look at our beautiful tree."

"There's a lot to do before three days are over," said Hannah, ever practical. "Life doesn't stop for a holiday. All the chores need to be done tonight before supper."

"Oh, Mama, you always remember the chores." This from Hans, who sat next to the fireplace with his mug cupped in both hands. It was his night to milk, and the night was cold, so Hannah could understand his reluctance.

"Just think, Hans, you can milk in our nice warm barn," laughed Frederick. "Think of last year in the old barn, when the wind came through every little crack. I'm glad we got that built this summer. "

"All right, boys," said Georg, coming in from the porch. "How about we stop visiting and get the work done while Mama cooks us something tasty?"

It didn't take the boys long to do their chores once they were bundled up. The cold air made them hurry, and Georg went along to make sure no one did a sloppy job in the rush for a warm cabin and hot meal. Once the cow was bedded down and the chickens roosting in the barn, everyone sat around the table. Biscuits and gravy were on the menu again, but there was no complaining. Everyone knew that before spring, food could be in short supply, so they enjoyed whatever they got now.

"I'm going hunting tomorrow," said Georg. "I'll take Samuel and Benjamin along. I've seen some deer signs down by the creek lately, and we could use more venison."

"They're probably still fat from stealing out of our corn patch too," said Samuel. If you wait another month to shoot them, they'll be skinny."

"True," said his papa. "And the weather doesn't look like snow yet. Perhaps we can bring home two."

The days were short now, and everyone went to bed early to save candles and to keep warm. Bed was always warmer now that all of the beds had snuggly featherbeds in addition to the hot bricks.

The children slept several to a bed for warmth. Margaret and Magdalena slept with Daniel in the middle; Hans, Frederick, and Johann slept in another bed. Benjamin and Samuel often slept on the floor near the hearth. They would keep the fire burning during the night, and they often mentioned that this toughened them up to be "real men," so Georg let them sleep downstairs while secretly confiding to Hannah that it saved him the trouble of getting up every night to feed the blaze.

Hannah was tired oftener now too and never minded retiring early. Some nights she and Georg lay in bed and talked of their dreams for the children—both of them had skirted around their struggles of fall, and an uneasy truce lay between them. Lately she had fallen asleep almost as soon as she got under the covers.

Once in a while, Georg would complain about her quickness to fall asleep, but her answer was always that soon enough she would be big and uncomfortable, and then she wouldn't sleep well; and after that, the new baby would keep them both awake, so she must get her rest now while she still could. Secretly, she was still wrestling over her mixed-up emotions and her inability to communicate her real feelings so Georg would understand her.

Hannah figured she had less than three months left until their new little one joined the family. She planned to spend the next day sewing.

By the time Hannah got up the next morning, Georg and the boys had left already, taking a horse along to help carry home the venison they hoped to track down.

Daniel followed Hannah all around the kitchen, asking, "Why? Why? Why?" to every chore she started.

Hans, Johann, and Frederick began their morning by chopping a large pile of kindling and carrying it into the kitchen for the fire, while Margaret and Magdalena took turns churning butter. Once that chore was done, Hannah planned to start them on some Christmas baking. They hadn't invited anyone over this year, although there were always travelers that got stranded or lost or stuck in a snowstorm around this time of year, and she planned for extra just in case.

The boys rushed in and claimed they were freezing, so Hannah warmed some milk up for them. At least when all the other food ran out, they usually had milk available, and she was thankful for it. While she stirred it over the fire, the baby kicked and sent her mind spinning around all the things she needed to have done before spring. Clara had always been such a big help when the last couple of babies arrived. She also enjoyed babies so much. Before she knew it, Hannah was in tears again over their autumn that had been so full of heartache.

I wonder how Mary could stand being the mother of Jesus, she thought. Did she know he would have to die and she would have to watch him? And did she feel as terrible as Hannah as she watched her child die? Surely she must have, so how did she go on day after day after that?

All the turmoil Hannah had buried in the past few weeks resurfaced whenever she thought of Clara. Anger and grief swirled inside, and now, just when she thought she had dealt with it, here it was again. "Oh, God," she whispered. "I cannot go on like this. Give me grace to make it through today. And somehow help me to be cheerful for my children."

She straightened up from the hearth and wrapped her apron around the handle of her kettle. Setting it on the table, she called for the boys to bring their cups for a warm drink. As they gulped down their milk, she brought out her knitting. The mittens were long since finished and hidden away, and now she planned to make a baby blanket. She didn't have much left, but all her old blankets were worn and tattered, and this baby was going to get a new one unless she ran out of yarn.

The kitchen was already beginning to smell like the bakery Hannah had walked past almost daily when she was small in New York. She could remember holding her mother's hand and looking in the window at the delicious treats inside, and her mother had always laughed and said, "Hannah, our cook can bake for us. We've no need to buy bread from a bakery."

Hannah's fascination with fresh bread led to her spending many days in the kitchen with their cook, learning the art of crusty loaves, and now she was glad for those skills. She hadn't married a rich man like her mother had, and her girls were rapidly learning the kitchen arts well, even at their young ages.

Suddenly she jumped up and went over to where Magdalena was trying to knead the bread. "Here, do it this way," she said slamming the lump of dough around and around, folding it and slamming it again, until some of her anger eased as she pounded the uncomplaining dough. The children watched in astonishment as she pounded until Hannah noticed them all watching her and was ashamed at her outburst.

"There, that should get all the air bubbles out." She set the bread back in the bowl to rise in the warm kitchen.

Without any other explanation, she resumed her knitting and contemplation of this celebration of a baby's birth. How had God ever picked this method of saving mankind? Her thoughts were interrupted again by Daniel, looking out the window.

"Mama, Mama, something's on the porch. Mama, it's eating the porch. Mama, come quick."

Everyone jumped up and ran to the small window. Sure enough, on the porch was a prickly creature, and he was gnawing the post that held up the railing.

"Daniel, that's a porcupine," said Frederick. "They don't come out often in the day."

"Mama, the—what is it?—is eating our porch. Can I go out and scare him away?"

"Oh, no, you don't!" Hans grabbed Daniel by the wrist as he headed for the door. "See his fur? That's not fur, its spikes, and he will poke you, and it will hurt."

"Really bad?" Daniel wondered.

"Yes, really bad. We have to leave him alone."

"Oh, that's why he called a pokey pine. Why does he want to eat our house?"

Johann laughed. "Papa told me," he said. "Porcupines like salt. Some kinds of wood are salty. We could sprinkle salt on something else, like a different piece of wood, and put it out on the ground. Maybe he would like that better."

"Well, just be careful," said Hannah. "It's miserable getting quills out, and they hurt and get infected, and I surely don't want any of you having to heal up from getting poked."

Hans laughed too. "Mama, we'll wait until he moves and then put it out for next time he comes back. If Papa were here, I'd ask him if porcupines are good for anything. Then we could shoot him."

"Maybe we should shoot him anyway before he wrecks the porch," said Frederick.

"Just wait for your papa," said Hannah. "Watch him out the window. Not many children get to see a porcupine this close."

It wasn't long after the noon meal that they heard the sound of a horse along the track. It was Samuel, Benjamin, and Georg returning, and they had two deer loaded on a litter. Benjamin walked proudly by the side of the horse and carried his rifle like a soldier returning from war.

Samuel couldn't wait and began running toward the house, whereupon Benjamin threw aside his dignity, shoved his gun into Georg's hands, and raced Samuel to the cabin.

"You will never believe it," he gasped. "I shot both deer. Ask Papa."

Samuel, grinning widely, shook his head.

Benjamin's excitement glowed in his eyes. "Don't believe Sam. I did shoot them both."

"Indeed he did," said Georg, stepping up beside him. "And now he will help clean them both, but some of you other boys need to come help too. Hannah, I'll tan these hides for you, and you can make us men some buckskins for winter wear."

All the bigger boys threw their coats on and ran outside to the woodshed, where the older boys were hoisting the deer up in the air by the back legs.

Hannah watched for a moment from the window, glad of the meat and the prospect of leather but content to remain in the house with the girls and Daniel, away from the smelly, cold job of butchering.

The insides had already been removed before the deer were brought home, but each carcass still needed to be skinned, and then everyone would help cut up the meat. Georg would hang it up in the smokehouse, and some they would dry for jerky. Venison roast would be a wonderful Christmas dinner, Hannah thought. She was glad Christmas fell early in the winter when they still had plenty of vegetables in the root cellar to have a feast. Since tomorrow was Christmas, she had already gotten out a bowl of dried corn, and it had been soaking all day to be soft enough to cook tomorrow.

By this time, the bread had risen. She helped Margaret and Magdalena form loaves, which they set on a flat stone to rise again, and then they shoved the stone into the edge of the hearth where no flames directly touched it. Some settlers baked only once a week, but her bread disappeared too quickly for that.

Someone always had to watch the fire, or the bread would be burned. The girls sat close by, and Magdalena told a story while they watched. She had quite an imagination and loved to make up stories for Margaret and Daniel.

The boys and Georg made swift work of the butchering, hanging most of the meat in the smokehouse, and Benjamin brought a large roast in for the Christmas dinner. Once the venison was stored safely away, Hannah got out her tub and announced that everyone would take a bath, even Georg.

"Tomorrow is special," she told everyone. "We are celebrating the birthday of the Christ child, not just a feasting and gift day. I want you always to remember that."

"Yes, Mama," several children said in unison. They all knew bath night came on Christmas Eve, and the boys had already started the wash-water kettle boiling before they finished up the evening meal.

After every one was clean—or in Daniel's case, at least cleaner than he had been—Georg got out the Bible and read everyone the account from Luke chapter 2.

Hannah had always loved the Christmas story. While she knew people didn't become angels when they died, she could picture Clara looking down at them as they snuggled together around the fireplace and listened to their papa reading. The thought brought her comfort. Finally, every child had been tucked in or sent to bed. With a desire for one last look into the peaceful night, Hannah went over to the door and pulled it open. "Oh, Georg, come here," she whispered.

Outside, a gentle snow was falling. "Look at that. Won't the children be excited tomorrow?" They didn't often have a white Christmas in this little valley. More often, it would just be cold and brown, and the snows would fall in January and February. Georg had built the older children a toboggan this year after he'd carved the toys for the little ones.

"I don't know if we'll get enough for sledding," he said, "but it sure is beautiful to watch."

They stood together silently, and Georg's arm stole around Hannah's shoulders. They watched the snow fall until Hannah began to shiver and then closed the door and went to bed themselves.

Contrary to Georg's prediction, by Christmas morning the snow lay thick on the ground and showed no signs of stopping. The sky was so cloudy that the little children never realized how late it was and slept past their usual waking hour. Hannah, grateful for a late morning, let them sleep.

Once she and Georg got up, they woke the older children. By the time the animals had been taken care of, everyone was awake and ready for the excitement they had anticipated for at least a week (not to mention the snow), although Margaret claimed they had been waiting forever.

Hannah had been saving eggs carefully. Her hens did not always lay as faithfully in winter, but she had plenty for a breakfast of scrambled eggs, and Georg fried up the venison tenderloin from the day before. With full stomachs, the family gathered next to the fire again.

Hannah had saved the paper from any parcels she had since the fall and had carefully wrapped each child's mittens in a package tied with scraps of her yarn left over from her many knitting projects. Each name was written clearly in her precious store of ink. Georg had simply made a tag for each gift and placed the toys under the tree, while the two sleds he had made for the older children were propped up against the wall. The children had been eyeing up the tree since breakfast began, but no one had commented yet.

Georg grinned and finally asked the long-anticipated question, "Who wants to open gifts?"

"I do, I do" was the joyful response.

Hannah always got to hand her gifts out first.

"Benjamin and Samuel, these are for you." She gave each of them a brown paper parcel.

Both boys laughed. They knew what was inside but pretended to be surprised at even receiving a gift. Then it was Johann, Hans, and Frederick's turn. They held onto their packages, waiting until everyone had a gift.

"Mama, Mama." Daniel was jumping up and down. "Don't I get sumpin'?"

"Oh, I don't know." At his disappointed look, Hannah reached behind the tree and pulled out a package for him and one for each of the girls.

Finally, all the children ripped their paper open to see what their mother had made this year. The boys got brown mittens with dark green stripes, since they always wanted to look manly, but the girls were thrilled with yarn dyed in every shade Hannah could find in nature; yellow from onions, red beet juice, and even blueberries soaked in vinegar made a lovely purple-blue, all contributing to a cheery striped mitten. The children always wondered when Hannah found time to dye her yarn.

Once everyone had tried on the mittens, it was Georg's turn. Daniel received a large black bear carved from a flat piece of wood. With wheels added to the base and a piece of string attached, he could pull it around and around the house.

Margaret and Magdalena each got a small carved bed for the dolls Georg had gotten them on his spring trip, and Margaret promptly asked Hannah if she had scraps for them to make doll quilts.

Johann and Frederick were the proud recipients of beautifully carved horses complete with flowing manes and tails; while Benjamin, Hans, and Samuel excitedly claimed the two sleds, although they knew they would be called upon to share them with the rest of the family. Although it was obvious the children were dying to get out into the early winter snowfall, both Samuel and Hans stopped to ask where their Papa had found such nicely carved toys.

"Believe it or not, I made them." He smiled.

"Papa, we didn't know you could carve," said Benjamin. "When did you learn that?"

"Oh, I have been carving since I was very small." The flicker of painful memories darkened his eyes for a moment, making Hannah's heart ache for all he had endured, and then he took a deep breath and let it out slowly. "I just gave it up since I came to the colonies, and I think I will take it up again. I missed it."

"It's wonderful," said Magdalena. "I want to learn how. Can you teach me, Papa?"

Georg was speechless. Hannah knew he'd been hoping one of the boys would ask that question.

"I'll have to think about that one," he said. "In the meantime, who wants to go sledding?"

In two minutes, the house was empty, and the sound of children shrieking with joy echoed around their little valley.

"And now, Mama," said Georg, "a present for you." He rummaged around in his saddlebag, which Hannah knew always kept his secrets safe. He pulled out two packages. The first held a beautiful woven shawl, which Hannah hugged. Hers was threadbare by now, and this was a wonderful replacement.

The second package was flat and rather heavy. Hannah shook it, but no sound revealed its contents, so she ripped it open. Before her eyes was a beautifully carved plaque with ornate swirls around the writing. It read, "The hurrier I go, the behinder I get."

Hannah laughed. "Where did you find that saying?"

"It reads better in German." Georg chuckled too. "I saw how much you liked my carving and thought I'd make something for you to hang in the kitchen and remind you to slow down once in a while."

In the absence of any witnesses, Hannah kissed Georg and then produced the shirt she had sewn and hidden under the new baby clothes, along with a new pair of mittens.

"Just what I needed." Her husband smiled. "My work shirt was looking as holey as the boys'."

Seeing her husband in such a cheerful frame of mind, Hannah prepared to broach the subject of Georg's war experiences. She was sure discussing it would help him. Before she could open her mouth, Georg spoke up. "How do you think the sledding is going out there?"

They both walked out on the porch and looked up the hill to where the joyful cries of children indicated the fun was taking place.

Daniel didn't last long. Two spills into the snow, and he was returned to the house by Hans with his fingers red and his mittens missing.

Hannah sighed. "I knew I should have put strings on those mittens to keep them attached to each other. Hans, tell everyone to look out for Daniel's mittens and bring them into me when you find them. I'll fix them so they can't get lost."

It wasn't very long before Samuel brought in one mitten, and shortly after that, Magdalena found the other. Hannah had already braided a long strand of yarn. Deftly she attached each end to a mitten, and when Daniel was warmed up, she threaded one mitten through each sleeve of his coat. Now they could fall off his hands but not get lost. He grinned and went out for two more trips downhill before quitting for the day.

The rest of the children wore themselves out traveling up and down the hills, and Hannah laughed as she recalled the spring past when she wondered why on earth they lived on a farm with so many hills. Now she knew why. It brought so much enjoyment to her brood.

By the time twilight was falling, the children had all come in, one by one, shivering, and Hannah had made each of them a cup of hot tea laced with honey from the bee tree Georg had found in summer. She gathered them all around the table, and they spent the remainder of the evening singing old carols and talking about the birth of the baby Jesus and what it meant to them. All in all, it had been a good Christmas, even with the loss of Clara still fresh in all their minds, and Hannah dropped gratefully off to sleep with a verse of one of her favorite hymns echoing through her thoughts.

> Fear not, I am with thee; O be not dismayed!
> For I am thy God, and will still give thee aid;
> I'll strengthen thee, help thee, and cause thee to stand,
> upheld by my righteous, omnipotent hand.

She could sense God's presence with her, strengthening her all through her autumn of distress. What she would have done without that hope she could not even imagine.

21

WINTER'S TASKS

January followed hard on the heels of the Christmas celebration. The air grew colder, snow was more frequent, and the children were not quite so eager to sled as they had been Christmas Day. It was hard enough keeping the fire fed, the cabin warm enough to be bearable, and the animals comfortable without getting cold on purpose. The boys used the sleds to pull in loads of wood for the fireplace and to take Daniel for rides when he ventured out; and on occasion, they would all play outdoors, but winter was such tiresome work just to keep life flowing.

Hannah grew heavier and heavier with child and began to long for spring. Winter had never been her favorite season. The deer hides from various hunts were well cured now, and she began making buckskins for the older boys and Georg. The hides were difficult to sew but quite durable once they were finished and held up better to winter's hard work and cold weather than much of the clothing the men normally wore.

Georg had learned to make moccasins in his travels and was teaching the boys how to make their own and save their shoes for occasions when they needed to go to town.

"We'll soon look like Indians," Samuel observed one day, watching Hannah struggle to cut yet another pair of pants out of the unwieldy hides.

"At least we'll be warm Indians." She paused, laid the knife she had been using on the table, and flexed her aching hands. "I need a rest from this job."

"I'll do it, Mother," offered Benjamin. "I've been watching you. I can take a turn."

With Benjamin carefully cutting, Hannah turned her attention to the girls, who had been painstakingly quilting a new cover for their bed. They had each made a tiny quilt for the doll beds Georg had made them and now were trying their hand at something bigger and more useful. Seeing that they were progressing well, Hannah turned her attention to her own project.

She had gathered all her scraps of fabric into a pile and was busy braiding a rag rug for the kitchen. The old one was almost worn through, and a new one would help keep their feet warm. As everyone worked contentedly, Hannah watched the firelight dance across their faces and found her thoughts turning again and again to their financial situation.

Only this morning, before they were even out of bed, she had tried to ask Georg how they were going to solve the problem of paying off the farm.

"I'm thinking of apprenticing Benjamin and Samuel," he had answered curtly. "I may take a trip to Fort Augusta when the weather changes to see about finding them places there."

"Oh, Georg, you can't!" Hannah cried, aghast. They had moved to a farm partly to avoid such an event. "We need the boys, and I can't bear it if our family is divided. I won't let you do it." She grasped his arm as if by holding on to him, she could keep her boys at the farm.

Georg jerked his arm away. His eyes had a hard shine in them. "Hannah, it's not up to you. I thought and thought over a solution. The younger boys can step up and learn the work. And if Benjamin and Samuel are apprenticed, they will be learning a trade, not just farming. You will just have to learn to accept it. I'm not happy about it either, but it is the only way we can work through this problem."

"As if these were not my children too," Hannah said angrily. She wrenched the covers off, letting the cold air blow around her bare feet, yanked her dress over her head, grabbed her shoes, and finally turned to face her husband. "You were planning this and never even talked to me? I should help you make this choice, not find out about it later."

"Well, we have talked about it from time to time. And this is my choice. I am the boys' father."

Hannah stormed out of the room rather than say something she would regret. Georg followed her downstairs, and neither one talked to the other all morning. The air still seemed tense, but Hannah could not bend or forget her anger over such an important decision. There had to be another answer somewhere.

And then it came to her; a mother's job was to protect her children. She would have to leave with them and go home to New York. It didn't matter that it was the dead of winter, and she was expecting a baby. She would make a way to get home, and Georg would eventually follow them. Her father would take them in, and then they could start over. She couldn't have her family split up.

Even now as they all sat quietly sewing and cutting, her thoughts would not leave her in peace. Finally she flung her rug and scraps down and went to her room. She shut the door and threw herself across the bed. Somehow she had to get to New York and make things right. If she stayed here long enough, she would think out an answer. She knew it.

After a while, she pulled out her ongoing letter.

January 1799

Dear Emily,
I can hardly believe I am writing this. I am trying to find a way to come home. Not just

me, but all the children too. Georg wants to
apprentice the big boys out. I know, Emily,
everyone does that. But I cannot. I cannot
lose any one else in the family. We have to stick
together and weather this storm. I don't want
to leave Georg. He's my husband, and I love him
dearly; but he is wrong in this, and I can't see
any other way than to take the children and head
home. He will come eventually—I know it—and then
we can start again. It's not such a bad thing to
lose our home, but I can't lose my children. It's
a mother's job to protect her children, isn't it?

   Oh, Emily, I need to find someone to mail this to
you. Send me some good advice, please, but don't be
surprised if I am already on my way to you.
   As always, I love you!
   Hannah

As she read over her letter, she knew without doubt that this was
the right choice. Carefully, she folded it up and placed it deep under
her clothing where Georg wouldn't find it. He must not know her
plans until she left, and there was still a lot of figuring out to do. It
would be safe under her things until someone passed by, and Georg
knew she wrote to Emily all the time. That wouldn't surprise him. He
just couldn't read *this* letter.

   She pushed the drawer shut guiltily. She had never hidden anything
from her husband before, but this was different. She had to protect their
family. The idea that she would be leaving Georg in the middle of winter
with all the farm work, and making life harder for him than it already
was, entered her mind, but she refused to listen to it. There were other
niggling thoughts fleeting through her mind that this was wrong, but
she pushed them firmly away and went downstairs to rejoin her family.

Her rug project was lying on the table right where she left it, and she picked it up again, but there were so many thoughts chasing around her head that she simply held it and thought until finally the children noticed her.

"What's wrong, Mama?" asked Frederick. "You usually braid faster."

"Oh, nothing, I'm just thinking" was the sort-of-truthful reply.

Maybe she could get Andrew Dunkleberger to give her a ride into Sunbury. No, that wouldn't work. He would be bound to ask questions, and Georg would find out. If she weren't expecting, she could saddle up and ride by herself, but she would need a wagon to transport all these children and warm clothing. And if a storm came up, they would need protection and money for the trip, and even Philadelphia was several days' journey in good weather.

She sighed and thought about Georg, out in the cold even now. How could she leave him here? But how could she stay if the children had to begin leaving long before they were grown up? Crossing the room to the door, she opened it the smallest bit and peeked out at the snow. The windows had been covered with old blankets tacked all around to help keep out drafts, so their only light came from the candles they had burning, the fireplace, or the door if it was open. Icicles hung long from the roof all around, mute reminders of the warmer weather of last week.

This time of year, Hannah always wondered what would happen if spring never returned. This spring there would be a new little one, and she still needed to prepare, whether she were here or back in New York. There were probably only seven or eight weeks left before the new arrival.

She shut the door quickly before too much cold air snuck in, and two minutes later heard the tramp of Georg's boots across the porch. He came in rubbing his hands briskly and blowing on his fingers to warm them and spoke as if no harsh words had passed between them.

"Boys, I set some traps this morning down by the stream. I'm hoping to catch some beaver. Pelts should be bringing a good price right now." He rubbed his hands again and held them to the fire. "Your job is to check the traps twice a day and skin the beaver when you bring them home. If we get enough, I'll snowshoe over to the road and see if there are any traders. Otherwise, we'll take them ourselves up to Fort Augusta."

"Oh, boy," cheered Daniel.

"Not you, little man." Georg rumpled his hair tenderly. "You are going to have to grow a little before I send you out in the snow to trap beaver. Everyone who has a pair of snowshoes can go and help out."

If Georg could act like no harsh words had passed between them, so could she.

"Wear your new mittens," said Hannah. "It's so cold out these days."

The short day was drawing to a close already. She heated milk in her iron kettle, poured it out into bowls, and they all dipped corn bread in it for supper. It wasn't much, but it was warm and filling. The little girls washed up the bowls, and then they gathered in around the hearth. It was too early for bed, but it was dark out, and Georg had been telling them stories every night of his childhood and life in Germany.

Hannah sat and watched him with the children, and as hard as she tried, could not imagine her life without the older boys. She could not conceive how Georg would manage without them and knew he would also miss them terribly. She would have to act soon. Once he took furs to Fort Augusta, it might be too late. He might take the boys along and leave them there. She shook her head. There was no way she could get away at this time of year and this far along in her pregnancy. She would have to think of something else.

So deep was she in her thoughts that she never noticed Georg asking her a question.

"Mama, did you hear us?" Margaret asked. "Tell us a story about when you were little."

With an effort, Hannah brought herself back into the little room. "All right, I'll tell about when we were all little girls.

"Father would take us one at a time on his trips. When we were small, they were just short trips into town, but as we got older, we got to go farther away and stay in a hotel with him. One year, I was walking through . . . hmmm, I think it may have been Philadelphia. It was the first time I went away overnight. Anyway, he was holding my hand, and we were looking in all the shop windows. We stopped by a bakery, and somehow I let go of Father's hand. He didn't notice, and suddenly I was all alone. I was so short and couldn't see him anywhere."

"Oh, Mama." Magdalena jumped up and gave her a sympathetic hug. "What did you do? Did you cry?"

"Well, as you can see, someone found me." Hannah laughed. "No, it wasn't your Papa. I met him on a different trip when I was much older. And yes, I did cry. A kind, grandmotherly lady saw me and helped me find your grandfather. I was so glad to see him, but my mother didn't let me go away for quite some time after that trip."

"Well, I'm glad she didn't keep you home forever, or you never would have met Papa," said Johann. "If it wasn't for Papa, none of us would be here."

"You are so right, Johann. Thank you for reminding me of that." Her heart thumped a little harder. Was running the right choice?

Georg spoke up. "I am responsible for all of you here, and I will try to always make the right choices for you." He looked directly at Hannah as he spoke.

So he hadn't forgotten their quarrel this morning. Hannah felt uncomfortable under his gaze, and pretending to be tired, suggested that it was bedtime.

"Go ahead," said Georg. "I know you're tired. The children and I will tell a few more stories."

Flustered now, because she had to leave, Hannah went upstairs, crept into bed, and tried to sleep. Even the warm brick at her feet brought no comfort. She finally got up, pulled their big Bible up onto the bed, and began paging through it. She wished that God could help her through this struggle, but she couldn't find the words to talk to Him, and she couldn't seem to find anything comforting in the Scriptures.

Her thoughts whirled around and around. Should she try to leave? Could she even make the attempt? Were there other options besides apprenticeship? Where was her answer? Did God even hear her?

The children were laughing downstairs with their Papa. Feeling weary and sad, Hannah crept under her covers and waited for sleep.

She dimly sensed Georg climbing into bed later that night but was too sleepy to acknowledge him and not sure she was ready to open up a discussion. He slept with his back to her, leaving an invisible wall between them all night.

Morning brought yet another snow. Hannah looked out the door and shut it quickly. The more snow that fell, the less chance she had of leaving with the children—but also the less chance for Georg to ride into Fort Augusta and make arrangements for the boys to leave home.

They still had plenty of cornmeal, so she stirred up a pot of mush. They would have it hot for breakfast, and most likely for supper, she would slice it and fry it, and they would have it again. There was bacon yet, hanging in the smokehouse. It seemed no one ever tired of bacon.

As she stirred the mush to keep it from burning while it thickened, Hannah thought about stories her father had told her about her grandfather crossing from Holland to New York. The ocean crossing had been rough, and mealtime included only biscuits and salt pork. She would remind her children to be grateful for cornmeal mush if they complained today.

For the first time in a week, no one commented on the breakfast choice, and Frederick and Hans even asked if they could take Daniel sledding. The sight of the smooth white blanket outside was tempting, and soon all the children were outside, making tracks everywhere. There was always some competition to see who could be the first to walk up the hill and mar the perfect white or who could sled down the fastest or go the farthest, and Hannah felt a rush of thankfulness for her children as they played together.

Georg spent the morning mending the harness for the plow horses in readiness for spring. It seemed even in the slow season, there were so many things to do. The children came in chilled and laughing, and after the noon meal, Georg took Benjamin and Samuel out with him to do some blacksmithing work. He was encouraging the boys to learn this skill too, although Hannah hoped he would not consider apprenticing either of the boys to a blacksmith. That was such hot, heavy work any time of year.

She felt like she kept coming back to the same issue, and Georg didn't seem likely to change his mind. It was frustrating to feel like her family was slipping away and she had no say in the matter, no control over the direction her children would take. Her feelings of powerlessness angered her—she thought again of the little bird in the cage that she had set free this past summer. Hannah knew she could no longer be that bird. She was going to get out and soon.

Hannah set the girls to sewing their quilt patches again and washed the dishes and swept the floor herself. It took her mind off the situation for a few minutes, but her thoughts soon wandered back to how she could get home to New York with all the children.

To distract herself, she thought about Georg's wood carving and his careful hands bringing toys and treasures out of wood. He had been whittling almost every evening since Christmas, and the children also loved to watch him work. It was a hobby they all were amazed by, and Magdalena was especially fascinated. Hannah knew Georg thought it was not appropriate for a girl to be carving, but she thought he was quite aware of all the attention she gave his tools and hands whenever he took up a piece of wood.

It did seem funny that all the years they had been married, Hannah had never known Georg was an artist. Now suddenly it was pouring out of him. I wonder, she thought, if he could make an income with his skills, maybe teach the boys and Magdalena—well, maybe not Magdalena—but perhaps his long-hidden skills could help instead of apprenticeships. Maybe when he came back in, she would talk about it with him, and they would find resolution for this nagging problem of how to survive.

Now she had even more to think about at night when she couldn't sleep with the big baby kicking her. Should she go? And how could it happen in several weeks before it was too late? Or should she stay and find a way to help Georg's skills bring in additional income? Why was life so confusing?

It was dark before her husband and the boys came in from the forge. They seemed to be developing such a close bond as the boys grew. Apprenticeship would be as hard for Georg as for her. After supper, he sent everyone to bed early and sat down at the table next to Hannah.

"I know you're angry at me," he began curtly. "I would have discussed the boys with you, but I can't see any other way out, so a discussion seemed pointless."

"I'm not angry at your thoughts." Could her husband finally be willing to discuss this, the most important decision they had ever made, with her? "It does seem like one way to help, but surely I'm entitled to have some input." Before she could lose her courage, she plunged forward. "What about carving—you have such a gift, and it's been hidden all these years. Couldn't you do something with wood carving or furniture? What about all the people moving into the area? They didn't bring all their furniture, they would buy your work—I know they would. What about a store like you mentioned last fall? The older boys could help run it, and you could teach them. It would be like you were giving them apprenticeship, but they wouldn't have to leave us. And what about—"

"Whoa up there, girl." Georg held up his hand to stop her flow of words. "All those things would cost money to start up, and I don't even have anything to barter right now in place of cash. Remember when your father was here and we floated boats downstream? A couple of them got caught in a whirlpool and sucked under."

Hannah nodded mutely.

"I feel like I'm caught in a whirlpool. It's sucking me down. I'm sinking, I can't get out, and there are people hanging on me, you and the children. I'm responsible for you all, and you are sucking me under. When I go under, everything goes with me. Can't you see? This weight all hangs on me. I don't know if I can survive it."

Hannah frowned. She had never thought she was a burden to Georg. *Could he really feel that way?* She shook her head to clear her thoughts. She and Georg had pledged themselves to each other years ago—to help each other. Neither one should be a weight.

"So include me when you feel that way. I want to help you. I want to feel part of this, not like I'm just helping drown you. Georg, can't you let me share this with you?"

"I don't know, Hannah." He got up, pulled on his boots and coat, and went out into the cold night. Hannah knew he was going out to the shed again. She raked the coals together and piled more logs on to keep the fire going and made her way upstairs.

When they had gotten married, she planned to be the best wife as well as the godliest woman she could be. Somehow marriage was beginning to feel like a terribly painful way to die to herself and be that godly woman.

22

SUGARING TIME

Winter was interminable. Hannah felt she had been pregnant forever, and still the baby kept growing. Spring seemed forever far away. Try as she might, she hadn't yet come up with a plan that would work to change Georg's direction for the family. The weather continued to thwart any chance of her leaving the farm with the children. If it didn't snow, it sleeted; the roads were impassable even with a sledge, and so Georg too had no opportunity to travel anywhere. The tasks of keeping family and farm animals fed and warm took up everyone's time.

Finally, in the middle of February, a breath of warm air blew through their little valley. Samuel was the bearer of eagerly anticipated news.

"Mama, the sap is rising. Papa said so."

"Oh, maple syrup time!" said Hannah excitedly. The sap rising meant spring was on the way, and even though there would be more snow and cold winds, sugaring time always led to spring.

Georg and Benjamin retrieved the small sap buckets they had stored away in the barn last winter, and Hannah washed all the little metal spigots that Georg had crafted over the years at his forge. The first year they lived here, he had bought two and then copied them. Every fall, they would go out in the woods when the leaves changed, for it was then that the brilliant scarlet trees revealed that they were not ordinary maple trees but sugar maples. Many trees all over the mountains were marked now for maple-sugaring time.

All the boys but Daniel went out with Georg to locate the sugar maples, Georg drilled a hole into each of the trees, and the smaller boys took turns inserting the spouts. Benjamin and Samuel then drove a spike into the tree and hung a small metal bucket under the spout to catch the sap.

It took several days of hiking before they were sure they had located all the trees, especially since Johann and Frederick were not very skilled on snowshoes yet, and Hans wasn't much better. Then they had to empty the small pails every day into a large pail and haul it home.

When they'd collected enough, Hannah was ready to start the boiling. This was an exhausting job even when one wasn't pregnant, so she wasn't looking forward to the long hours stirring the kettle while the syrup boiled. It could take fifty gallons of sap to make a gallon of maple syrup, and it often took four or five weeks from the time the sap started running until it was done, so she knew there were long days ahead. Still, it was a nice change from honey on the cornmeal mush.

Once the syrup was collected, it was poured into the largest kettle they owned, put over a fire, and stirred constantly to prevent burning. Some larger farms boasted a sugaring house for this part of the project, but Hannah and Georg just took turns outside, stirring and stirring. Fortunately, it wasn't the coldest part of winter, but it still was a chilly job, even next to a fire. Benjamin and Samuel were old enough to help also, but even so, day and night until the sap boiled down was exhausting; and then they would begin again with another collection of sap until finally, if the trees held out, they had a year's worth of maple syrup.

Hannah stood her turn, stirring and stirring and watching the girls play in the snow with Daniel. It had melted a little, and the snow was perfect for rolling into balls and creating a snowman. The ball they had rolled was so large, they could hardly move it, so they started on a smaller one for the middle. Daniel screamed with pleasure and ran round and round in the snow and was no help at all. By the time the second ball was finished, it was too heavy for the girls to get on top of the first ball, and they hollered for help.

Hannah laughed at their antics as she stirred. Suddenly a pain shot through her. She knew that feeling, but it was too early for labor. The baby shouldn't come until at least the end of March. Must have just been a muscle twinge, she decided, and kept stirring.

Several minutes later, she had another "twinge," and then later on, another. By the fourth one, Benjamin looked at her oddly as he walked past.

"Mama, what's wrong?" he asked. "You look like something hurts."

"I guess something does hurt." She gritted her teeth until it passed. "Go find your Papa. I think he's up in the field checking on the trees up there. And send Samuel out to stir this syrup while I go lie down."

Samuel returned in several minutes and eyed her thoughtfully.

"Is it the baby, Mama? I thought the baby wasn't coming until spring."

"Well, it's not supposed to," Hannah snapped. Immediately she regretted it. "I'm sorry, Samuel, I don't feel well. Watch this doesn't burn. Benjamin went to get Papa."

She walked slowly indoors and climbed the steps to their room and lay down on the bed. This was not supposed to happen to her.

She hadn't lain there long before she heard Georg's steps running up toward their room.

He burst in the door, concern written all over his face. "Hannah, is it the baby already? It's too early, isn't it?"

"Yes, it is too early. I think maybe I've been doing too much. If I lie down awhile, I should feel better." There was a chance that was true, even if it was a slim one.

"I'll go help the boys with the syrup. Now you rest here. Don't get up and don't worry about us. We can manage just fine. I'll be back in a little while to see how you are."

"Yes, dear," Hannah said obediently. She was more concerned than she was trying to let her family know, but she did hope maybe a rest would solve the problem.

Georg closed the door.

Hannah got up, grabbed her Bible and her letter-writing materials from the drawer and propped her feet up in bed. She wasn't sleepy and might as well get something useful done. She wished she had a book to read that she had not already read ten or fifteen times, but all the books were in places like New York or Philadelphia, not in settlers' houses.

She opened her letter to Emily. There were her wishes to run away from home and take all her children someplace safe. Well, it didn't look like that was going to happen. She folded it up small and hid it under her pillow and began a new missive.

Dear Emily,

It's hard to believe it is February already. You must soon be making final wedding preparations, and I am lying in bed today hoping this little one is not on his way too early. I have propped my feet up and am trying to behave, and I am praying that no baby shows up before it is ready. Not that I would mind being one person again instead of two, but I think we need a few more weeks.

I wrote to you thinking of bringing all the children home. It's so hard to explain, but I could never work out how to do that. Sometimes I am frustrated being a woman. A man would just jump on his horse or hitch up a wagon and go do what needs to be done.

I, on the other hand, am terrible at hitching wagons, not too much better at riding a horse, and if anyone saw a lone woman with a bunch of children traveling in the dead of winter, they might lock her up somewhere. And now the baby is soon ready to come. So I am going to tear up my other letter and burn it before anyone sees my foolishness.

Oh, Emily, I do long to see you and Father. I love my home, but sometimes it is just too far from your home, and life here is so much harder.

Whenever you get this letter, pray for me. We may already have a new baby, or I may be just on the brink of enduring another labor—which I do gladly, by the way. I am excited to see our new little Zartman face-to-face.

My next letter will most likely give you all the news about your new nephew or niece. In the meantime, I seal this up with a hug and a kiss for you and for Father. I know he doesn't like too much display of emotion, but give him a hug for me. I will see if Georg can get this sent soon.

I love you,
Hannah

That letter finished, Hannah took up her Bible. She had been so busy lately; she hadn't taken any time to read Scripture. Perhaps that was why she felt so downhearted. Her encouragement was all in this big book, and she hadn't even opened it for more days than she could count. She wondered what God thought about her lack of faithfulness.

"Oh, God," she said suddenly, "You must be angry at me. Don't bring this baby so early because I have been unfaithful."

She stopped then and reconsidered. God was a loving God. Surely He wasn't punishing her just because she was too busy to spend time reading the Scriptures; but He must be disappointed in her.

"God," she started over. "I feel like I just can't manage it right. I try and try, but it seems I could always be a better wife, a better mother, and just a better person all around. Can You help me?"

There, that felt better. She just needed to start fresh. She was beginning to feel better too. The pains seemed to be getting further apart.

She could hear the children banging around down below and running in and out the door as they worked on the maple syrup. Now and then she could hear Georg's deep voice directing some part of the process. As she felt better, she fell asleep and only woke at the sound of Georg opening the door to see how she was doing.

"I feel much better," she said before he could even ask. "I think I'll come downstairs."

"I don't think so. You'll never rest down there."

"Oh, Georg, I can't be up here alone. Isn't there someplace I could lie down and watch everyone?"

"Wait here," Georg said. "I'll be back to get you."

Hannah heard him go outside and then a short while later come back in. She also heard Daniel say quite loudly, "Daddy, is that the surprise you were makin' for Mama?"

Everybody laughed.

Georg said, "Shhh, it's a little early, but I think this is a good time."

When he came up the stairs, she pretended not to be able to hear everyone downstairs. She followed Georg down and was indeed surprised to see a lovely rocking chair sitting in front of the fire with a matching footstool next to it.

"But I already had a chair," she blurted.

At that, all the children giggled.

"This one was made by Papa," said Magdalena.

"And we all got to help," added Margaret.

"It's beautiful." Hannah rubbed the arms. The wood was sanded so smooth, it was soft to the touch.

"And a footstool too. I guess there *is* somewhere I can sit down here."

"Well, it was going to wait until the baby came, but I guess it's still for the baby. He just can't see it yet."

"You mean *she* can't see it yet," laughed Hannah. "Very well, I'll sit right here and knit, and you can carry on with all the work."

The rest of the afternoon and evening passed quickly. Georg had decided there would be no more syrup gathering. They were almost done with the boiling down anyway.

In honor of their finishing this project, and since it was a yearly tradition, he decreed it was time for a taffy pull. With loud cheers, the children began to get ready.

"What's taffy, Mama?" asked Daniel, who was too young to remember last year's frolic.

"Watch and see darling," answered Hannah cheerfully. She was feeling so much better, but no one would let her get up, so she rocked and watched.

Georg bustled about, seeming to enjoy his turn in the kitchen, although he couldn't locate anything he needed.

"Hannah, where's that small kettle?"

"It's sitting by the sink, dear. I just washed it out this morning."

"Oh, and where is that small wooden stirring spoon? Benjamin, go get me two pails full of snow, but leave it sit out on the porch until I get the syrup boiled."

Samuel bustled about in Georg's shadow, trying to look important; and Hans, Frederick, and Johann watched all the commotion with big smiles of anticipation. Candy was rare, and they only made taffy once a year.

Finally everything was assembled, and the process began. Georg filled the small kettle with several cups of their freshly made maple syrup and hung it over the kitchen fireplace. The amber liquid had to be stirred constantly to keep it from burning—much like the sap-boiling process, but this time the heat needed to be more intense. Finally, with sweat rolling off Georg's forehead as he stirred and stirred, the syrup began to boil. After it had boiled awhile, Johann fetched a glass of cold water, and Georg dropped several droplets into the tin cup.

"Nope," he said, "not yet," and continued stirring.

Daniel could hardly stand the waiting. "What is it, Mama?" he kept asking. "What's Papa making? How come you aren't cooking? Can we eat that stuff?" His questions seemed endless, but no one minded.

After several attempts with cold water, Georg pronounced the syrup ready.

"Benjamin, bring those pails in here so Mama doesn't have to go outside tonight," he commanded.

The pails were brought in, brimming with cold, fresh snow. Georg dumped the snow into a large, flat dish and then drizzled the syrup slowly over it. The syrup cooled immediately and became thin strips of candy.

"Wait two or three minutes so you don't get burned," he instructed, "and then grab a piece."

The children were soon shrieking with delight as they gobbled up their maple taffy. No one even wanted to try pulling it as they sometimes did but ate it as soon as it was cool enough. Georg finished pouring out his pot and then brought some over to Hannah where she was still rocking.

"You'd better get some before it disappears," he said, handing her a sticky piece.

She laughed and popped the whole thing into her mouth.

"Oh, you're as bad as the children," he said. "Eat it slowly and make the fun last."

"Nope, fast is the best way, I've always thought." She licked her fingers.

A few minutes were all that was required to devour all the candy.

"More, Papa, make more," urged Daniel.

"No, my little man. Enough for tonight. This was just a little treat for working so hard the last couple weeks. The maple syrup is for using all year long. We can't make it all into candy for you. Besides, it's bed-time. One warm spring morning your Mama will make you pancakes, and you'll be happy for maple syrup to pour over them."

"Night, Papa," said Daniel a little reluctantly, but Margaret took his hand and led him off to the washbasin to clean up for bed.

One by one, the children washed their sticky fingers, hugged Georg and Hannah, and made their weary way to bed. The sugaring process had been as long and arduous as ever, but also as rewarding as ever.

"If we get any more sap next year, we'll need more places to store it," observed Hannah.

"Well, let's just see if we are still here next year."

The festive mood evaporated.

"You're tired too, Georg." Hannah suggested, "Let's go up to bed. Tomorrow will be soon enough to clean up all this sticky stuff."

"I agree. Let's leave the mess. I'll go make the bed ready. You rest here, and when the bricks have it warm enough, I'll call you."

Hannah agreed even though she felt perfectly capable of getting the bed ready by herself.

Georg carried several bricks warm from the fire and wrapped in cloth up to their room and placed them in the bed. He hadn't been there two minutes before he called down the stairs.

"Hannah, what's this paper under your pillow?"

Oh no, she had forgotten to tear up her letter to Emily!

"It's just a letter to my sister," she called back, hoping he wouldn't look at it. "Just put it in my drawer."

"Hannah!"

Hannah flinched as if he had hit her, and she felt as if all her strength drained away. Judging from his tone of voice, he must have looked at it. How would she ever explain her rebellious missive to him?

Sure enough, his face reminded her of a thundercloud as he stomped down the stairs.

"What is this supposed to mean?" he bellowed.

"Georg, shhhh, the children are in bed."

"Don't shhhhh me." His eyes blazed at her. "I want to know what this is supposed to mean. You were planning to leave? I can't even believe my eyes. I mean I can't believe what you wrote here." He shook the letter at her, his voice ragged with hurt.

Hannah cringed. She'd never thought he would see her inner thoughts. Yes, she had planned to take all the children, but she had never once stopped to consider how deeply that loss would affect Georg. Her eyes filled with tears.

"You don't understand, Georg." She twisted her apron and willed him to understand her heart. "The boys were leaving. You were taking them. I can't lose any more children. I felt like I couldn't stay here if it was the last house on earth."

"So you'd rather lose a husband?"

"No, of course not. I didn't think . . . I mean . . . I was just . . ." There really was nothing she could say, and maybe now she had just ruined everything.

Georg turned around without speaking, threw the letter in the fireplace, and stormed upstairs. Hannah was afraid to move. She twisted her hands in her dress and listened to Georg upstairs, stomping across their bedroom floor, but she couldn't imagine what he was doing. Probably just pacing around, and soon he would cool off and they could discuss this sensibly. She heard him go into the boys' room and could hear a murmur of sleepy voices responding to something Georg said.

The sound of boots on the steps drew her eyes. Georg had a bag and his extra coat. Still without speaking, he took his gun off the pegs where it hung near the door.

"Where are you going?" Hannah hated to hear his answer, but she had to know.

"I don't know." Georg wrenched the door open, letting in a cold chilly wind. "Maybe I don't care."

Without another word he opened the door and went out into the dark night, leaving Hannah alone with her fears and her regrets.

23

STRONGER TOGETHER

For the next week a gray cloud hung over the little cabin in the valley. Hannah thought most likely the older boys knew where Georg had gone, but she hated to break their confidence with their father, and there really was no emergency in their house—providing the baby didn't make another attempt to arrive early.

As one day passed into the next without his return, she began to wonder if he had abandoned them.

Then illness struck their little home. Daniel was sick first. He coughed up phlegm and ran a fever, and at night his cough sounded like the barking of a dog. Hannah was familiar with croup and many of its remedies, but as one after another of the children got sick, she began to feel overwhelmed.

One morning she woke up, knowing even as she opened her eyes that she had a fever. It was difficult to cough with her big belly, and she worried this illness would bring on labor.

Finally she called for Samuel. "If you boys know where your Papa went, please go and find him. We need some help here."

Samuel's face turned red. "Papa said not to tell you."

"I know, but we need some help. You don't have to tell me, just go get him and tell him we are all sick."

Samuel nodded. "I can find him," he said and ran out the door.

Hannah wished she were in bed, but too many children needed her attention to retreat there now. How she wished Clara were here. She was always so patient with the little children when they were sick.

Well, she couldn't turn time back. She would just have to manage as best as she could. The boys took turns helping her wring out cool cloths for the smaller children with fevers, and she stirred honey into many, many cups of tea, hoping to stop the coughing. Her mother used to take them outside when they had croup, but Hannah didn't have the energy and was afraid it might make the children worse.

It was late in the afternoon when she heard Samuel's horse coming up the road. Brown Betty had been limping a little since autumn, and Hannah always knew the sound of her gait. She could only hear one horse though and wasn't sure Samuel had been able to find Georg.

Several minutes later he burst in the door. "I found Papa and he's coming. He went to get Esther."

Hannah hugged Samuel weakly. "Thanks. I knew you could find him."

Before too much more time passed, she heard another horse, and close behind it, the sound of a wagon. There must be more help coming, she thought tiredly. Normally she would have refused help. After all, a mama should be able to care for all her own children, but she was too sick to care what people thought of her today, and she was concerned her illness might endanger the new baby.

Georg approached her hesitantly, looking as if he wanted to say something, but before he could, Esther came in and began bustling efficiently about the kitchen. She took one look at Hannah and shooed her up to bed, and Hannah was only too grateful to comply.

Hannah couldn't decide if she was hot or cold, finally settled on cold, pulled the covers up to her chin, and drifted off to sleep. Somewhere off in the distance, she could hear Georg talking to Esther and the children, but her fever made her feel like she just didn't care what was going on downstairs. Her own raspy cough woke her in a few minutes, and when the spasm subsided, she tried to sleep again.

Much later, there was a knock on her door. It was Benjamin with a bowl of soup.

"Can you eat, Mama?" His voice was thick with concern.

"I'll try." She pushed herself to a sitting position. "Maybe it will help me feel better."

"Esther says you need to eat for the baby," he said. "I'm supposed to make sure you eat all this soup."

"All right, Georg." Hannah smiled but then remembered that Georg was still angry and hadn't even come up to see her.

She took the spoon, ate half the soup, and gave the bowl back to Benjamin. "I can't eat any more just now. Tell Esther it was good but I think it will make me sick to my stomach to eat more."

"Should I ask her to come up here?"

"No, I just want to sleep." Hannah pulled the covers up again and then decided she was too hot and threw them off, even as Benjamin tiptoed out and shut the door.

She wished she didn't need to think about Georg.

Surely he would come up and ask how she was.

Puzzling over his behavior, she drifted off to sleep again and then came awake with a jerk. What had woken her? And then she knew. It was labor for sure. What time was it? The room was dark, but she could hear voices downstairs, so someone must be up yet.

After the pain eased, she crept out of bed, wrapped her blankets around her, and opened the door.

"Georg," she called.

No one answered.

"Esther?"

Still no answer.

Her voice was so hoarse from coughing that perhaps no one could hear her. She started down the steps, and the walls began to spin around her. Thinking she had better rest until the spell passed, Hannah began to sit, but the fever made her misjudge exactly where she was, she tripped on the blankets tangled around her and fell headlong down the rest of the steps, landing painfully on her shoulder and surprising Georg and Esther, who she vaguely noticed were sitting at the table talking quietly.

Esther jumped up and ran over to Hannah and gently helped her to sit up.

"Careful, Hannah, you've had a bad fall," she said shakily. "Why are you out of bed?"

"It's the baby. The baby is coming right now!" Even as she spoke, she could feel the beginning of another contraction. "Where's Georg? I need him."

"He's here, honey." Oh, that was right. She'd heard his voice a moment ago as she was falling, hadn't she? "Now just lay still on the floor a minute while I get some things ready. Georg will help you upstairs then."

Somewhere in the back of her mind, Hannah knew what was happening, and yet the fever made her mind so fuzzy, she couldn't think clearly. Georg picked her up as if she were weightless and carried her easily upstairs. He laid her gently in the bed, but Esther shooed him out before he could say anything to Hannah.

Another contraction gripped her.

Hannah hated to cry out and scare the children. When her other babies were due, Georg had found someone to care for the children, or she had gone elsewhere where there was a woman to help her. With everyone sick, Georg wouldn't take them anywhere at all. She knew Esther was bustling about, taking care of things for her, but still she kept thinking about everyone . . . but thinking was too hard right now. As the pain eased, she felt a little more coherent, but it seemed scarcely any time passed before she felt the beginning of another contraction.

At this rate, the baby would be born quickly, and she could just think about getting over her fever. Normally Hannah spent a week or two thinking about the process of bringing a baby into the world and preparing herself mentally, but she didn't have that luxury this time, and she felt completely unprepared for the task ahead of her. Before she could suppress it, she moaned out loud. Esther jumped and hurried over.

"Hannah, how close are your pains? I thought we would have some time yet."

Hannah shook her head. She couldn't speak.

"Now lie still, I need to see if the baby's head is down. You do understand, don't you?"

Hannah nodded and gripped the bedposts behind her head. If only this baby would hurry up. She couldn't remember labor feeling this bad before. She heard Esther sigh heavily and saw her turn back to her preparations for the baby.

If only she had strength to ask how the baby was. Suddenly a sharper pain grabbed Hannah, and she screamed, "Georg, where are you?"

Esther ran over again. "Hannah, can you hear me? The baby is facing the wrong way. He's pressing on your back. That is why it's so painful. My mother delivered many, many babies, and she knew how to turn them. I'm going to see what I can do."

"I need Georg," Hannah cried hoarsely. "Please get him."

"Hannah, men are no help at a time like this. Let me help you." She gave Hannah a handkerchief. "Here, bite on this when the pains are so bad. It will help you not to scream, and your throat won't be so painful. Can you drink a little tea with some honey?"

"Just water," Hannah croaked. "I'll try not to scream. It scares the children."

"This is not the time to worry about your children," Esther said sternly. "Let's worry about you and your new baby."

Agonizing minutes passed, during which Hannah endured pain like she had never experienced. No wonder some women were afraid of childbirth. She'd secretly thought them cowards, but she'd never imagined it could be this horrific. She was so out of control of the situation.

"Esther, please, I need Georg. Please just call him!"

"Hannah, you are all right, trust me," Esther replied.

"Esther, what if I don't make it through this? I need to tell Georg I love him. Please get him. When he left, he was so angry. I have to talk to him."

"Hannah, it's just your pain talking. You are not going to die. I know you don't drink, but I brought some whiskey. It will ease things a little bit. The baby is not going to be born for a while, and you need your strength."

"No, Esther, I cannot drink that." She shook her head and waved her hand wildly in the air.

Esther scurried out of her way. "Hannah, look at me. Really look at me. You have to drink this. It's going to be a long, long night, and when it's over, you'll look at your new little child and rejoice, but this pain is too strong to handle without some help."

Finally Hannah gave in and choked down the whiskey Esther offered her. It burned her already raw throat, but after a few minutes did give a little relief to the contractions that gave her no rest.

Soon she found she could think better. "Esther, I'm sorry I was so rude to you."

She was ready to weep now. "Georg and I had a big fight, he has such hurt feelings, and I have hurt feelings, and I do so need to talk with him."

"Hush, all women say crazy things in labor. I can't be insulted so easily, and you can talk to Georg in the morning with a baby at your side. Now just lie still and rest if you can."

Hannah closed her mouth. This was useless. She would never get Esther to call Georg, and she was too ashamed to explain to Esther just how bad it had gotten between them and that it was all her fault. But what if she would die? Women died all the time in childbirth, and even though she had already had nine children quickly and not too painfully, this one was clearly different.

"God," she prayed silently. "I need Georg. Please send him up here." Between contractions, she prayed over and over, but he still didn't come. Although she knew in her heart that God heard her, her mind kept saying the opposite. "Where are You, God? And where is my husband? Doesn't anyone know I need him?"

The night wore on and on. Hannah bit her handkerchief and prayed and wept quietly, and the wedding clock chimed the hours past, and from time to time when she couldn't beat it any longer, she screamed. Esther was always there to hold her hand and offer words of comfort, and Hannah was grateful; but she so wanted her husband to be with her.

Somewhere in the midst of all this, Esther left the room, but Hannah was scarcely aware of it until she returned.

"Hannah, I was just downstairs to see Georg," she began.

"Oh, is he coming to me?"

"Let me finish. He took all the children out to sleep in the shed, and Benjamin and Samuel are sleeping in the barn. It's not very cold, and there's a fire in the shed stove. He was just out to check on them, and they're all sleeping soundly."

"What time is it? Oh, I knew I shouldn't scream so."

"Hush, Hannah. You didn't scare anyone. It's somewhere around three in the morning, and no, I don't know how much longer this will take. Now just rest when you can and stop worrying. I'll do all the worrying," she said under her breath.

Now what did that mean? Fear gripped her again, along with a contraction. Where was God when she needed Him?

"Esther, get my Bible from the drawer please. There is a hymn in there on a piece of paper. Will you read it to me?"

"Of course I will. Just a minute."

Esther found the Bible and sat next to Hannah, holding her hand in one of her own and squinting at the paper in the dim candlelight.

How firm a foundation, ye saints of the Lord,
is laid for your faith in his excellent word!
What more can he say than to you he hath said,
to you that for refuge to Jesus have fled?

Fear not, I am with thee; O be not dismayed!
For I am thy God, and will still give thee aid;
I'll strengthen thee, help thee, and cause thee to stand,
upheld by my righteous, omnipotent hand.

When through the deep waters I call thee to go,
the rivers of woe shall not thee overflow;
for I will be with thee, thy troubles to bless,
and sanctify to thee thy deepest distress.

When through fiery trials thy pathway shall lie,
my grace, all sufficient, shall be thy supply;
the flame shall not hurt thee; I only design
thy dross to consume, and thy gold to refine.

The soul that on Jesus hath leaned for repose,
I will not, I will not desert to its foes;
that soul, though all hell shall endeavor to shake,
I'll never, no, never, no, never forsake.

"Hannah, that is beautiful. I never heard that hymn before, but hold onto it tonight. Esther's eyes glistened with concern. "I'll be honest. I think this is going to get worse before we are done here."

"Esther. I cannot take much more. I'm not just a silly woman in the midst of childbirth. I've had nine babies. Don't you think I would know if things are not right? Please get Georg for me. I don't want to die and never speak to him. He can't go on if I die tonight knowing we never resolved this. Please, Emily, please get him."

"Who is Emily?" Esther stared at her for several seconds. "He shouldn't come in here, but you won't rest until he comes, so I will go find him." She left, and Hannah could hear her running down the stairs, calling, "Georg, come quickly!"

At last, her weary mind said. "Thank You, God, finally, someone will listen to me."

Before Georg and Esther returned, another pain gripped her and released and then another one. The knowledge that the children were outdoors finally released all Hannah's pent-up distress. She wailed and then screamed with contractions that seemed like they would wring the life out of her.

Soon she heard footsteps coming toward her little room, and then Esther was speaking outside the door.

"Georg, she won't rest until she talks to you. I don't know what happened between you two, but please resolve it. She's afraid this baby is going to die and herself too, and I need her to focus and give her strength to this labor so we don't lose her. I don't know how much more she can take, but an easy mind with you will go a long way toward helping her cope."

Georg burst through the door before Esther even finished her speech and knelt beside Hannah's bed. He grabbed her hands and wept as he looked at her. "Oh, Hannah! I am so sorry I left. I was furious at you, but mostly I was hurt, and I should have just left all that go and been here to help you. Maybe this wouldn't have happened."

Hannah gasped and gripped Georg's hands. Sweat beaded her forehead. "I'm going to die," she shrieked.

"No, you are not!" Georg said firmly. "Hannah, I will stay here with you, and you are not going to die."

As the pain eased, Hannah's mind was clearer.

"Georg, I am the one who is sorry! I wrote that letter when I was upset, and I reread it right before you found it. I thought I should never have been so foolish." She gasped and waited a minute as yet another contraction peaked and then eased. "I was going to tear it up and burn it, but then I got distracted, and you found it and never even let me explain. I've thought over and over in my mind how I could have handled it differently. I can just say I'm sorry." She started crying then and Georg patted her awkwardly.

"I'm sorry I left, Hannah. I should have been here for you, and I should have realized that everything hits you harder when you are pregnant. Plus Clara died. I don't think either of us coped with that very well."

Hannah tensed up as another contraction swept over her. As its grip tightened, she said breathlessly, "Georg, remember how I said so many times that I wouldn't do this or that if this was the last house in the valley?"

"Of course, you are always throwing that at me. But I choose to overlook it most times." He squeezed her hand.

The pain eased gradually, and so too, her mind cleared somewhat. "Georg, I will not say that anymore. I love this place. I love the way you have worked so hard to make life for us here. I get angry when you talk about selling it or leaving or apprenticing out the children. Surely we can stick it out . . . ohhhh." She gasped and then screamed. "Get Esther."

Esther must have been right outside the door, because she ran in. "Georg, you must leave."

"No," they both said at once.

"I've birthed calves, piglets, and colts," he answered. "I'm not leaving my wife when she is this bad off.

By now Hannah was beyond caring.

"Please get this baby out," she cried. "God, please help me."

Esther rolled her sleeves up again and said calmly, "I think maybe it's time. Georg, hold her hand and talk to her. Hannah, you must push now. I know you're exhausted, but this baby needs your help if he's going to make it into the world quickly."

Hannah didn't even answer; she just tried her hardest to help her little one make an entrance that he seemed determined not to make. Finally she heard Esther tell Georg, "I can see his head, it won't be long."

The news gave her heart, and she gripped Georg's hand with all her strength as she pushed.

"Here he comes, Hannah," cried Esther, while Georg just held her and whispered, "I love you," against her hair.

Sure enough, after what seemed years of work, the newest Zartman made its way, yowling lustily, into the world. Esther laughed with relief and practically threw the baby at Georg.

"Quick, wipe her off, keep her warm. I have to attend to Hannah, and then we'll take care of your new little one."

"Hannah," Georg spoke tenderly even as he wiped off the squalling infant. "We have a beautiful baby girl with lots and lots of black hair."

"A girl?" Hannah said wonderingly. "For some reason, this last week I was sure he was a boy. What shall we call him? Her."

"Nothing right now. You need to sleep, and Esther will take care of her. I'll be downstairs if either one of you needs me, and when the children wake up, they can see their new sister. You can name her later on."

Hannah was almost asleep already as Georg tiptoed out. Drowsily she began to think about names, but sleep soon overtook her.

EPILOGUE

GRACE

Dear Emily,

I never made it to your wedding, but I guess maybe you never thought I would. At one point this winter, I was so sure I would be there with you to celebrate, but now I know my place is here with Georg and the children. Whatever comes our way, we have to face it together.

You are just married, so this may sound funny, but I am amazed by how two people who are so much in love can quarrel over such silly things and bring ruin to all they have worked so hard to build. Remember that when you are angry at Jacob.

Emily, we have the most beautiful little baby. I was so afraid she would never see the light of day and that I would die with her; but Esther, my friend, is a wonderful midwife, and God has spared us both.

We named her Grace because God has truly been gracious to us, and while she will never take

Clara's place, she does remind me so of Clara when she was newborn. The children fight over who will get to hold her so I can scarcely get my own turn in unless she is hungry.

Oh, Emily, life is a wonderful thing, and while I know we have many hard days in front of us, I have renewed my commitment to be a helpmeet to my husband. Surely life is never easy, and we are fools to think it would be, but I want to grow old here in my little cabin with my husband, see my children grow up, and encourage them to be faithful in their commitments too.

Emily, remember how I used to say that when I died, I wanted to be remembered as a godly woman? I almost gave that up this winter, but I am holding fast to my faith and waiting for the day when God will say to me, "Well done, good and faithful servant."

You'll never believe this, but Georg has set up a wood carving shop in the shed, and he's teaching Benjamin and Samuel to fashion simple furniture. One day he may make it into a business. I'm trying to get used to the idea that my big boys will be going out as apprentices soon, though I wish they didn't have to; but they are big boys and even seem excited about such a grand adventure. Georg will miss them too, of course, and I do so wish they could stay home and just be boys for a little longer. I suppose life must go on for every mama.

While I don't know when I will see you, I do hope it will be sometime soon. You can hold my

new little daughter, and perhaps I can hold one of
yours. I can't wait.

    I love you.

    Hannah

ABOUT THE AUTHOR

As the daughter of a jungle doctor, Miriam Ilgenfritz thought she had seen it all. But years later, Miriam found herself in a different jungle—as the mother to sixteen children. She earned two degrees from Crown College in Waconia, Minnesota, both of which turned out to be useful with toddlers: cross-cultural communication and elementary education.

Miriam lives on a small farm in central Pennsylvania with her husband, nine of her children, four golden retrievers, a milk cow, and a plentiful garden. Like Hannah, her main character in *Letters to Emily*, she has delivered baby piglets—and, more recently, twin calves. Miriam estimates that she has changed more than 99,000 diapers over the past three decades, and she is usually found ankle-deep in laundry, cooking, or dishes. In her free time, she reads and trains for long-distance races. Running affords her the creative time to turn her vast collection of family misadventures into written stories. She hopes to one day learn to play the oboe.

Follow Miriam's blog at: miriamilgenfritz.blogspot.com

E-mail: storycraftsmom@gmail.com